Alicia Bewitched

The Alicia Trilogy – Book Three

by

Nick Iuppa & John Pesqueira

This book is a work of fiction. Names, characters, places and incidents are either the product of the author's imagination or are used fictitiously. Any resemblance to actual persons, living or dead, or to actual events or locales is entirely coincidental.

ALICIA BEWITCHED

Cover designed by Nick Iuppa
Cover Photo: Persians iStock # 623347764

Preview Cover:
Cover designed by Nick Iuppa
© Gerald French/CORBUS/AX010441
© 123rf.com/maxfx/8621645

Visit the author's website at www.nickiuppa.com

Paperback ISBN: 978-0-9863241-2-3

Printed in the United States of America

10 9 8 7 6 5 4 3 2 1

Dedication

To all my past and present relatives from Mexico whose history and stories have informed so much of my life and creative endeavors.

— John Pesqueira

To my grandmother, Michalina Gorecki who gave me a great appreciation of my Polish heritage... and witches.

— Nick Iuppa

Novels by Nick Iuppa & John Pesqueira

Alicia's Ghost
Alicia's Sin
Alicia Bewitched
Avenging Adelita
Esteban's Quest
The Battle for the Alamo Taqueria

Novels by Nick Iuppa

Taken By Witches
The Witch Within Her

Bloody Bess and the Doomsday Games

Praise for Alicia's Ghost

"Incredibly imaginative!" — Chuck Reedy, Author

"Who could have guessed that ghost sex would be so hot?"
— Janey Baker, Actress

"Every time I thought I had it figured out, there was a new twist to the story. I couldn't put it down. Great read!"
— C. Gallagher, Agent

"Interesting, engrossing, with lots of action and twists."
Veronica Del Rosa—Author

"Funny & fun to read! Kept me wondering what would happen next."
— Eric Dueker, Filmmaker

"The storytelling is excellent. Can't wait for the sequel."
— Elke Hitto, Writer/Journalist

"I couldn't put it down until I finished it. So, when will the next one be out? Please don't keep us waiting!"
— WW, Constant Reader

"A haunting tale of ghostly struggles for love, power and revenge!"
— Bob D, Author

"Carlos is lucky, he has some ghost friends who come to the party and make it an amazing, chilling, and just plain enjoyable adventure."
— James Loftus, Author

"I love the characters, and Alicia ... these guys have the Latina in her down to a science."
— Becky Escamilla, Constant Reader

"Fabulous story... a pleasure to read."
— Linda Todd, Constant Reader

Praise for Alicia's Sin

Acknowledgments

We'd like to thank all the people who helped with the creation of this book, especially Norma Cervantes, Kimberly Behl and Lauren Ayer. We also appreciate the exceptional design and layout services of Laurie Douglas, and the great editorial support from Janet Grady, Tara McNabb, and Debbie Thrush.

"We are only man and ghost. Who are we to stand against witches and demons and devils?"

Alicia Mann

The Major Characters

THE LIVING

Mexico

Dr. Carlos Mann (Mancowski) – Leland University logic professor

Fernando de Cervantes (Señor Popcorn) – El Rey del Maíz (The King of Corn)

Eva Córdoba de Cervantes (Señora Popcorn) – His wife

Enrique Córdoba – Director of Anti-Narcotics Operations for the Mexican government

Yolanda Córdoba – His wife

Miguel Carillo – de Cervantes's right-hand man

Victor Estephan – de Cervantes's lieutenant

Doña Cuca – A curandera

La Bruja – A witch of the Yucatan

Maclovio Renta – A rival drug lord to Señor Popcorn

Marty Marinara – FBI agent

Ancient Maya Citizens and Lost Memories

Akhushtal – Maya name for La Bruja

Chac and Ikan – Ballplayers vying with the sisters' family

Ichik – Doña Cuca's lover

Ixchel – Doña Cuca's great, great granddaughter – Carlos's great grandmother

Conrad Mancowski – Carlos's great grandfather

Los Altos

Assad Madani – Part owner of the Torquemada Record Store

Veronica Joy Madani – His wife and adopted sister of Tiger and Amy Joy

Chinatown

Amy Joy – One of Carlos's Logic Students

Helen (Tiger) Joy – CEO of the Joy Lum slave trade empire
    and Amy's adopted sister

Florence (Bunny) Joy – A submissive and Tiger's twin

Kathryn (Kitten) Joy – Tiger's adopted sister

Albert and the Joy boys – Enforcers for the clan

THE DEAD

Mexico

Alicia Maria Mejias Mancowski Mann – Ghost wife of Dr.
    Carlos Mann

Sylvia Morales – Professional model and friend of Alicia

Padre Hidalgo – A priest and revolutionary

Chinatown

Mr. Lum – Founder of the Joy Lum slave trade

Mother and Father Joy –Slave traders, adopted parents of the
    Joy girls

Mr. Fu – Ancient worker from the days of the railroad

Los Altos

Carlyle August – Former wealthy entrepreneur, proprietor of
    the bookstore, and head of Ghosts Anonymous

Mr. Friedman – Once an elderly gentleman and safecracker

Jenny Beck – Once a teen Goth skateboarder

Royce Brilliant – Once a gay biker

Prison

Mistress Fea – Ghost inmate at the correctional facility in
    Chowchilla, California

Roxanna – Another ghost inmate

Table of Contents

4

5

6

7

Detailed Summaries of the Previous Carlos Mann Novels

(Spoiler Alert — It's all here.)

Alicia's Ghost Summary

I'm Carlos Mann.

I find my beautiful wife Alicia lying slashed to death on the floor of our little apartment in Los Altos, California. She's the girl I fell in love with when I was growing up in a Mexican village.

I call the police. At first they think I did it. I'm a Professor at Leland University, but they still suspect me of taking a butcher knife to my wife.

Eventually, I'm cleared. But then my mind starts playing games with me, forcing me to hide inside compulsions, making me obsess about dangers that aren't even there. It's better than facing the fact that I've lost Alicia forever, isn't it?

But then she's back from the dead... and she's pissed! I can tell because all of my books have been thrown across the living room. Pictures of our life together are scattered everywhere. She's used mustard, ketchup, and mayonnaise to do a Jackson Pollack on the kitchen wall. Alicia never could control her temper, but I know what brought her back.

One of my students, a pretty Asian girl named Amy Joy, snuck a pair of her panties into my desk drawer yesterday morning. I try to think of it as a call for help, but I'm sure it doesn't look that way to Alicia.

Still, I need to save Amy. A sinister pair of human traffickers named Mother and Father Joy *own* Amy and her sister, Veronica. They buy young girls in China and sell them in the US as victims, submissives, dominas, or (if the girls are smart enough to make it through Leland University) as obedient wives for cruel and demanding businessmen. Problem is, Amy and Veronica are flunking out of my class, about to move from prospective wives to certain victims. So, the girls tell me everything.

Mother and Father Joy find out about our conversation and send a couple of thugs to kill me. That's enough to get Alicia to show up and save my life. She appears at her horrific best and scares the hell out of the bad guys. What a show! And when it's all over and she's restored to her natural ghostly beauty, Alicia makes love to me. Let me tell you, ghost sex can be amazing!

But still I have to convince Alicia to let me help Amy and Veronica, because Mother and Father Joy have just sold them to a surgeon who gets off on sadistic mutilation. I rescue the girls. Mother and Father capture them back, and in the end Alicia and I have to call on Ghosts Anonymous to help save the Joy sisters.

We have to find a safer place to hide them.

I am Alicia Maria Mejias Mancowski Mann.

And I cannot believe my husband is risking his life for these Joy girls just because I am dead. So, I tell him the story of how I was murdered. He knows that I became a model when he went off to study at the university. He knows I met Señor Popcorn, a wonderful older man who let me live with other models in his home in Mexico City. Señor Popcorn is a drug dealer, but he protected us and never asked for favors.

When Carlos did not have the money for his PhD, Señor Popcorn said that I could earn money by going to El Paso and buying guns for him. It was a simple job except that he sent a bad guy named Luis along to *protect* me. Instead of protection, Luis tried to rape me out in the desert. But then a nest of rattlesnakes attacked him. I escaped and eventually completed the mission. Señor Popcorn was so pleased that he gave me all the money Carlos needed for his degree.

Carlos and I were married, moved to Los Altos, and lived happily ever after... until Luis (who somehow survived the rattlesnakes) found me and murdered me! Now, I am going to get even: scare Luis into craziness, and then kill him myself... very slowly.

While Carlos is saving his Joy girls, I have fun terrorizing Luis. I appear as a store window mannequin who turns into an ugly witch; then a hospital worker who bloodies him up and tosses him down the garbage chute; next I'm a motorcycle cop who chases him off a cliff. But Luis ends up in Sinaqua, Arizona, where there are places called Dread Zones that turn ghosts into nothingness. I am almost destroyed, but the Purgatory ghosts find me and take me back to Los Altos. There, I recover so I can help Carlos take those Joy girls down to Mexico City where Señor Popcorn will keep them... *forever, I hope.*

When we get to his estate, el Señor is waging a drug war with an enemy who has partnered with Mother and Father Joy. They throw Chinese dragons, demons, and even DEATH ITSELF at us, and it is only the sudden arrival of long-dead Apache warriors that saves us.

Once again Carlos goes off, this time with the FBI, to confront and kill Mother and Father Joy. But the pair have an evil daughter named Tiger who escapes and starts planning the rebirth of their slave trade and the death of my Carlitos.

Alicia's Sin Summary

I'm Carlos Mann.

Amy Joy says that her evil, sexy sister, Tiger, holds me personally responsible for the death of her parents, and she plans to make me pay with my life.

Fortunately, before the Queen of Human Trafficking can set her evil plans in motion, Señor Popcorn whisks Alicia and me off to Cancun. He wants us to help him win the love of Eva Córdoba, the daughter of Mexico's top anti-narcotics agent and the popcorn man's long-time enemy.

We have to outwit witches, dodge gun battles, and find a new (legal) career for Señor Popcorn before Eva will consent to marry him. Unfortunately, by the time it's all over, Alicia's temper gets her into so much trouble that she's sent to Vienna, to the ghost of Dr. Sigmund Freud, for anger management training.

While she's gone, Tiger Joy comes after me. With the head of the Leland Philosophy Department and the crazy wife of a long-dead poet, Tiger charges me with plagiarism. I lose my professorship, have to struggle to find a new job, and when I do, I'm captured by Tiger's Joy Boys.

Meanwhile, under Freud's psychoanalysis, Alicia relives her childhood and discovers the source of her terrible temper. She also meets the ghost of a lecherous prince who tries to seduce her. He tells my wife that she and I are no longer married because of the ceremonial words, "till death do us part." Alicia is dead; so, how can we still be married?

In the end I'm able to escape from Tiger's Boys and head to Vienna where I find that the prince has sold Alicia to the gypsies. They put her on display in the Ghost Chamber of their traveling carnival. But Alicia's anger boils over and blows apart the Chamber, releasing all the spirits that the gypsies have captured. I arrive just in time. Alicia and I are reunited. But now, to get around our ridiculous marriage vows, Alicia insists that we re-marry.

I agree, but at our wedding, ghosts of Spanish Inquisitors suddenly appear and announce, "This is a great sin. The dead shall not marry the living." A battle ensues and we escape, only to have Tiger finally capture Alicia and sell her to the Inquisition... to be burned at the stake in the Dread Zones of Death Valley.

The ghost of renegade priest, Padre Hidalgo, remarried us. Now he and I arrive just in time to call upon the spirits of all those who have suffered at the hands of the Inquisition to help us save Alicia.

It's months later, and we're attending the wedding of Señor Popcorn and his bride Eva, when we learn that the FBI has finally captured Tiger and sent her to prison. It's just what she deserves, I think. But then I find out that the case against Tiger will take years to settle, and she may get off scot-free. In the meantime she's turned her prison cell into a pleasure palace with guards who worship her.

I think it's time to take matters into my own hands, don't you?

I'm going to kill Tiger Joy myself.

Alicia
Bewitched

Prologue

I'm standing in a prison cell that looks like a suite at the Ritz Carlton Hotel. Two years ago I stayed at the Ritz in London when I won the Seaforth Prize for an article I'd written. I was alone then, just as I am now, because I can't have Alicia with me... not here, not tonight, not with all the deadly work I have to do.

On the wall opposite the cell bars hangs an enormous painting of a tiger. The big cat is realistic enough to be in a photograph. And yet there are brush strokes there, I know it, I can see them... sort of. I refocus, move to change the reflection, and there they are... hundreds of them... thousands of them. The image becomes a pattern of light and dark, colors and shadows. I want to lose myself in those tiny brush strokes, stay hiding in there forever. But I can't. I've got work to do. So, I force myself to take in the whole picture. And suddenly the tiger seems about to jump right out of the painting and attack me. I tense my muscles ready for the cat to lunge, and then feel stupid when I remind myself that it's only a picture hanging on the wall.

Just below the image of the tiger are couches and chairs upholstered in blue velvet. They form a large sitting area around a rosewood coffee table. Across from them is a 72 inch flat-screen TV. Beside it is a large rosewood bookcase that holds famous novels and stacks of anime comic books. Beyond the bookcase is a king-sized bed.

The lights outside the cell have been dimmed. Still, their soft glow casts the shadow of iron bars over the prison bed, over the pink silk sheets and pillowcases, over the slight form of the young woman who lies sleeping under the covers.

Her long black hair fans out onto the pillows as if some glamour photographer arranged it, but her face is turned away from me. It doesn't matter. I can tell who she is by the six-inch stiletto heels placed neatly together at the edge of the bed, and by the leather jumpsuit slung over the dragon-carved hope chest just below it. She's sound asleep, doesn't know I'm here. More importantly, she doesn't know that I've come to kill her.

I'm not good at any of this, not the bribery that I had to use to get myself into this place and certainly not the cold-blooded murder that I've been planning for over a year.

Still, I have to do it. It's only logical.

I think back to a conversation I had with Marty Marinara of the FBI. We talked about the fact that the agency had actually captured Tiger Joy, the CEO of the Joy Lum Slave Trade Empire, the girl who now lies sleeping in front of me. Marinara told me the government's case against Tiger would unfold slowly: They'd charge her with human trafficking; they'd hold preliminary hearings; Tiger would get out on bail … no matter how high the cost. But eventually she'd be tried for everything *except* the hundreds of murders she's commissioned. If convicted there'd be more appeals, more trials; she'd be in and out of jail for years, and when she was behind bars she'd have this kind of cell: velvet furniture, plush carpeting, a private bathroom. I can see the door to it standing open on the far side of the cell. There's even a Jacuzzi in there.

Given her underworld connections, her undeniable beauty, and ravenous sexual appetite, I figure that Tiger Joy could just move her kingdom in here, start running things from her cell and having a great old time. I'm sure the guards treat her like the empress that she is.

See what I mean? By the time Marinara and I had worked our way through the possible outcomes, I knew there was only one logical way to see that justice was done. I'd have to find a way to kill Tiger myself.

I guess you know that I was a prizefighter when I was younger. I'm not a violent guy by nature, but I had a great boxing instructor and became very good at it. Once, before we were married, Alicia attended one of my bouts. The guy I was fighting started teasing her from inside the ring. She was humiliated, and it made me so angry that I almost killed the guy. They had to drag me off of him or I might have. So, I have the chops to take a life, I guess.

Except, this isn't quite the same, is it? This is premeditated murder, and no matter how logical it is, I actually have to *do* it... carefully and rationally. Tiger's a small girl really, and I know I can just snap her neck if I want to, but still ...

I close my eyes, and the first face I see is my beautiful Alicia, last year ... in Death Valley. A horde of crazy monks were tying her to a stake so that they could burn her as a heretic because she was a ghost and wanted to marry me again ... while I was still alive.

"The dead shall not marry the living," the monks chanted over and over. Tiger sold Alicia to the ghosts of the inquisitors so that they could burn her out of existence. That's the kind of bitch Tiger is.

"I'll get you, Carlitos," she mumbles in her sleep.

Yeah. She's vowed to murder me too. She knows that I helped the FBI kill her parents in a mammoth sting operation. Tiger and her infamous "Mother and Father" had captured Alicia and were holding her in some obscene ghost trap. My attempts to rescue her led to a shootout. Mother and Father were gunned down. Somehow Tiger escaped, took over her parents' business, and made it even more successful than it already was. Now Tiger wants revenge ... on me and everyone else. So, this is self-defense, really: assassinating a true sociopath, sort of like killing Hitler early in his career.

I stand and move as quietly as I can, past the bookcase and up to the head of the bed. I grab those pink silk sheets.

"You can do this," I whisper to myself.

For just a minute that great painting of the tiger catches my eye again, and I'm distracted by the pattern of the brushstrokes that make up the image. I could study those for a lifetime. I really want to. Then I feel the girl on the bed begin to stir.

"I'm going to torture you before I kill you, Carlitos," she says joyfully.

I throw the covers back, grab Tiger by the shoulder, and spin her around. She's wide-awake instantly, looking up at me with those dark, dangerous eyes.

"Why, Dr. Mann," she coos. "How nice to see you."

I reach for her throat. She doesn't pull away, doesn't even blink.

"Naughty, naughty," she says.

And just then a heavy hand falls onto my shoulder.

1
Alicia

Chapter 1

Carlitos is missing.

I run from room to room in our little apartment wringing my hands on the apron I wear around my waist. It says, "Kiss the Cook," which is something I want Carlitos to do. But, when I call my husband for kisses and supper, a supper that I have made with great love and spices... he is not here.

He was supposed to be home by six thirty... or at least call me. I thought for a moment that he *was* here, but, really, I did not hear him come in. I chopped up fat chicken pieces and threw them into the mole sauce. I sang loudly as I cut the cilantro and onions and jalapeño peppers. I danced around the kitchen while I set the table using my best Mexican plates and silverware. I poured a big margarita that I made myself by squeezing limes and mixing everything else.

During all that noisy work, my husband did not appear. He did *not* return from his appointment by six thirty as he said he would. And now it is nearly nine.

Maybe he stopped to get me a bouquet of roses for the table, I think. But would that delay him for two hours?

"Don't worry. Carlitos will be home soon," I say to myself as I stir the sauce for the very last time... I hope.

It is an hour later. "Carlitos!" I call into the courtyard through the window above the kitchen sink. No one answers. So, for the next two hours I pace and stir and pace some more. I cannot eat the dinner of course. I am a ghost. Ghosts do not eat. We *wait* mostly. So that is what I do. I wait... and it gets later and later.

#

I have never been obsessed with time the way my husband is. He has clocks in every room of the house, and not just regular clocks. These, he tells me, are *atomic* clocks that are in tune with the great world clock that is somewhere in England. Every single one of these clocks tells me the exact same thing... that Carlitos is now four hours late for supper.

I hate clocks; I hate telling time. Ghosts should have no sense of it. And yet tonight I do, and all these clocks remind me again and again that my husband should have been here a very long time ago.

I walk up to my husband's desk. I look at the telephone that is sitting in the corner. Even the phone has a clock built into it. And then I wonder, "Why am I so stupid? Why do I not just call him?" And so I pick up the phone and push the button that dials him directly, knowing that my special ring will tell him that I am calling.

The phone rings and rings. I do not like this. Carlitos always has his cell phone with him, always answers on the second ring when he knows that I am calling... but not tonight. Tonight I get his answering message:

"Mann here. IF this is important... THEN leave a message."

That is some kind of logical joke, I guess, some *syllogism*. That is a word Carlitos uses all the time, which I do not understand. But tonight I am so mixed up I am using the word too. What is important is that Carlitos is not answering, and that is not a syllogism. There is nothing logical about it.

"Please call me, Carlitos, and tell me when you'll be home," I say to the voice mail as sweetly as my fear will allow. Then I hang up and decide to do something to fill the terrible time while I continue to wait.

I go into the kitchen and throw out the Margaritas that have now grown watery from sitting in their shaved ice. And I start all over again, squeezing limes and adding the other ingredients. I tell myself that by the time I am through, my husband will walk through the front door with a big bouquet of flowers, and even bigger kisses for me.

I take my time. I wash all the margarita glasses, stir the mixture together and wish that I had some ghost-margaritas that I could drink myself. But I do not. And now it is 11 p.m., and my husband is *still* not home.

I go back to the phone and call again. I close my eyes and feel tears. My hands shake as I hold the phone to my ear. My lips switch between hopeful smiles and sadness. And then, on the fifth ring, there is an answer. It is Carlitos, but his voice is tragic... and heartbroken.

"Alicia," he says sadly.

"Carlitos, what is it?"

He sighs, struggles to say something and then, finally whispers, "I won't be home."

I flinch.

"Tonight? You will not be home tonight?"

"Not tonight," he answers, in a tragic voice, "not for a very long time."

And then I hear a voice I know well, a woman's voice, insulting him, calling him names. These names are too terrible for me to repeat.

"Carlitos," I say trying to be the only one who is calm. "Tell me. When will I see you again?"

I hear my husband's heavy, desperate breathing. This is not a man who is coming home to share kisses and margaritas.

"I don't know," he answers at last. "Maybe... never!"

Chapter 2

It's now midnight, a perfect time for ghosts. But I am shaking with fear. Something terrible has happened to Carlitos. I go out into the night pacing, racking my angry brain for ideas on where to find my husband.

I am sure you understand that Carlitos really *is* my husband even though I am dead and he is not. I will not let you remind me of the words, "Till death do us part!" I do not want to hear them. The ghost of Padre Hidalgo married us again... *after* I died... while Carlitos was still alive.

Padre Hidalgo is the Father of Mexico. I never paid much attention to history class, but every Mexican schoolgirl knows that much.

I wish I knew how to contact Padre Hidalgo right now and ask him about my Carlitos, but I am sure the old priest is haunting some holy place in Mexico. I cannot contact him, and so I go to the only spot I can think of where ghosts gather to talk all night and share information: The Purgatory Bookstore in downtown Los Altos, California.

I zoom through the streets and am at the store in minutes. I pass through the locked door, up the stairway, and into the attic where I can hear ghosts talking. They turn to me when I show myself. I expect them to smile, but they look as terrified as I am. Do they know what I know? How could they?

"Alicia, sweetheart," sighs Royce Brilliant. He's the ghost of a gay biker. He sits there with spiky hair and silky biker's shorts and shirt. Beside him is the Goth shadow of Jenny Beck, who died in a skateboarding accident. For once she does not have a blank stare in her eyes. Her look is tragic. She sits there twisting her stringy hair, saying the word "hopeless!" over and over.

Carlyle August is the leader of the group. He stands and comes up to me. He looks like the ghost of Cary Grant, the star whose old movies I loved watching on television when I was a little girl. Of course, now that I am all grown up, I am only in love with Carlitos.

But Carlyle really loves me, I think. So I try to be nice to him. Who knows when I may need to take advantage of that love? Maybe right now, because my ghost-body suddenly flames with anger.

There, right in the middle of this meeting of ghosts, sits a living person, and worst of all, she is my enemy.

"What is *she* doing here?" I ask Carlyle, turning my most hateful eyes on him.

"Please, darling, don't upset yourself," he says. "She's just begun to tell us something very important."

"I don't want to hear it."

"You need to."

"If it is from her lips... then NO!"

"It's about Carlos," my rival says, and even my angry stare cannot make her go away. "He's in terrible trouble."

My anger abandons me. "I know," I whisper sadly as I slump into a chair amid the other ghosts and this one living person.

She is Amy Joy, a sad victim of human trafficking, which is a Chinatown business run by her sister, the terrible, evil, wicked, and nasty Tiger Joy. Even though Tiger is younger than I am, she is the boss of a great worldwide empire of buyers and sellers of young women who are trained to be wives and slaves to men.

"Where is my Carlitos?" I ask.

"I don't know," Amy answers. "But I know that he vowed to kill Tiger, and he went after her last night."

I stare at her. Carlitos did not mention killing anyone when he left yesterday morning. He just said that he had important business.

"I don't believe you, Miss," I say.

"Perhaps then, you will believe *me*," a disembodied voice suddenly interrupts.

We all look around knowing that this is a technique often used by ghosts who want to catch everyone's attention. And so it is. A wispy, old Chinese gentleman suddenly flickers up at the table.

"Mr. Foo," I say, giving my best smile to the man who has helped me save Carlitos over and over again.

"Alicia, my dear. I am so sorry," he says. He shakes his head and takes a seat among us.

"Tell me, please," I beg him. "What happened to Carlitos?"

"I was there," he answers. "I saw it all. But... how can I describe it?"

Again he shakes his head and closes his eyes.

"Please, Mr. Foo," Carlyle says as he steps forward and puts an anxious hand on my shoulders. "You can see that the lady is suffering."

"Yes, of course," Mr. Foo answers. "But it is all so tragic and terrifying."

He pauses again, nervously.

"I beg you, sir, speak up," Carlyle adds far too politely for me. Mr. Foo must see my growing anger, because he lowers his head, thinks for a moment, and then begins his story.

Chapter 3

"I haunt Tiger's prison," Mr. Foo begins, "the women's correctional facility in Chowchilla, the place where they have the capability to *execute* women for their crimes. I watch her as she lies sleeping in her cell. It's after midnight when a new guard suddenly makes his way toward her.

"'Hey there, handsome,' one of the inmates calls out. 'Never seen you here before.'

"She's a scrawny old woman whose tangled hair makes her look very much like a cat from the alleys of Chinatown.

"'Shhhh,' the new guard hisses and motions for the woman to be quiet.

"'You going to see the empress?' she asks as she slinks up to the bars of her cell. 'If you are, then fuck her for me, will you?'"

"I'm so sorry, beautiful lady," Mr. Foo tells me with some embarrassment. "But I want to be accurate."

I reach across and squeeze his hand.

"It's all right," I say. "I need to know exactly what happened. Please continue."

"The guard turns and catches the woman's eyes. He is so handsome, young, and intelligent looking, with a great Aztec nose and blue Polish eyes. He's your Carlos, Alicia.

"He moves quickly, ignoring the chatter from the other inmates who are still awake. Tiger is not. She's sleeping soundly in her regal bed.

"He seems rather nervous as he lets himself into her cell, which looks like a suite in some grand hotel. He sighs, hesitates, and must be asking himself, 'Do I really want to do this?' The picture on the wall distracts him. It is a painting of a hungry tiger.

"It must remind him of an important question: 'Can the world be safe with Tiger in it?'

"That's enough to bring him to the edge of her bed where he flings back the covers, spins Tiger around, clasps one hand over her mouth, reaches around to the back of her head with the other, and then...."

Both Amy Joy and I lean forward, not breathing, needing to know if Carlitos has become a murderer.

"Was he able to kill her?" Amy asks hopefully.

"If you mean was he *capable* of killing her," Mr. Foo says, "we may never know."

"Oh." Amy Joy and I say the word at the same time. Then we look at each other in anger. We do not even want to share our feelings for Carlitos.

Thankfully Mr. Foo continues.

"Before Carlos can act, four guards grab him and drag him back across the cell. They slap a piece of duct tape over his mouth to silence him. And so the only sound anyone hears is that old alley-cat woman from across the way begging, 'Give him here; give him to me. I can make pretty use of the boy.'"

I bury my face in my hands and begin to sob. I think I can hear Amy sobbing too, which would make me angry except that I am really too heartbroken to care.

"And then the phone rings," Mr. Foo adds. "Carlos's cell phone.

"I can see the look in his eyes. He asks himself, how could he be foolish enough to leave it turned on? I don't know, but Tiger nods her head, and the guard rips the tape from his mouth and hands him the phone. He answers it and talks to you, Alicia, and tells you that he may never come home again. He hangs up, but you call back, and Tiger flies into a rage.

"She screams, grabs the phone away from your husband, and throws it wildly across her cell. She runs up to it and stomps that spiked heel of hers into its heart, killing the phone and any way you might have of reaching your husband again. But it may not matter. Carlos now looks so defeated that he barely even looks up. Even when Tiger strides right up to him, knee to knee, and stares at him.

"'I'd love to fuck you, Carlitos,' she says, 'but there are just too many people around. Besides, I don't dare give you another chance to kill me. This time you might succeed.'

"'Jimmy?' she calls to one of those guards. They have all fallen in love with her, it seems.

"'Shall I strangle him for you, Mistress?' asks a muscle-bound ape who waddles forward.

"'No, sorry... I'd love to watch that... but no.'

"'He came here to kill you,' Jimmy growls as he cracks his knuckles.

"'I know,' Tiger says, 'wasn't that cute? Still, I need him in one piece.'

"She turns back to Carlos, smirks, and blows him a sexy little kiss. Then she licks her lips invitingly.

"As much as the sight turns him on, Jimmy does not approve. He grunts. Tiger turns back to him. She purrs as she struts up to him, flashes her claws, and rakes them harmlessly down the front of his shirt.

"'Yes, Jimmy. Let's beat him up. Beat the living shit out of him. It'll serve him right, and I'll enjoy the show. Just don't kill him. I have big plans for our murderous little Carlitos.'"

Mr. Foo looks up at me sadly now and sighs. "I'm sorry."

"But what happened next?" I ask. "What did they do to Carlitos?"

"The guards put on a show for their mistress," he says. "They all lust after Tiger. She provides them with astounding sexual favors, so they do whatever she asks. And this night they beat on your husband with their fists, with the butts of guns, with pipes, until he looks like a piece of well-pounded chuck steak."

I jump to my feet.

"Take me to la puta!" I shout. "I will scratch her eyes out like a jaguar."

"The guards won't let you," Mr. Foo tells me. "She owns them."

"It's a tragic state of affairs," Amy says. "Tiger's in prison, but she lives like an empress, giving orders, having servants. The guards provide her with anything she wants. It's disgusting."

"Anything disgusting she wants," I repeat, understanding at once.

"Mostly she wants revenge," Amy continues.

"Every time she tries to take revenge on Carlitos, it only makes things worse for her," I say.

"But she has new and more powerful allies now," Mr. Foo says. "She's building a vast empire right from prison."

"Then, I will go see her there," I say. "And I will scratch her eyes out."

"Believe me, beautiful lady, you don't want to haunt a prison," Carlyle interrupts, "especially not that one."

"Mr. Foo did it successfully."

"But at great and terrible risk," the old man answers.

"I will go there anyway."

"Do you have any idea of the kind of ghosts that haunt Chowchilla?" Mr. Foo asks. "The ghosts of inmates long dead are still there; they're monsters, villains, and killers."

"But I have friends in the FBI," I say with a smile.

"That's right," Jenny Beck speaks up. A happy memory suddenly pushes away her look of despair. "That cute agent, Marty Marinara. I almost scared him out of his mind convincing him that ghosts really *do* exist. It was so cool."

"Then you'll come with me, Jenny?"

"That's my job, Alicia," Carlyle says firmly.

"The job is mine," Mr. Foo says.

"I appreciate the offer, but you have to protect Miss Amy Joy," Carlyle tells Mr. Foo. "And you know that Tiger will learn of this visit, and she'll try to punish you for it. Better stay behind while we keep her occupied."

My mind is going in circles. Men fight over the job of protecting me when I know I can take care of myself. Finally I give in... sort of.

"If you think you can help, Carlyle," I say at last, "you are welcome to come. But if you get in the way, I will have to ask you to leave."

Carlyle simply smiles and nods. "Of course, beautiful lady, of course."

"So then, Amy," I say as I turn to her and give her my warmest false smile. "Thank you for your information. Now, please take Mr. Foo with you and go away leaving me and my husband alone... forever."

She nods, and I can see that tears are filling up her stupid eyes. What does she expect, that I will allow her to rescue my husband and then take him away from me just because she is alive and I am not?

"We are remarried," I remind her. "Man and ghost! Now excuse us. Carlyle and I must go and rescue my husband before Tiger has him for supper."

Chapter 4

Marty Marinara sits behind a big desk in the San Francisco Federal Building and stares at my breasts. I have chosen to wear my passport dress, which I think is very businesslike, but there is a small opening at the top that offers a little peek.

"You're lucky I happen to be visiting the West Coast today," he says without looking up.

"If necessary I would have traveled to Washington to ask for your help."

"Well, then I guess I'm the lucky one."

He is still inspecting my chest.

"Señor," I say.

"Yes?"

"My breasts are not talking to you."

"*Oh yes, they are*," he murmurs before he even knows what he is saying. And then he blushes bright red.

Señor Marinara is big and cute. When he smiles he has dimples. He is smiling now... in embarrassment.

"I'm so sorry," he says softly.

"So am I, Señor," and then I realize that I really *am* sorry. "None of us are really lucky today."

"No?"

"Not when Tiger Joy is still able to have her revenge against my husband."

Señor Marinara tilts his head and looks as though he is trying to understand my words. Finally he smiles. "I guess you're right."

He picks up a stack of papers and looks at them until the redness in his face goes away. Then he tosses the papers aside, leans back, and just stares into my eyes.

"So, what do we have to do?"

"You have to help me visit Tiger in her prison with no interference from guards or gangs or anyone."

He nods while he thinks.

"Promise me that you won't look like a ghost when you visit?"

"There are many forms I can take."

"Good. I can make a call that will get you in to see Ms. Joy. Just don't look too... too... you know."

"You want my death face?"

"Of course not. Just don't look so goddamn..."

"Scary?"

"No! So goddamn *beautiful*."

"I am a professional model, Señor, so being beautiful is my business."

"And you're very good at it."

Señor Marinara allows his eyes to wander all over my body again, and I am surprised, and sorry, and I wish my husband were here to beat him into bloody raw hamburger, which Carlitos could do with ease, because he is a prize-winning fighter.

The FBI man sees me staring back at him in anger. He realizes the sin his eyes are committing, and he blushes again.

"I mean no disrespect, Mrs. Mann."

"You were just admiring my view," I cross my legs deciding to smile and be nice. I need his help.

"It is okay," I say. "I should be used to it. Making men stare at me is what I do best."

I have decided to flirt with Señor Marinara a little bit. It is the least I can do if he can help me save Carlitos.

"Just dress it down a little. If you go in there looking the way you do right now, the inmates will go nuts... maybe the guards too."

"Is it not a *woman's* correctional facility?"

"Definitely, but believe me, women prisoners get every bit as horny as men."

"Then perhaps I should *not* bring my handsome gentleman friend along," I say. "It might make things worse."

I motion for the ghost of Carlyle August to show himself.

Carlyle materializes, smiles, and says, "It's a pleasure to meet you, Agent Marinara."

The FBI man laughs at both of us.

"Two handsome ghosts," he shakes his head. Then he just sighs. "You guys will probably start a riot."

He does not know how right he is.

Chapter 5

So now we are in some very small town in the San Joaquin Valley. A great, gray prison looks down on us. A driver from the local police brings us into the prison compound. We talk to the warden, are told what we can and cannot do, and now we wait in a little room where we will have our discussion with Tiger Joy.

Locks clang, bolts crash, doors open, and in walks Tiger, dressed in a black latex jumpsuit and high heels. There are zippers all over her clothes.

"This is not a traditional prison uniform," I say to Carlyle.

"No, but you have to admit it's exciting."

"You admit it; I am not interested in such excitement."

Tiger takes a seat on one side of the window that divides us. The opening is covered with a wire screen that reminds me of the chicken coops we had in our back yard in San Lucero, Mexico. Carlyle and I sit on the other side of the screen.

"I don't believe I've had the pleasure of meeting your friend, Alicia," Tiger says. "Won't you please introduce us?"

"Where is my husband, pendeja?" I growl back in anger. There is no point in beating around the bushes. Right? But Tiger does not answer me. She just turns to Carlyle.

"Alicia is always *so* rude," she says. Then she gives him her killer's smile and begins to toy with her long black hair.

"How do you do, my name is Helen Joy."

"I'm honored to make your acquaintance, Helen," Carlyle says, "but I thought your name was Tiger."

"Just a nickname. Though I *do* prefer it to Helen." She says her real name as though it has a sour taste. Carlyle continues like an excited little boy.

"And I also understand you own a real Bengal tiger."

"No longer," she says with a pout. "Unfortunately, he was killed when the FBI burned our Chinatown home to the ground. My people are out searching for a replacement, one who is appropriately *ferocious*!" And when she says that last word, she lunges toward Carlyle who falls away laughing at her in pretended terror.

I'm growing tired of all this.

"Where is my husband, you bitch?"

Tiger answers... but only to Carlyle.

"See the kinds of nasty things your friend says to me, Mr. August. It's distressing."

"Call me Carlyle."

"I'd like that."

I turn to Carlyle throwing daggers at him with my eyes.

"Whose side are you on?"

He looks at me with apologies and then turns back to Tiger.

"Would you be kind enough to tell us where we can find Alicia's husband?"

Tiger begins toying with one of her zippers. It goes right across her right breast. I am fearful that she is going to unzip it and something is going to pop out and make Carlyle go crazy with sexiness. She bats her eyes at him as the slow unzipping begins, but I growl loudly and she stops.

"Why would I tell you where Carlitos is?" she asks.

"Carlitos is *my* name for my husband," I hiss. "Do not call him that."

"You're right," Tiger answers with a sexy smile. "I have a better name for little Carlos. I like to call him SLAVE!"

She stands when she says the word, and I stand right with her. I lock my eyes on hers and growl like a wild jaguar. Tiger may be her name, but she is not from the same jungles that I am.

"Ladies, please!" Carlyle calls like some soccer referee. Tiger and I both take our seats again, but we both have our arms crossed as we continue to stare at each other and growl and hiss. At least Tiger has stopped playing with her zippers.

"Can you at least tell us if Dr. Mann is still alive?" Carlyle asks.

"Of course he's alive," Tiger says. "Why would I want to kill him before he's been properly tortured?"

"I will torture *you!*" I scream at Tiger, and suddenly the skinny guard seated by the door, someone we had not even noticed before, gets up and rushes over to me and tells me to control my voice or he will have me taken away.

Tiger giggles when he does this, and – as soon as the guard goes back and sits down – I turn to her and let my eyes tell her all the hatred I am feeling. I do it without saying a word.

"Alicia you are so damn beautiful," Tiger adds. She's toying with that zipper again. "Do you have any idea what someone like you would be worth in my business?"

"Your business?"

"Of selling love slaves."

"More than any man could ever pay," I say proudly.

She laughs. "That may be true, but you lack the proper training. Anyway, I will never tell you where Carlos is. I will only tell you that he is alive and being tortured to pay for his sins."

"My husband HAS NO SINS!"

"I'm afraid your time is up," the skinny guard says as he jumps to his feet and runs up to us again.

I am about to shower more curses on Tiger Joy, when Carlyle grabs me by the arm and squeezes it.

"Not now, Alicia," he whispers.

I growl at Tiger.

She hisses, as one of the guards comes up to her, takes her by the arm and begins to lead her away. She smiles, turns, and looks back over her shoulder through those long dark lashes.

She purrs out a sweet, "Goodbye, handsome," to Carlyle. And then she struts through the door and back into her prison.

"Let the haunting start right now," I whisper to Carlyle. But before I can begin to rot right there in front of the skinny guard, Carlyle whispers, "No!"

"Please be careful, Alicia. We have to find out where she's holding Carlos so we can rescue him. We'll strike tonight at midnight, okay?"

I nod. And then I smile with evil in my eyes.

Midnight is a wonderful time for ghosts to strike. Is it not?

Chapter 6

The haunting does begin at midnight. But we do not begin it. The ghosts of long dead inmates of the prison, not quite bad enough to go straight to hell, start screaming through the place.

As Carlyle and I move down the hallways, we see spooky ghost-figures flying everywhere. Many zoom up to the tops of the high walls and throw themselves down onto the stone floors with terrible cries and curses. They splatter like unholy water only to form back into horrible shapes and fly up the walls again.

Inside the cells we see ghost prisoners doing prison things: writing letters, scratching words into walls, trying to carve escape tunnels and hiding them behind pictures of movie stars.

We move on, and now things get even worse. Some ghosts chop up the bodies of others as though their victims are chicken or lobster being diced for stewing. Puffy shapes hang at the ends of twisted bed sheets, which are tied to the overhead beams. Theses ghosts have broken necks and terrible dead faces because they have hanged themselves in their cells.

Ghost women are being brutally raped... by other ghost women. I look away. So does Carlyle. There is nothing sexy about it.

Through all of this, the living inmates sleep their troubled sleeps. They do not see or hear the sorrows and the screaming, but perhaps these horrors visit them in their dreams. Even Tiger, whose cell is filled with the most ugly painted women I have ever seen, sleeps right through it all.

We stop outside of Tiger's cell to watch what is happening. Inside the bars a fat ugly woman sits on Tiger's couch and talks to her friends as though the cell is really hers. They chatter like birds sitting in their own private treetop.

As we stare at the women, a gruesome ghost-guard steps up behind us.

"Enjoyin' the viewin'?" he asks in a voice like sandpaper. I turn and jump backwards because he is so ugly. He is slapping a nightstick into his hand and it scares me, but not Carlyle.

"Have you ever seen anything like this in your life?" my friend asks.

"Every night," the ugly guard answers. "And what do you think, Miss?"

"These women frighten me."

"Interesting," the guard answers, "but you really should be more afraid of... ME!" and his eyes bulge out of his head as he says the words.

I step back right into the arms of another ghost-guard who pulls my hands behind my back and handcuffs me. When Carlyle raises his fists to defend me, other guards step forward and snap handcuffs onto him. Then they drag both of us through the bars and up to the fat old ghost woman who is the center of attention.

"Found these intruders, Mistress Fea," the guard says to her. She is dressed in a tattered old gown, which may have been very beautiful a hundred years ago. Her giant bosoms are covered with many nasty moles, and they are nearly spilling out of her low-cut top. She has red hair, and is smoking a ghost-cigarette. It is already making my eyes water and my stomach swim.

"Dread Zone em," Mistress Fea says to the guard.

It must mean take us to the nearest Dread Zone where our powers will disappear, and the forces of nature will murder us. We have learned that there are such places on this earth, and they can squeeze ghosts out of existence very quickly.

"No, Mistress," I say stomping my spiky heel right into the foot of the guard. It hurts him so much that he lets out a wail that stops all the ghost-business in the prison and draws all the other ghosts to gather outside of Tiger's cell.

"I have come to save my husband," I say.

"Let him take care of himself," Mistress Fea answers.

"But he cannot, he is alive."

"The dead can't marry the living," Fea says. "*Till death do us part*, remember?"

Those words make my eyes blaze and my muscles tighten. I think I may be able to break my handcuffs with anger if I want to.

"We have been remarried, in a ceremony performed by Padre Hidalgo."

Mistress Fea shakes her head and gives me a questioning smile. "A living person consented to marry a ghost?"

"Yes. My Carlitos still wants to be married to me even though I am dead."

"There's just no end to the stupidity of men, is there?"

The ladies around her now begin to giggle and nod.

"What are your crimes, ladies?" I ask when they have quieted.

They all answer at once, saying things like prostitution, robbery, and murder. Carlyle and I are in a cell full of thieves and killers and putas, together with Tiger Joy whose crimes are worse than all of them combined.

"If you are murderers, then why are you not all in hell?" I ask.

Mistress Fea winks at me. "Extenuating circumstances," she says with a smile of pretend innocence, and the others start giggling again.

"And repentance, sugar," says one of the others as she steps forward. This ghost is very tall, young, thin, and moves like a man. She also has a deep man's voice, but the body of a woman.

"I'd like to make you my own little sugarplum," she says to me. "Bet you taste delicious."

Her hair is black and short and combed into the style of a boy I once saw in a movie called <u>Grease</u>. She wears no make-up at all, but her face is clear, her cheekbones high, her lips are full, but hungry it seems, as are her teeth, which are enormous, wide, and sparkling. Her lips smile around them, and for a second I think she is going to take a bite out of me.

She slams the guard in his side.

"Gimmie the keys, numb-nuts," she says to him.

"Come on, Roxanne," he begs, but she slams him again, harder this time. He doubles over and, after a moment, he hands her the ring of keys. Roxanne glides up behind me and undoes my handcuffs getting only a *little* fresh with my backside as she does. Then she undoes Carlyle's handcuffs.

"Ghost handcuffs," he sighs rubbing his wrists for a moment. And then he turns to the women.

"Pardon me, beautiful ladies." The women fall silent as they stare at my handsome companion. "Let me explain why we are here and why you should not drop us into the Dread Zone."

"You can stay," Mistress Fea tells Carlyle. Then she shrugs. "We'll just kill the girl."

"Me?"

"Not this tasty morsel," Roxanne says as she comes up to me and puts her arm around me. She spins me to her, lifts my face, and looks into my eyes. "I'll bet you're delicious, aren't you, sugar?"

"I do not know what you are saying."

"Just that I find you so... yummy," she growls the last word. "So, why don't we step into the bathroom over there, and you can give me a little taste."

This brings more giggling from the other women in the cell. Half of them are in love with Carlyle and the other half want to eat me alive. I am not trying to cause this, believe me.

"She does look delicious," Mistress Fea adds.

"Scrumptious," Roxanne answers. She is wearing a long white robe that is partially open so that I catch glimpses of her shapely figure and long, long legs.

These are all putas, I am sure. Many have said their crime is prostitution, and like all prostitutes, I imagine that they place more value on the money they charge for their services than for the sex they sell. This makes me wonder if I can bribe them with something they think is more valuable than sex. But what would that be?

Many women now begin reaching for Carlyle, running their hands over his body, occasionally grabbing and squeezing quite hard. He looks like someone who is about to be dragged underwater never to rise again. He pulls himself above this sea of women's hands, turns to me, and screams a silent, "Help!"

"Ladies, please," I say. "My friend and I would be happy to be your lovers."

"What?" Carlyle whispers at the top of his voice. "What are you saying, Alicia?"

"Of course we would, amigo," I answer boldly. "But perhaps there is something we could trade, Señoras, that you would like even better than our love."

Roxanne, the hungry ghost who wants to have me for supper, has already unzipped the back of my dress, and now she leans into me and whispers, "I don't think so, sugar."

I feel her fingers sneaking around under my dress. And for some reason I am curious as to where they want to go. It might not be too unpleasant.

"I will give you all of myself," I sigh to her. "But I may be able to offer you something more spectacular."

"You're saying there's something sweeter than this?" and her hand slides under my panties and pinches my bottom. I giggle. *Oh, my.*

"Of course there is," I sigh.

"What could it be?" Mistress Fea asks, and suddenly all her friends are asking the same question.

"*You* know exactly what it is you want," I tell them.

The other women are staring at me now. So is Carlyle.

Suddenly Mistress Fea's eyes brighten.

"You don't mean that you can get us...?"

"I do."

"We can have...." Roxanne suddenly zips up my dress and moves away from me.

"That's right. Say it, ladies," I command. "Tell us what you really want." (I have no idea what it is. But they all answer me in one word.)

"Movies."

"Not just any movie, of course," I dare to say.

"Our favorite."

"A copy for each of us."

"The ultimate chick flick," Roxanne says as she comes up to me and rubs my backside enthusiastically.

"That's right," I say to all of them, "a separate copy for every one of you."

Carlyle stares at me in unbelieving.

"Alicia, what the hell are you talking about?"

"It is simple, is it not?"

"No, it's not."

"But it is. These señoras will let us invade the dreams of Tiger Joy to find out where she is hiding Carlitos. And all we have to do is give each of them a DVD of their favorite movie."

"Right!" they all answer.

"Which has to be...."

"*Thelma And Louise!*" Roxanne and other ghosts shout in a united voice... but not all of them.

"<u>Ghost</u>," Mistress Fea says at the same time.

"*When Harry Met Sally*," say others. "*Sleepless in Seattle*," shout still more. "*The Philadelphia Story,*" add several others. "*Titanic.*"

WOW! I'm glad they told me. I never would have guessed.

"In Blu-ray," a new chorus begins. "Just regular DVD for me." "I still have VHS!" "Can I get the 50th Anniversary Edition?" I look at Carlyle with crossed eyes. Who knew it could be so complicated?

There is a shouting match going on in one corner of the cell. Roxanne and Mistress Fea are pulling each other's hair. Two fat old putas are slamming their ugly ghost bodies into each other, bouncing back and almost destroying the real furniture. I'm suddenly sorry I started all this. And that is when Carlyle August walks coolly into the middle of the battling putas, and smiles.

"Ladies, please," he says. "We will fill each and every one of your requests. Just form an orderly line and tell me what you want. I'll take detailed notes, and I'll give you each a receipt with my personal guarantee that you will all be satisfied."

"Or...." Mistress Fea demands.

"Or I'll give every disappointed customer a personal, patented Carlyle August *foot* massage."

I roll my eyes. Massaging the feet of some of these grimy ghosts will be most unpleasant. But then I know that Carlyle is some kind of hi-tech genius, and so I let him make his promises. In the end even nasty foot massaging is worth it if we can save Carlitos.

Chapter 7

Torquemada is the name of "The Best Used-CD-DVD-Record-&-Tape Store in Silicon Valley®." It is named unfortunately after the Grand Inquisitor who sentenced two thousand Jews and Muslims to be burned at the stake during the 15th Century. A Jew and a Muslim run the store together. And Assad Madani, one of Carlitos's best friends, is one of the owners.

I steal into his bedroom late that same night dressed in a casual pink plaid dress that is perfect for asking favors of a good friend. I sit in the corner and think of how long I have been away from my husband, which of course starts me crying, and my tears awaken not Assad, but his wife... Veronica. As you may know, she is one of the Joy sisters, and almost a victim of one of the worst crimes ever committed.

"Alicia," Veronica whispers. "What are you doing here? And why the tears?"

I do not really like Veronica because she is the sister of Amy Joy, the girl who wants to marry Carlitos and is my rival. Still, I answer her.

"I am crying because I have to ask you for a favor," I say sniffling back a nose full of tears.

Veronica has always been kind to me, and Assad has also been wonderful. Now she comes to me and gives me some tissues to wipe my eyes. And then she says, "Of course we'll help you. Let me wake my husband." And she puts both hands on her husband's shoulder and starts shaking him.

Without even opening his eyes, Assad jumps to his feet, swings back and forth, and punches the air, like he is a very unsuccessful Carlitos in the prize-fighting ring.

After a moment he stills, and Veronica, who I must admit is a very tender woman, comes up to her husband, puts her hand on his cheek, kisses him, has him open his eyes, and whispers, "It's all right, Assad. Alicia has come by because she needs our help tonight."

"I do," I say, and then I tell them the whole story ending with my need for a hundred copies of romantic comedies in every format imaginable as noted on a list made by Carlyle August.

"Blu-ray, 50th Anniversary Editions?" Assad asks. "So, we are dealing with high tech ghosts."

"Just very great fans," I answer.

"They are all wonderful movies," Veronica adds.

"Chick flicks," Assad groans as he shuffles into his slippers and out the door to his car. He is still wearing his blue and white striped pajamas, and even a little pointed cap on his head. The point flops over so that it hangs foolishly by his ear. But I think it is very cute.

Veronica wears a silken nightgown that is most glamorous; she pulls a wrap around her and comes out to the car too.

"I have to stay with little Carlos," she says. She is talking about her baby who is named after my husband.

"No worries," Assad answers as he starts his old Toyota. "I'll just run to the warehouse and gather up everything that Alicia needs. I'll be right back."

"Drive safely," Veronica says.

I hop in the car right beside Assad. "He will be fine," I tell her, "I'll take care of him." She smiles and nods, Assad blows her a kiss, and we are off.

#

Is it just bad luck or does someone know something of my plan?

34

I wonder this when Assad and I drive up to his warehouse in South San Francisco. A robbery is happening. Police are there, yellow tape is everywhere, and they won't even allow Assad near his own building.

While he argues with the policemen, I make myself invisible and go into the warehouse. Inside, a tired-looking detective is talking to two slight teenage boys who must have broken in and tried to rob the place.

I see that they are both Chinese, dressed in black slacks, turtlenecks, and designer tennis shoes. A little logo on their shirts gives them away. It is a small image of a Tiger's head baring its fangs. These are the employees of Tiger Joy. I know it. But I cannot understand how anyone could know what I am planning to do. And then I figure it out.

Tiger has her own ghost friends, and they are very powerful. Among them is Uncle Lum who founded the slave trading business in the 1850s. He called his family the Joy Lum Clan, and that is what they are still called today.

Uncle Lum is powerful enough to have heard of my visit to his niece's cell, even though Tiger was asleep at the time. He may also have heard of my talk with the ugly ghost-women, and my plan to get into Tiger's dreams. He does not want the prison ghosts to be on my side, so he will try to stop me from getting Blu-ray, DVD, VHS and 50th Anniversary copies and taking them back to the prison.

I look into the backpacks lying at the feet of the boys. They are stuffed with all the movies I have come for.

I want to grab the backpacks and disappear. Of course, the movies will not disappear. As I take them from the room, they will seem to be moving of their own power.

A little distraction is all that is required, I think... but how to do it?

At times like these I miss Carlitos so much. With his logic, he could figure out the best way to distract my enemies.

I try to be logical too:

The living are afraid of scary ghosts

All these people are living

So all I have to do is show them my scary ghost face, and they will run away

QED

I can do that, I am sure. But right now everyone is looking the other way. So, I simply grab the backpacks, and start flying toward the back door.

The quick movement of the backpacks catches the eye of the boys and the cops, and all of them start chasing me.

As a ghost I quickly pull away from them, race through the door and out into the open. I can see Assad's car in the distance. But suddenly a fat old Chinese gentleman appears right beside me. I recognize him at once as Tiger's Uncle Lum. Of course, he is still old and fat, and I have been a famous high school soccer star only a few years ago. So, I quickly leave him behind. But then something else happens that I did not expect. I hear a roar, and an enormous tiger-ghost begins chasing me.

This cat is vicious and faster than I am. I know this because its great paws are right behind me getting closer and closer. And then it takes a swipe at me with claws that are so huge that I can't believe them. Luckily I am a ghost and the claws pass right through me. But the backpacks are not ghosts and if the tiger catches one of them he will rip it open, probably making it impossible to fill the details of our order, and Carlyle will have some nasty feet to massage.

The tiger swipes at me again. I make a quick soccer move, feint left and turn right. The cat goes sprawling on its side.

Good. I cut away from it, but it is up on its big paws again and pounding after me.

"Assad!" I shout.

He sees me and rolls down his window.

"Open the car door."

"Which one?"

"Not yours. The other one!"

"The passenger side?"

"Yes!"

The tiger takes a great swipe at my heel and almost reaches through me and grabs one of the bags, but that is when I hurl the first bag way ahead of me and begin to run even faster.

The tiger roars. I kick the backpack just as Carlitos taught me to kick a soccer ball when I was a little girl. I send it flying, like one of my famous high school goals, right into the front seat of the car.

But that's when the tiger catches the strap of the second backpack.

I trip forward and manage to wrestle the backpack away from the tiger's claws, but the bag opens and the Blu-rays almost spill out. Still, I throw the other backpack in front of me, and – putting on a burst of my famous speed – I kick this backpack too. It flies high in the air, but one of the Blu-rays flies even higher. The tiger jumps, catches it and falls to the ground. It begins tearing the package apart.

I don't even look behind me. I merely catch the backpack, and rush with it into the front seat. Assad snatches it from me and throws the bag into the back.

"Let's get out of here," I shout as the tiger finishes tearing up Thelma and Louise, and begins charging after us again.

Assad floors it, and the car peels out. We drive away from the tiger, the warehouse, and the police who saw nothing more than a pair of backpacks flying out of the warehouse by themselves.

The cops and robbers also saw the packs jump into the car by themselves. They are now looking at the torn up Blu-ray, and wondering what could have destroyed it.

"Ghosts, maybe," one of the cops says to the others.

"Who believes in that shit?" one of the boys asks.

"No one," the other kid answers.

"Will my warehouse be haunted now?" Assad asks as we drive off. I try to explain what has happened. But I am so out of breath that it may not make any sense. Also I am very troubled that we will be returning with one less Blu-ray than we needed. I vow silently that I will perform the deadly foot massage on Roxanne or whoever demands it, and then I answer Assad's question.

"Perhaps your warehouse will be haunted," I say at last. "But only haunted by my friends, who will be your friends too. Anyway, I have to get back to the prison and find my way into the dreams of Tiger Joy."

"Very well," Assad says, though he is now even more shaken than I am.

"Please, let me out *right here*," I say.

"Along the side of the Bayshore Freeway?"

"It will be fine."

What a long night this has been. And it is not even over.

"Thank you again for your help, Assad," I say. "Give my love to Veronica."

The man is still very nervous. But he smiles at me.

"Good luck," he says.

I reach over and kiss him on the cheek.

"Everything will turn out well, trust me."

He nods. "For some crazy reason, I do," he says. Then he shakes his head and almost laughs.

I smile.

And then I am gone.

Chapter 8

We are sitting in a café in Paris, Carlyle August and I. Each of us has a glass of champagne and two small cookies, which also contain champagne. They taste delicious, and I am surprised that I can eat them. But then I see that I am not really tasting or eating... and this is not really Paris.

We are inside Tiger Joy's dream. All the inmates of the prison have their movies... the right titles in the right format and there are even a few left over.

"Contingency," Carlyle tells me, and I can only admire his planning skills. No foot massaging necessary for either of us.

The ghosts have retired to watch their favorite editions of their favorite films. Tiger is sleeping unprotected. And so we have entered her dreams.

I spot the evil woman sitting at a table in the far corner of the café. She is alone with her own champagne and cookies, and she looks so innocent. She is dressed in a thin flowery dress and a big hat and sunglasses. The skirt flirts with the breeze and allows her long legs to reveal themselves to every young man who walks by. The boys all turn their eyes to this summery girl and admire her. She giggles. She is having fun. And I have to ask, where is the evil bitch who captured Carlitos? Where are her high heel boots, latex skirts, and whips and chains?

"I'd like to talk to her," Carlyle says. "May I?"

"But she already talked to us this morning," I answer. "And she didn't want to tell us anything. Won't she remember that?"

39

"Hopefully not," he says. "It's a dream after all, and who knows what one remembers in dreams."

I am doubtful, but I think Carlyle looks so good in his blue French suit, that I have to say, "Go then."

And so he moves in on Tiger Joy and I can tell by the look in her eyes when she sees him that she does not remember the conversation we had this morning. What luck.

"Greetings, lovely Miss," Carlyle says as he makes his way up to Tiger. "How are you this fine day?"

She raises her sunglasses for just a minute to look at him.

"Très bien, merci," she answers.

"Going French then, are you?"

Tiger giggles. "Was it my pronunciation that gave me away?"

"Not at all. Your pronunciation is magnifique; your looks are magnifique. And your legs, Mademoiselle. May I say, 'Ooh là là!'?"

Tiger giggles, rocks forward in her chair and then back again.

"You're very gallant, monsieur."

"Et vous êtes très belle."

Carlyle is seducing Tiger with French words that I do not even understand. It makes me giggle.

"Merci." Tiger answers and blushes.

Now, young gentlemen are giving *me* the eye, walking slowly by me and then by me again, smiling, flirting; it makes me angry because I am supposed to focus on Tiger. Soon, my anger shows in my eyes, and the young gentlemen all disappear very quickly.

"May I know your name?" Carlyle asks.

"Helen Joy," Tiger answers with a smile.

"Miss Joy," I like that. "Is that what you bring to the lives of your friends?"

Tiger is falling for all this romantic nonsense, and I cannot believe it.

"I like to think that I bring people joy," she says.

I want to gag.

"I'm Carlyle August."

Tiger stops cold as though she suddenly does remember him and this morning's conversation.

"Haven't we met recently?" she asks.

"I'm certain I would remember someone as lovely as you," Carlyle sighs. "But you may know me by reputation."

"The famous Silicon Valley entrepreneur?"

"That's me."

"Wait! Didn't you die in a car accident or something?"

"Would I be here talking to you if I had? That was my brother."

"Oh, of course."

She takes a sip of champagne and flutters those long eyelashes at him.

"But why are we talking about me?" Carlyle asks. "Tell me something about yourself."

"Just an American girl in Paris."

"And your hometown is...."

"San Francisco."

"Chinatown? Were you Miss Chinatown?"

"Hardly."

"You could have been... probably *should* have been."

Tiger lowers her eyes modestly, and now I want to scream. She is playing the sweetheart. And it seems so wrong to me. I am about to stand, run up to both of them, and shout, "Where are you hiding my husband, you bitch?" But then I think of my anger management counselor, the ghost of Dr. Sigmund Freud, and I control my temper... for now.

"Let me see if I can guess your profession," Carlyle says.

Before Tiger can say "no," he guesses. "You are a professional model, right?"

Tiger giggles, "No."

"Not high fashion... bikinis, lingerie?

Tiger smiles. "Thank you, but no."

"Oh, but you could, you know," Carlyle says. "You have the figure for it."

"I'm a professional woman."

"Of course, a bank manger?"

She shakes her head.

Now, Carlyle is leaning in toward her, making her feel very special, I think.

"Software engineer?"

"Guess again, silly boy."

"I'll go out on a limb and guess that you're the CFO of a high tech start-up."

Tiger crosses her legs and that wind plays with her skirt again, lifts it up so high that I can see that she is wearing thigh high silk stockings, the kind that turn all men into guacamole.

Carlyle August turns red.

"You're getting close," Tiger says.

"You're a CEO?"

"Chief Executive of the Joy Lum Family Association."

Carlyle slides his chair even closer to my enemy.

"A social club?"

"A billion dollar corporation."

"You run a billion dollar corporation?"

Tiger takes off her big floppy hat, and her sunglasses so she can look more closely at my friend. "Seem impossible?"

"Of course not. You could be a very powerful chief executive." He gives her a silly curious smile. "What's your product?"

"Joy," Tiger answers with pride.

"Joy?"

"The kind you receive from a beautiful woman."

Carlyle's eyes drift back and forth as if between two different choices. "That means you're either a matchmaker or...."

"Let's call it matchmaking," Tiger says. "We find eligible young girls in China and pair them up with interested men."

"For the purpose of..."

"Matrimony, of course."

Carlyle looks relieved. He wraps his arm around the back of Tiger's chair. She does not pull away. Instead, she smiles slyly.

"Or anything else our clients want." Tiger turns her face toward Carlyle and her lips are no more than inches from his.

Carlyle swallows hard. "What else would your clients want?" he asks nervously.

Tiger pauses; their lips are almost touching now.

"Submissive or dominant partners, mistresses or love slaves."

"You train them?"

"We offer the finest education of its kind in the world."

Carlyle pulls back and stares at her, even though he knows all of this.

Tiger puffs up her chest with pride and the sight is amazing since Tiger's chest is already puffed up with silicone and implants.

"But how did a sweet girl like you...."

"Get to be the CEO?"

Carlyle nods like a little puppy.

"The business was almost destroyed several times and the leaders were murdered. Finally, I was next in line, and I was able to restore our credit, our reputation, and our profitability."

Tiger does look like a CEO as she rattles off these words.

Carlyle takes a sip of champagne and smiles. "I find you most impressive, Helen."

"Call me Tiger."

"All right then, but are you really a tiger... when, for example, you have to deal with your enemies?"

Tiger is smiling. But her eyes narrow and her lips pull into a hard line when she says, "I can be more than a tiger. I can be a real *bitch*!"

Carlyle looks as though he is suddenly thrilled. "I find this all incredibly exciting," he says as he pulls even closer to her. Now, their knees are touching. Their hands are very close. He is giving her a hungry look as if he just has to know just how much of a bitch she can really be.

"Give me an example," he says.

Tiger leans in and takes his hand.

"There's a man," she says as she turns his palm up and massages it with her thumb. "He's my archenemy. He's responsible for the death of my mother and father at the hands of some hideous federal agents."

Carlyle's look shows such concern, as though he is feeling very sorry for her loss.

"I've tried to capture him for years. Finally, I trapped him. And now that I have him, I'm going to make him *suffer* terribly... before I have him executed."

Tiger still wears that sweet summery dress. The big hat is sitting beside her on the table. So are the sunglasses. The champagne is nearby. But she is not the same woman any more. Her eyes tell me that inside she is a complete monster. But Carlyle looks as though he is thrilled with this new Tiger Joy. "Tell me more," he breathes.

Tiger says, "I needed to send him somewhere, a place where no one would ever be able to find him. Somewhere where there are few laws to control the kind of torture I can inflict."

"Mmmm," Carlyle says as if he is a great fan of torture. "Brainwashing, waterboarding, whips and chains?"

Tiger's eyes light up as though she is so very proud of what she has done.

"Better than any of that," she says. "I sent him into the depths of Quintana Roo, to the home of one of the great witches of the world, who will drive him mad with her witchcraft... before she finally makes him destroy himself."

2
Carlos

Chapter 9

I wake up, and the first thing that comes crashing down on me is that I've failed... botched the entire job. I set out to rid the world of Tiger Joy, and instead she's gotten rid of me!

I had it all planned out before hand, all the way down to the snapping of Tiger's neck. I just never realized that Tiger could win over the guards so completely. Never realized that she would see me coming and be ready.

Amy warned me, told me exactly the kind of lifestyle Tiger had set up for herself in prison: the Executive Suite at the Chowchilla Correctional Facility. So now I'm M.I.A., probably so far out of sight that....

There's a wicked hissing coming from a corner of whatever hole Tiger's buried me in. Truth is, I haven't even raised my eyes to look around.

My head pounds with the fact that I've failed, didn't get the job done, and in the process got myself captured. I may never see Alicia again.

Hissing...

It slithers into my consciousness like some overzealous python.

My eyes jump to the far corner of the room, barely registering the slimy bars of the cage that holds me. I'm looking out over the muddy floor in some kind of cave, over pools of blood and what look like the stubs of fingers hacked off and scattered everywhere in the slime.

The vision is terrible and there's a deadly sick smell to go with it, but it's mixed somehow with the sweetness of flowers.

HISSING!

In the far corner of the room there's an archway that leads to a tunnel... a way out. But filling it completely is a churning tangle of enormous black water snakes.

I hear another hiss, but this isn't from any snake I've ever heard. It's more like a sucking sound coming from the opposite corner. I turn and see two slim, sinister young men crouching against the far wall in the darkness. They look like they'd be ready to slit my throat on the slightest whim of their bitch goddess, Tiger Joy. And then, they both start giggling, they roll over laughing, and they can't stop. It's as if their laughter will strangle them if they can't catch their breath, but unfortunately they do.

They're passing a joint back and forth. That sucking sound is really their deep drags on the joint. One of them slaps the other on the thigh, struggles to his feet and then slumps back down into the lotus position. The other giggles and does pretty much the same. They're stoned out of their minds.

They sense my awareness, raise their eyes to me, and give me that blank, heartless stare... tempered only by the silly grins that soon return to their faces. I still can't lower my guard though. Just because they're wasted doesn't mean that they're not as deadly as the snakes.

I look around the rest of the cave. To the far left of the tangled snakes are statues of religious figures: the Virgin Mary, Santa Theresa, but outnumbering them by far are statues of some ancient Maya goddess... a crazy mix of Catholicism and dark native spirituality.

There are bowls full of blood in front of the statues. Individual severed fingers stand upright in some of them. I can make out a bloody heart in one of the larger bowls, and to my horror I start to think that it's maybe a human heart. The thought sets off a terrible idea: that there are other body parts floating among the deadly offerings? I'm sure there are: an ear, a woman's breast, a liver, some toes, a penis, a brain! My eyes search the scene, scan the statues, all the puddles of blood, all the bowls filled with severed body parts that stand as offerings before saints who never wanted such sacrifices. I start to catalog them in my mind until I realize what I am doing and start to feel so dizzy. I close my eyes... press my eyelids tightly together, and when I do the smell of the place begins to overwhelm me. It's putrid. The stench of rotting flesh combines with snake shit. The only thing that makes it all somewhat bearable is the scent of the weed hovering over everything... and that sweetness of fresh cut flowers that tries to overwhelm the ugliness of it all.

I lower my head, put my hands to my eyes, and hold them there. The smell of flowers is even more intense when I turn to the left, and so I do, and through my opening fingers I see a monstrous statue of a woman, tall, dressed in white lace robes with a garland around her head and a death mask for a face. She's holding a sythe. Smaller statues of the same woman are all around her. The statues of the saints are interspersed with these terrifying forms. And then I see the flowers... fresh cut, scattered almost everywhere on this side of the cave: in pots, in vases, in coffee cans, strewn freely across the muddy floor. Here, their sweet scent mingles terribly with the smell of the blood that's pooling in the cups and bowls in front of the great figure. Cut-off fingers and toes are even more numerous on the ground before this monster. Directly in front of her, there's a mound of them, and I know who she's supposed to be: the ancient Maya goddess, MICTECACIHUATL, Queen of the Land of the Dead.

I reach forward and take hold of the slimy cell bars and try to figure how long this cage has been here. Centuries? Even longer? Is this where Tiger's decided to have me executed?

I'm not much for talking to myself, but it seems that this is the time for some kind of pow-wow. Tiger has sent me here to be punished for trying to murder her. She wants me worked over by whatever sick fuck inhabits this place. Something tells me it's a tall, death-faced woman who looks just like Mictecacihuatl, that eight-foot monster outside my cell.

I think about Alicia and immediately realize that I have to escape, if only to be able to see her again.

Something tells me that if I die down here, I won't see her in the next life either... not for planning a murder. That's as big a sin as doing it. But I do have a chance, I realize. If I can stay alive, Alicia will find me and rescue me again. She's done it before. Of course, she always takes her own sweet time about it. I know that. But it's still well worth it when she does come through.

So, I have to stay strong, be willing to put up with a lot of nasty shit, survive no matter what until Alicia finds me.

My wife is nothing if not resourceful. And she's got the whole damn ghost network to help her. The thought gives me new confidence. Get tough, survive, and be ready for the big getaway.

I look through the cell bars, at the tangle of water snakes, at the stoner tough guys Tiger has sent to keep an eye on me, at the terrifying statues surrounded by pools of blood. In spite of all that, I start to think, "Yes, I can handle this. I can make it."

And then I hear humming.

Chapter 10

A woman's voice is crooning an old melody that I seem to know very well.

It's been tucked away in the back of my mind for as long as I can remember. The humming is sweet, almost hypnotic. I move, almost in slow motion, turn around so that I'm looking at a part of the cave that I've never seen before. And what I find there stops me cold.

There's an enormous black cauldron suspended over a fire pit. Directly above it, a narrow chimney must run a thousand feet up to the jungle above us. The chimney's probably there to allow the smoke to escape, but its effect right now is to focus a sharp beam of light directly onto the cauldron giving its tarry surface a sparkle as though there are real diamonds embedded in the gritty muck along its rim.

Stepping out from behind the big dark pot is an old woman wearing the same ugly clothes as the statue of Mictecacihuatl. Her face is just like the statue's too: deathlike, a centuries-old nearly bald head with dead-white skin and purple-gray blood vessels zigzagging across her temples and forehead. Her hair is so sparse that I can see bugs crawling over her scalp. Her lips are paper thin, and yet they smile at me as she begins to sing to me in Spanish. The words match the melody that she was humming, and I can't believe my ears.

You're my little baby
You're my little boy

You're my little grandson
The treasure of my world
When you're sick and tired
And you begin to cry
Dziadzio will sing to you
His Polska lullaby.

The words, as I say, are in Spanish except for two of them: Dziadzio and Polska. I have no idea what the first word means but the second is pretty damn obvious. So's the conclusion I have to draw. Here (wherever the hell I am) in a cave where Christian and Maya icons mix, this ancient witch-woman is crooning a Polish Lullaby... in Spanish.

"Mancowski," the ancient woman teases, "odd name for a Chicano boy, dontcha think?"

She leans forward and I see that her skin is pulled so tightly over her scalp that she has more of a skeleton head than a face.

"How come you have a name like Mancowski, boy?" the creature asks. "Down here in Quintana Roo, how come you have that name?"

This woman's breath smells like a rotting corpse in a moldy coffin. She has worked her way around to the other side of my cage, and now I can see the enormous statue standing right behind her. They look almost identical.

"Yer name, boy," the death-faced woman cackles. "Where'd it come from?"

I'm stunned. Instead of being able to speak, all I can do is slouch down and shrug.

"I see," she says as she studies me with eyes that are far too bright for the death-whiteness of her face. "All right then." And she scuttles behind the huge statue and out of sight.

God, what a trip this is. Distractedly, I glance around the cave picking up snatches of details: snakes, cauldron, statues, flowers, blood, and bad guys.

A black cat darts out from near the snake pit and runs into the shadows behind the great statue. It's gone for only a beat before it returns leading the old woman who is now lugging a five-foot square mirror framed in dark wood. She drags it to the edge of my cage and then forces it through the bars, tipping it back against them so that it's looking up at me.

The wood frame is carved into the shape of the water snakes that are wriggling around in the pond across from my cell.

"Have a peek here, boy," the woman cackles, "and see if this will loosen your tongue."

This creature sounds like a witch, and whether she is one or not, she's sure acting like one. As the black cat begins to twine itself around her legs, a syllogism starts forming in my mind:

If she acts like a witch,
And talks like a witch,
Has a black cat,
And a black cauldron,
Then maybe she is a witch.

Maybe, but that's no syllogism, is it? Some part of the proof is missing.

I turn to the mirror and then jump away from it. Over the edges of the frame, the carved snakes have come to life and are writhing around just like the live ones in the pit.

"Look into my mirror, boy," the old woman cackles.

So, I do.

The face of the mirror is cloudy, as though its backing has faded so completely that it barely reflects anything at all. But then it begins to clear, and there's an image there.

It's a young man. He's wearing a rather battered wool suit, standing at what looks like a blackboard. As he steps forward I can see that he's in a classroom. About a half dozen high-school-age students sit at uncomfortable desks looking at him. Every one of them looks frightened. A round-faced boy is gnawing on a pencil way too enthusiastically. A girl with white-blond hair in pigtails has pushed herself back hard against her chair and her eyes are wide with surprise. A pimply boy is trying hard not to look up; he's scratching at his desk with the point of his pen. He holds it like a knife, and his scratches leave deep zigzag pattern in the surface. The teacher looks scared. His words are slow, barely audible, but determined. Suddenly, there's a pounding at the classroom door. Gloved hands push it open, and members of what look like the Nazi SS step into the room. The teacher turns immediately and in three long strides he dives through the open window. The students stand in a group and try to block the police from getting to him. The Nazis muscle them out of the way. The pencil chewer is belted with the butt end of a rifle. The towheaded girl is thrown against the far wall where she slams her head and slouches to the floor. The Nazis are firing out the window.

I turn to the witch. She's standing just outside the cell, studying the look on my face, smiling, and still humming, only now it's a frightening tune, something that goes very well with the scene I've been watching.

I turn back to the mirror. Now the young man is running through darkening city streets. Guns blast all around him. Rushing SS are not too far behind. I can hear them. Bombs fall, blowing out whole sections of the road on which he's running. The guy ducks into a doorway that's set into a solid wall of houses; my eyes follow him as he rushes through dark hallways, almost into total blackness.

"Chod tutaj," someone whispers. The guy hears it and turns.

An interior door opens, he moves through it, and the door closes behind him.

Inside, three people are sitting around a table: a very old couple and a young woman who looks remarkably like the young teacher.

"Conrad, musisz wyj wieczorem," the girl says.

I don't understand her words but I can see that they upset the teacher, Conrad. He shakes his head as if to say, "Hell no!"

But then the old man grabs him by the arm.

"Musisz," the old guy says.

The girl pulls a bundle from the corner and hands it to Conrad. He takes it, trying desperately to choke back his emotions.

"Wróc do ciebie," he murmurs.

The others nod. There's an oh-so-brief glimmer of hope in their eyes. It ends when a massive explosion rocks the outside of the building.

"Id teraz!" the old woman says as she shoos the boy away with her hands. He staggers backward shaking his head, and then he seems to give up. He steps back to the table, hugs each one of them, tosses the bundle on his shoulders, and rushes out the door, whispering once again, "Wróc do ciebie."

I stare at the mirror saddened by the scene I've just watched, but still wondering what any of this has to do with me.

"That was your great grandfather, escaping from the Nazis just after they'd taken Poland," the old woman of the cave tells me.

"What were they saying?"

"Wróc do ciebie," she answers. "I'll come back for you." Then she smiles, but this smile gets more and more witchy.

"Of course, he never did come back to save them. The Nazis targeted Conrad because he was a teacher, the leader of an opposition cell that formed even before the Germans had conquered Poland. He had to get out of the country before they found him and executed him... and everyone he knew. He was saving not only himself, but also his compadres. You saw him promise his father, mother, and sister that he would come back to save them. Of course, return became impossible. The three of them eventually died in concentration camps.

"Now, Dr. Mancowski," she says with a cruel smile, "you will soon have the same terrible realization that Conrad's family had as they were worked to death in the Nazi prison camps."

"What's that?" I dare to ask, even though I know.

"*No one is going to come back to save you either*... no one living or dead."

She begins to cackle wickedly, and as she does the snakes that frame her dark mirror come to life again and begin to glide around it.

I fall back against the far wall of the cell and stare at the monstrous woman.

"Just who are you?" I ask.

She smiles, bats her eyes as coquettishly as an ancient woman possibly can, "La Bruja."

Need I really translate that one? "Bruja" is the Spanish word for witch.

I lower myself to the dirt floor of my cell.

Is that what all this is about, that I'm her prisoner, and there's no way that I can be rescued?

La Bruja turns and hobbles off into the shadows, and her cat follows.

I close my eyes and recognize that my obsessive-compulsive disorder is kicking in. I decide that I need to know exactly how many bars there are in my cage. Also, better figure out how many snakes are in the pit over there, how many statues, how many stumps of fingers, how many bowls of blood.

I'm so damn tired. But somehow I need to start counting.

Chapter 11

Before I can double-check my count of the number of lopped-off fingers that are scattered across the floor of the cave, the witch's mirror begins singing to me... or at least someone in the mirror's reflection begins to sing the same words the old witch was singing.

You're my little baby

You're my little boy

You're my little grandson...

But the singer is an old man with a decidedly Polish accent.

Now, I'm an infant, I think, inside the mirror. The kid is me.

I see strong hands holding me carefully as we move through the evening streets together. The small Main Street shops of the village look like a place I visited only last year, where we fought a great gun-battle. That was the city of Tizimin, a city that may not be too far from this very cave. I can't really tell. All I know is that, in the mirror's image, I'm being carried through the streets on a warm summer night, and the man who is carrying me has great, strong hands, and he's singing that Polish lullaby.

I get blurry infant's images of the golden sunset reflecting off storefront windows as we pass by them. The man is bouncing me up and down, nodding and smiling to people as we pass: a pretty young woman in an old-fashioned hat, a young man wearing military gear, an elderly couple walking ever so slowly.

"What a sweet baby," the old woman sighs.

Everyone's smiling and nodding as we go, but the man keeps singing, even louder now as though he wants the world to know that I'm his little grandson.

And then I jump and start crying loudly. I've heard a shot.

The man jerks. His smile falters. He drops to one knee, reaches behind his head with one hand while he holds me with the other. When he pulls his hand in front of our faces, his fingers are covered with blood. Still, he keeps on singing.

When you're sick and tired...

And you begin to cry...

Now the words come much slower and with far greater effort.

Dziadzio... will... sing... to... you... his... Polish...

The man lowers me to the ground gently. I hear another shot, and start crying even louder as he falls face down on the earth beside me.

There's screaming everywhere.

"Dziadzio, Dziadzio," I hear a young girl's voice calling. She runs up to us, looks at the man, then at me, and then she gathers me up.

"Oh no, Carlitos," she sobs. "Oh, no!" And now she's the one running through the streets carrying me and screaming over and over again, "Dziadzio is dead, Grandfather is dead."

Inside the witch's cave I stare into the mirror in disbelief. I remember the moment when my grandfather died. I remember the scene. How old was I, six weeks? It seems improbable, but it's true. I remember being carried away by my Aunt Teresa only seconds after my grandfather was gunned down on the streets of Tizimin nearly thirty years ago.

Chapter 12

The mirror now shows me the interior of a waterfront bar. It's more than alive. Everyone is shouting, partying, and generally raising hell. The language is rough; so's the clientele: tough guys... girls who are even tougher. Everyone is crowding up to the bar, waving money at the bartender. There's dancing and groping everywhere, especially on the small dance floor behind a half dozen tables crammed with couples. At a pool table in the far corner, a few sailors are alternately playing pool, grabbing drinks, and feeling up the girls.

The clothing looks like something out of a '40s war movie. The music is big band swing. Most of the men are in uniform, but only a few are Americans.

One of the girls at the bar (I hear someone call her Rosalie) is flirting shamelessly with the little guy next to her. She has short-cropped brunette hair, heavy make up, lots of eye shadow, a birthmark (probably penciled in) on her upper lip. But – underneath it all – there's a very sweet face. The little guy wears a white t-shirt with a black vest and matching slacks. He has a pack of cigarettes rolled up in his sleeve. The guy on the other side of Rosalie doesn't like the way she's eyeing the little guy, even though he's been buying her drinks all evening.

Now, the big guy turns and says something to her; she laughs and goes back to flirting with the little guy. The big guy spreads a wad of cash in front of Rosalie. She turns and smiles at him. Her look is very encouraging... way too encouraging for the little guy, especially when the big guy reaches over and starts grabbing at her.

That's it! The little guy motions for Rosalie to step away, and then he starts giving the big guy a ration of shit. The big guy responds by poking his finger at the little guy, stabbing it into his chest over and over again. Rosalie clearly knows when to get out of the way; she scrambles out the door as the little guy reaches over the bar, grabs a bottle, stands, and smashes it against a nearby tabletop. He's very short but broad shouldered, and he holds the broken bottle like a butcher knife.

"Je vais vous tuer, vous merde!"

Right. They're French. The whole damn place is French. But, as I say, there are also British and American servicemen and even (for reasons that I have yet to figure out) quite a few Mexicans. Everyone is young and rugged looking. The girls look like they're mostly hookers who've dropped in to work the place.

Way in the far corner, I spot Conrad, looking as he did in my earlier visions of the bombed out streets. He's trying to be as inconspicuous as possible, which I guess is how he's managed to stay one jump ahead of the Nazi SS, escape from war-torn Poland, flee all the way across Germany and France, and somehow end up in a bar in some French seaport town, where a ship is soon leaving for Mexico.

The little guy with the broken bottle lunges at his opponent, who deftly sidesteps the attack, yanks the bottle from the little guy's hand, spins him around, and presses the broken glass to his throat. The little guy struggles, but the big man has him in a death grip, and it's clear that he's about to slit the little guy's throat.

"I wouldn't do that if I were you," comes an American voice that's almost too John Wayne to be real. The big guy with the bottle doesn't let go, so the American just lifts the little guy off the ground and spins both of them around so that he and his victim are facing maybe four or five American soldiers.

"What's it to you, Yank?" the guy with the bottle asks through a thick French accent.

"He's little, you're not. You grabbed his girl. He defended her honor. Seems unfair that you should kill him."

The Frenchman laughs, "There are five of you, mon ami, but the bar is full of Frenchmen. Are you sure you want to meddle?"

"I'm sure," the American soldier says.

"Okay then," and the Frenchman deftly slits the little guy's throat and pushes the bleeding body toward the Americans.

All hell breaks loose.

The place is packed with Frenchmen who now defend their fellow countryman. Glass breaks, women squeal, chairs fly up into the air and come crashing down on heads. Guys fall to the ground unconscious.

It isn't clear whose side the Mexicans are on, but they're in the fight just the same.

The one person not fighting is Conrad. He lays low in the back of the room, not necessarily wanting to stay out of the fight as much as to take advantage of it.

At this point half the bar patrons are down, and the other half are fighting even more wildly. Whores pound the hell out of each other. Then comes Conrad's golden opportunity. A Mexican guy is clocked in the head by the back of a chair and is sent sprawling unconsciously at Conrad's feet. Conrad is on him in a second, digging into his shirt pocket, pulling out his papers and his boat ticket.

One of the Mexican's friends sees what's happening and moves in on Conrad. But Conrad has the papers now, and he's up and on his feet spinning through the crowd, throwing punches, and smashing chairs as he needs to. Just as he gets to the door a chubby whore in a laced red corset steps in front of him.

"It is not too late for us, Monsieur."

"Sorry, no," he says as he tips his hat, gives her a slight shove in the other direction, and heads out the door just as the Mexican's friends come raging after him.

Conrad runs damn fast, I think. He cuts through the narrow streets and then jumps headlong down onto the docks. He finds a shadowy place behind some barrels. He crouches down and holds his breath. The Mexican's friends come running after him, but they didn't see him hide. So, they stop and begin rummaging around on the dock.

"If we don't find the guy," one of them shouts to the others, "Jose's stuck here forever. The Nazis already run the place. If he doesn't get out now, he's in some very deep shit."

The Mexicans pound through the dock upsetting barrels and shouting at Conrad wherever he is, "Get your ass out here, motherfucker!"

Conrad stays put. Prays. In the end they don't discover his hiding place. They give up. But as they leave, one of the Mexicans turns and shouts a warning:

"We'll find you, and we'll kill you! Got it, gringo?"

They don't find him that night or on the ship. They don't find him for many, many years. But they do find him eventually... as he's carrying his grandson through the streets of Tizimin... and they shoot him dead.

Chapter 13

As I said, the mirror shows me that the Mexicans don't find Conrad on the ship, but they do make the first part of his voyage a living hell. Jose's friends are constantly after him. The stolen papers get Conrad onto the ship, but he has to hide out through the entire voyage. He can't share passage with Jose's friends. They all want him dead. As it is, whenever Conrad needs to make any move at all, he sees them out there... watching for him.

On the tenth day out, Conrad is nearly starving to death. He's been living off scraps from room service trays and leftovers dumped into trashcans. He grabs them in quick bursts for those few seconds when no one seems to be looking. But now, Jose's gang comes prowling through the hold of the ship, and they flush him out of his hiding place. Conrad somehow avoids them and makes it onto the deck. But there he runs into crewmembers who have agreed to help track him down.

Jose's friends have gotten to the ship's captain, and Conrad is now officially listed as a stowaway. The captain puts the sergeant-at-arms in charge of finding him. The guy's tall, squarely built with an ugly scar-mangled face and a raspy voice to match. His name is Ed Squinkly, I learn from the conversation. Perfect name for the guy, huh?

Conrad's on deck, trying to play it cool as he moves toward the crew. He figures that they know he has papers and a legitimate right to be on the ship. The five crewmembers walking toward him smile and nod, but Squinkly's among them and his smile turns sour.

"That's the stowaway!" he shouts. "Get the son of a bitch!"

As they rush toward him, Conrad sees an open doorway with a big gilded sign above. It screams out one word: EXCLUSIVE! Sounds good to him, so he swings into the doorway and races into the unknown.

Conrad now finds himself in the hallway that leads to the luxury suites. But Squinkly and his troops come pounding in after him anyway. Then Jose's gang blasts through the doorway at the opposite end of the hall. Conrad's trapped. There's nowhere to go. He ducks into a dead-end passageway off the main corridor and begins trying to open the stateroom doors. They're all locked. But just as the bad guys are closing in on him, one of the doors does open, and he bolts inside, spins around, and locks the door behind him.

When Conrad turns back to the suite, he's amazed at just how luxurious it really is: enormous, with a huge bed, complete kitchen, dining area, sitting room, and a monster closet taking up one entire wall. There's also a private bathroom off the main cabin. Steam billows out of the half-opened doorway.

Conrad hears the bad guys tromping through the hallway outside, missing him, he hopes. He also hears bathwater running. It smells sweet, of jasmine and lilacs. He hears someone moving within the bath, and then, coming out through the steam, wrapped in a silk robe that makes her look like an angel on a holy card, is a sweet, graceful young woman. She's small. Her features are fine; her lips are smiling gaily; she's humming. And then something squawks:

"¡Usted es hermosa!"

"Why thank you," the woman giggles.

"I didn't say anything," Conrad blurts out in surprise.

The woman turns and sees him standing just inside the doorway; she freezes, but seems more confused than threatened. Conrad shrugs and tries to smile.

"I didn't say anything," he repeats.

"No, sir, you did not. I was talking to Pancho."

Another squawk. *"¡Usted es hermosa!"*

Conrad turns toward the kitchen area and now sees a huge multi-colored macaw strutting out across the kitchen counter top. The bird turns to Conrad and calls:

"¡Eres muy feo!"

Conrad turns back to the woman for a translation, and she starts to laugh out loud.

"Pancho says, 'you are NOT beautiful, Señor.'"

"No doubt about that," Conrad answers as the young woman focuses her attention fully on him.

"Are you here to deliver a package?" she asks. "Have you brought something for me?" Her tone is still far sweeter than Conrad thinks it should be.

"I have brought... myself?" he answers with a crooked grin.

"I see." The young woman doesn't stop smiling; in fact, she starts giggling again. "And just who is yourself?"

Conrad decides to skip the formalities. "Please help me. They're after me; they want to kill me."

The young woman now looks concerned, but her voice is still so gentle.

"They?"

"Friends of some guy named Jose Perez. I took his papers, had to; the Nazis have chased me all the way from Poland."

"The Nazis want to kill you?"

"I'm sure of it."

The young woman walks into the sitting area and lowers herself onto the sofa. The bird meanwhile struts back into the kitchen area and out of sight. *"¡No confiar en él!"* it caws. "Don't you dare trust him."

The young woman looks concerned, but still very confident.

"I'm sorry, but you can't stay here."

"Just for a few minutes. They're outside in the hallway right now."

The woman shakes her head and is about to say "no," when there's a not-too-polite knocking on the door.

Conrad raises his hands prayerfully. She smiles, turns toward the closet, slides open the door, and gestures for Conrad to enter it. As she does she holds one finger to her lips "Shhhh."

Conrad obeys.

The young woman goes to the cabin door and softly asks, "Who is it?"

"Sergeant-at-arms, Ma'am."

She answers without opening the door. "Yes?"

"We're looking for a stowaway, need to search your cabin."

She opens the door a crack, keeping the chain-lock in place, and peers carefully out into the hallway. Ed Squinkly stands there trying to look apologetic. Four crewmembers cluster behind him.

"There's no stowaway here," she says.

"We're required to search every room, Miss."

"Do you really think I would let a stranger into my room?"

"We have to check. Sorry."

"Not my room." Her eyes flash in a moment of challenge.

"I'm sorry, Miss Cordoba, but...."

"Please. I don't mean to be difficult, but I've had a very trying day. I've just drawn a bath. It's already getting cold. I'm tired. I need my privacy."

"*¡Usted es hermosa!*" The bird calls suddenly from the kitchen.

Squinkly's face twists into a confused frown. "And just who was that?"

"My pet macaw, Pancho Villa."

"Funny name for a bird belonging to a woman as high born as you are, Miss," Squinkly says.

"Pancho," the young woman calls, and the bird comes flapping through the air and lands gently on her shoulder. It takes one look at Squinkly and squawks. "*¡Eres muy feo!*"

Squinkly looks flustered for a moment and then pushes his foot into the doorway preventing the young woman from closing it. "Bird or no bird, Miss, we need to search your stateroom."

"No, Captain."

"I'm not a captain, just..."

"You seem like someone with a great deal of authority." She smiles sweetly. "I respect that, Mr. Squinkly."

The sergeant-at-arms blushes. "You know my name?"

"From the orientation. I was comforted by your brave assurance to all the passengers."

Squinkly twists back and forth on his heels like a little boy. "That's why we have to...."

"Mr. Squinkly, I give you my word. There is no stowaway in my room."

The sergeant-at-arms looks at the other men, then back to the young woman as she continues. "The ship's crew has been so kind to me. Please offer me this one added courtesy."

Her eyes beg for understanding. Squinkly melts. So do the rest of the crew.

"Of course, Miss Cordoba. Pardon our intrusion." He pulls his foot out of the doorway.

She nods to the crewmen, closes her door, and locks it again.

"*¡Usted es hermosa!*" Pancho Villa chirps.

Chapter 14

In my cell in the witch's cave, I see that the candlelight is dimming. The enormous statue of Mictecacihuatl still glowers down on me. The bowlfuls of blood still stink. The dismembered fingers still rot. The snakes still writhe in their slimy mud hole, but they keep their distance from me at least. Tiger's two sinister tough guys have passed out from their weed, and I feel like filing a complaint with their mistress. If they're here to keep an eye on me, they're doing a really shitty job of it. Of course, I have no way to contact Tiger, so I can't let her know. Still, it would be fun to see the kind of punishment she'd send their way... probably far milder than what she and La Bruja have cooked up for me.

The witch is out of sight, so's her cat. Still, I know she'll be around soon enough. The firewood under her cauldron is ready to light. All she has to do is strike a match, or maybe just flash a little lightning from her fingertips. The cauldron will begin to bubble, and the deadly spells will start.

In the meantime, the mirror keeps churning out the story of my grandfather and his encounter with this lovely young woman onboard a passenger liner heading for Mexico. I'm thinking that it's better to focus on that than to do another obsessive count of all the hacked off fingers and bloody bowls on the floor of the cave.

• • • • •

"I'm Conrad Mancowski," my grandfather says holding out his hand to the young woman who has probably just saved his life. He's emerging from her closet.

"Eva Cordoba," she answers as she reaches out, takes his hand, and shakes it. He notices that it's trembling a little.

The name is far more of a shock to me than it was to my grandfather since I know that it's the name of the woman who has recently married Alicia's mentor, Fernando de Cervantes (or Señor Popcorn as we like to call him). This may be his wife's great grandmother.

Conrad looks like he's about twenty-one now. Eva could be thirty maybe... an older woman.

"And what am I going to do with this... Conrad?" she calls to her macaw with a smirk.

"*¡Viva la revolutión,*" Pancho answers.

"Save my life," my grandfather adds.

"You want me to be Joan of Arc?"

"Maybe Florence Nightingale?"

"*¡Usted es hermosa!*"

"Quiet, Pancho," Eva tells her bird. Then she turns back to Conrad, "You think I'm as kindhearted as Florence Nightingale?"

"Generous, anyway. You've already proven that."

Eva moves to the couch and takes a seat. Conrad comes toward her but doesn't sit. He's keeping his distance. Pancho flies back into the kitchen.

"Okay. So, say I *do* want to be generous with you," she says as she tosses her long black hair gracefully behind her. "When will you be able to leave my cabin?"

"To be safe, I'd say just before we're ready to dock."

Suddenly, a glass flips up into the air from the edge of the kitchen counter. It spills seltzer water all over the luxurious carpet. Conrad looks at Eva in surprise. "Was that Pancho?"

"He's back in his cage."

"Who then, or does your glassware just fly around on its own?"

"It's my grandmother," Eva answers.

"Your grandmother's here too?"

"My chaperone."

"But you just told the sailors that...."

"She's a ghost."

Conrad shakes his head in disbelief.

"Just what I need, hallucinations," he says as he lowers himself onto the couch.

Another glass flips up in the air and crashes down onto the floor. The scene is starting to remind me of my first encounters with Alicia's ghost. Apparently female Mexican ghosts love to throw things.

"She's real, and very protective," Eva says. "We've been friends since I was a little girl. She died when I was eleven. It does not seem that she approves of you spending the rest of the voyage in my stateroom."

"I guess she doesn't know what a gentleman I am," he adds. "Is she scary?"

"Not to me. But if you were to be just a little bit less than a gentleman...."

"Tell her I won't be, honest."

Eva smirks again. "That remains to be seen, Mr. Mancowski. Let me confer with Grandma and see if I can talk her into letting you stay."

"Where do you want me to go while you... talk?"

"You don't have to leave. The bath's already drawn. In fact it's getting cold. I'll talk to Grandma as I'm bathing, and while I do, you can try to think of some other place to stay if she refuses to let you move into my cabin."

"I won't be a bother."

"That's for us to decide, isn't it?"

"I guess so, but believe me, you can trust my... discretion."

Eva smiles at the word. Then she stands and begins to move toward the bath. "There's some food in the ice box. Help yourself."

"Great. I'm very hungry," Conrad says as Eva makes her way into the bath. But as he turns toward the kitchen he catches a glimpse of a frightening old woman staring at him from out of the mirror that hangs over the sink.

I see her too. She looks a hell of a lot like La Bruja.

#

Now, I see La Bruja staring at me from outside my cell.

"I think it's time to mix up a little potion for you," she says as she makes her way to the cauldron. "Go back to your telenovela, if you like. I've got work to do."

"Telenovela?"

"The soap opera in the mirror; it's a tragedy. But you already know that."

As the old hag moves to the cauldron, a huge, black water snake slithers toward her out of the slime. In a flash she's grabbed it, jerked it over her head, and slammed it into the cauldron with such force that it doesn't come up for air even after she lights a raging fire under the pot.

#

In the mirror I see that it's days later. Eva and Conrad have begun to enjoy the best platonic relationship two such hot young people could ever have. She's feeding him well: steals leftovers from breakfast, lunch, and dinner and smuggles them back to her stateroom. Conrad eats it all and regains his strength and some of the weight he lost while hiding out in the hold of the ship.

They play cards and puzzle games. Even though they both speak English, Eva teaches Conrad some rudimentary Spanish while he tries rather unsuccessfully to pass on some basic Polish. The lessons are fun, if not very effective.

On the second to last day of the voyage, Eva decides that she needs to come up with enough food to get Conrad into the interior of Mexico. So, she heads into the noontime buffet wearing a very full gown with big pockets.

NICK IUPPA & JOHN P. MENDOZA

After an hour of thievery, Eva tucks half a chicken into the slit in her gown, then turns to leave. Unfortunately, Edward Squinkly, sergeant-at-arms, is standing right behind her.

"Miss Cordoba." His saccharine voice is starting to make Eva's skin crawl.

"Sir."

"Have you found the voyage comfortable?"

"Oh yes."

"A smooth passage, then?"

"Yes, very smooth."

Squinkly smiles like a cat who's just cornered a mouse.

"So smooth that there's been no sense of mal de mer?"

"Seasickness? No."

"Your stomach is quite comfortable?"

"Yes, thank you for asking, Señor. I'm feeling fine." Eva suddenly understands that she has to get away from this predator now. "If you will excuse me, please, I really must get back to my cabin."

Squinkly takes a step sideways so that he blocks her.

"Leave before the chicken turns cold?" and he reaches into her dress and pulls out the stolen food.

"I'm sure the busboy would have been happy to prepare a doggy bag for you."

Eva steps back in shock, looks beyond the chicken and flashes a deadly stare into Squinkly's beady eyes.

"How dare you, sir?"

"I wouldn't normally. But there's a stowaway still on board, and I'm forced to keep a keen eye out for anyone attempting to steal large quantities of food."

"I never would..." she begins. But he grabs Eva by the shoulders and begins to shake her until oranges, boiled potatoes, a loaf of bread, a bottle of wine, a dish of green beans, a bowl of pickled beets, and an entire custard pie fall out of the folds in her gown.

"You have a very large appetite for such a slight young woman."

Eva sighs. "I'm actually a very big eater. What of it?"

"It's just that your habits aren't so much those of a wealthy Mexican woman, as of a ravenous Polish stowaway. Let's go talk to the captain about all this, shall we?"

"But I'm feeling rather ill all of a sudden. I have to get back to my stateroom."

"Just a few words with the captain, and I'm sure you'll be able to do just that. This way, please."

Squinkly takes Eva Cordoba firmly by the arm and begins escorting her out of the dining room. As he does, he motions for one of his men to walk beside them.

"Will you please take Miss Cordoba to the captain and see that she remains with him while I search her room?"

Eva hears the words and bolts away from the men, but Squinkly grabs her and then passes her to his shipmate who holds her tightly.

"You're hurting me," Eva whispers.

"I'm very sorry," the shipman answers. But he doesn't loosen his hold on her arm. Meanwhile, Mr. Squinkly heads off toward Eva's stateroom, and on the way he gets four other crewmen to join him.

#

When Squinkly enters Eva's room, the window is wide open, and heavy sea breezes are swirling the curtains around like frightened ghosts. The furniture sparkles with a layer of mist.

"He might have tried to go out that window," he calls to the others, "but he'd be crazy to." Squinkly is grinning. Now that he's closing in on Conrad, he's starting to have fun. "We're too far off shore for that. Probably some kind of trick. Better give the place a good going over."

The men split up and begin searching Eva's stateroom. Several push their way into the bathroom, jerk open the closed shower curtain, and find nothing.

Squinkly opens the giant closet and tears armfuls of Eva's

expensive gowns from the racks. He rips several of them as he does, but there's no sign of a stowaway. Several of his men go through the dresser drawers checking out Eva's underwear and getting turned on by how sweet and feminine it is.

"What do you expect to find in there?" Squinkly calls to one of the men. "There won't be any stowaways hiding in her drawers." But just the same he scoops up a sheer pair of panties and stuffs them into his pocket.

The kitchen cupboards don't offer much hiding space either, but Squinkly tears them open and jerks their contents out onto the floor. "Damn!" he growls as he stomps around in cornmeal, diced potatoes and sugar. And then he sees a movement in the heavy drapes that hang on the far side of the open window. The sheer curtains are still swirling around them, and the sergeant-at-arms decides that maybe the window was opened to distract him.

He motions for his men to move in behind him as he heads toward the drapes. They all stop then, forming an arc around the mass of thick velvet fabric. There's dead silence in the room. Even the sounds of the sea seem to pause as the sailors hunch down and prepare to lunge toward the stowaway they are sure is hiding behind the heavy drapery.

"NOW!" Squinkly calls as he rips the drapes open and finds...

Another set of drapes; this time they're a scary shade of purple-gray.

"Damn!" Squinkly says, and he rips these apart too. More drapes.

He grabs these too and parts them... More draperies!

"This is bad," one of the men calls, but Squinkly pushes him away and grabs at the next set of drapes. These won't budge at all, won't move, won't part for him.

"Something damn evil's going on here, Mr. Squinkly," one of the crewmen says as the men all move to the door and then out of the room.

"Get back here," Squinkly rages, but the crew is gone.

The sergeant-at-arms now feels the first touches of fear crawling slowly over his shoulders and down to his fingertips.

"It's fuckin' nothin'," he grunts and slams his hand toward the draperies yet again. And now they do part, at least enough for Mr. Squinkly to reach into the opening and feel around. There's a harsh squawk and the sharp call of Pancho Villa. *"¡Viva la revolutión!"*

The huge macaw sinks the full force of his beak into the hand of the sergeant-at-arms, who jerks it back, and stares for a moment at the bloody chunk of flesh that the bird has ripped away. He turns and runs, tripping over the gowns that he's pulled from Eva's closet. He gets tangled in them, stumbles, falls forward struggling to escape as though the gowns themselves are reaching for him, trying to drag him back to those evil draperies and the bird that seems to want to eat him alive.

"¡Eres muy feo!" are the last squawking words Squinkly hears as he rushes down the hall holding his bloody hand high above his head. He will never be the same.

Mr. Squinkly will tell his tale over and over again to the captain, to the ship's doctors, to the rest of the crew, though none of them will support his lunacy.

The captain does everything in his power to repay Eva Cordoba for the destruction his men have brought to her cabin.

Eva's frazzled and furious pet macaw, Pancho Villa, will be found behind a very simple set of gray velvet drapes, which the young woman had arranged to protect him from the cold sea air. The bird stomps around back there calling, *"¡Eres muy feo!"* to everyone in sight... including his *mistress*. He's that pissed.

And while all this is going on, the ghost of Eva's grandmother spirits Conrad Mancowski off into the windy night as the ship passes the Yucatán. She leaves him ashore in a little fishing village in the state of Quintana Roo... very far, she hopes, from the vengeance of Jose's friends... at least for a while anyway.

Chapter 15

Conrad stands on the shoreline, watching sunrise flood the streets of a little fishing village. He's not at all sure where he is or how he got here. He's feeling dazed... almost dizzy. There's some vague sense of flying through the night. But it seems so unreal. Was he really lifted up by boney old hands with incredible strength? Ghost strength?

Conrad flinches at the thought of it.

Local sailors are heading down to their fishing boats this morning, and they look at him suspiciously. A few push right past him as though he isn't even there. But more and more of them stop and stare until there's a crowd of short, rugged men gathered a few feet in front of him. In his confusion Conrad steps toward them. The men step back; their eyes grow wide, and their look moves toward terror.

"¡Brujo!" one of them cries pointing toward him. Others repeat the word, sometimes in Spanish and sometimes in English: "Witch man!"

"Another one dropped here in the night!" one of the fishermen calls as he shakes his head and rubs his forehead in anger.

"Evil bastard!"

"¡Maldito Bastardo!"

One of the crowd draws a curved fishing knife from his belt and steps forward, asking, "What evils do ya bring ta us now, brujo?"

Conrad holds up his hands as though pushing them away. He shakes his head "no," and steps back.

The men huddle up. Conrad hears more words that suggest he's not the first to be dropped here by ungodly creatures.

"Whenever it happens, there's hell ta pay!" one fisherman says to the others.

Conrad doesn't really even know how he's gotten here. But it sounds like a ghost brought him. He's not the first, apparently, and whenever it happens the village suffers.

"No catch fer a dozen weeks."

"Si, es verdad."

"No fuckin' rain at all," agrees another.

Conrad shakes his head and starts to wonder if he's ever going to catch a break. But then an old guy in knee-high wading boots, with a deep scar down the side of his face, pushes his way though the crowd and walks right up to Conrad.

The gnarled little guy crosses his arms and begins walking slowly around him. He smiles and nods as he goes... sizing up this newcomer. He's speaking a strange version of English through a heavy Spanish accent.

"Who the hell are ye?"

"Conrad Mancowski."

The scar-faced fisherman tries on the name, "Man? – cow? – skri?"

Conrad nods and smiles. Old Scarface smiles back. But most of the others continue to grumble.

"Not a bad one," Scarface says as he points at Conrad.

Several of the fishermen spit on the ground in response to the comment. More knives are drawn.

"¡Todos son malos!" says one. "All bad," echoes another. "Let's slit 'is throat."

Luckily, Conrad can only understand a little of what's being said. The local accents make it almost impossible. Hell, as I watch through the witch's mirror, I can barely figure it out myself.

"No murder!" Scarface calls. He swipes his hands in front

of him like an umpire calling a runner safe. "NONE!" The others mumble and shake their heads.

"Wait right 'ere," Scarface says, and he squeaks back through the crowd in those high wading boots and heads back into the village.

Conrad stands there not knowing what to do or say. He still has no clear memory of how he's even gotten here... wherever the hell he is. And then he sees the crowd of fishermen moving slowly, carefully toward him. More curved knives are drawn.

"We'll teach yer witch not ta drop er garbage here!" one of the little men calls as he jumps up and takes a swipe at Conrad with his knife.

"¡Vamos a enviarle un mensaje!" calls another.

"Yeah! Let's send er a message," the others echo as they circle Conrad.

The circle tightens. One of the fishermen grabs Conrad's left arm. Another grabs his right.

An ancient, bug-eyed guy in bright green pants and an orange serape charges forward, stands on tiptoes, and presses his blade to Conrad's throat.

"Evil dies NOW!" he shouts.

The others are holding Conrad so tight that he can't pull away from the blade. It feels like it's going to plunge right through his windpipe.

But just then the scar-faced fisherman comes fighting his way back through the crowd. The others turn. Conrad sees that Scarface is pulling someone behind him: a small round girl who struggles to keep up? Even though Conrad only catches a glimpse of her, he knows that she's very young, maybe only fourteen or fifteen years old. She has chubby cheeks, a shock of long black hair, a round nose, and sweet lips that seem to mumble prayers as she's pulled headlong through the crowd.

Scarface jerks to a halt in front of Conrad.

"Wha's this?"

"Brujo!" one of the others shouts. "Witch dropping! Brings months without rain, weeks without fish."

"God hates a witch man."

Scarface shakes his head and frowns.

"Yer plotting murder then?" he asks.

While all this is going on, the young woman who has come with Scarface turns toward Conrad and studies him with curiosity and compassion.

"Señor," she whispers casting her eyes downward. "No se preocupe." Don't worry.

Conrad shrugs.

"You killed the last pair of innocents who showed up here on the shore," Scarface says. "A couple a children!"

"They were brought by a ghost witch."

"I saw her."

"¡La vi también!" says another.

"I saw them too," Scarface admits. "But just because we had a few weeks of bad weather afterward, doesn't mean that *those children* caused it."

"No fish!"

"Same thing, estúpido!"

"¡Brujería!"

"Witchcraft!"

"And what about the young girl who was brought here before them?" Scarface asks.

"A jaguar showed up and killed seven villagers!"

"¡Brujería!"

"Coincidence!" Scarface shouts, and he suddenly grabs the girl by the wrist, spins her around, and – in that single motion – she swings a rifle up from her side. She cocks it and aims it at one fisherman and than another and another. The men all scuttle backwards away from her.

"Are we not Christians?" Scarface asks now that the crowd is under control. "Did you forget the holy words?"

As I watch all this in the mirror I have only a small sense of what the scarfaced guy is saying. Conrad doesn't have much of a clue either... except maybe what he can figure out from the little man's tone. It's reverent:

"*Kindness to strangers! Be welcomin'. Blessed are the merciful.*"

A sudden hush spreads over the crowd. Knives slide back into sheaths. The grumbling dies.

Conrad can't believe what he's seeing, this strange-looking little guy in a tiny village on the edge of some *jungle*, is quoting scripture to save his life.

"Get out of here!" Scarface calls to the others. "There's work ta be done. Ixchel will care for him."

The girl gestures with the rifle, pointing with it first at the men and then in the direction of the harbor. Gradually, most turn and head down to their boats. A few others stand a little ways back and watch.

"She's a damned witch herself," bug-eyes calls.

The girl fires a single shot just over his head, and they all scatter. She reloads before they have a chance to look back.

Scarface smiles, reaches for the girl, pulls her in front of him, takes the gun from her hands, and pushes her at Conrad.

"Nieta," he says by way of introduction. "Ixchel!"

Conrad recognizes the word "Nieta," granddaughter. The girl's name sounds like eesh –chel, or even "seashell."

She'll take care of ya till I get back," Old Scarface says. "None'll mess with er, boy. She's a crack shot."

"Sir," she whispers to Conrad as she lowers her eyes shyly.

Conrad is stunned. The girl is so short, so compact, but that round face is very sweet, and those eyes are so compassionate and mysterious.

"Señorita," he says, bowing.

The girl claps her hands together. Her eyes flash with joy. Her smile sparkles.

"But what? How? Who??"

"It's a long story, son," Scarface tells Conrad, "who we are and how we came ta be, and speak the way we does and believe in what we does. Perhaps little Ixchel (seashell) here'll tell it to ya some day. Or maybe not."

"Take care a him," Scarface tells the girl as he grabs one of her hands and one of Conrad's and pulls the two together. And then the little guy in the big boots is gone, heading down to the boats, using the rifle to herd the rest of the crowd in front of him, leaving the couple staring at each other in confusion, and gratitude.

Most amazingly – they're holding hands.

Ixchel blushes. She turns away, then back to Conrad; her smile gets even wider if that's possible. "Ven por aquí, Señor," Come this way, sir, she says with more perfect pronunciation than anyone in the village has used before. Conrad nods and follows as though he's been hypnotized.

"Witchman," Ixchel whispers to herself as though the word itself is delicious. I hear it, but I'm not sure Conrad does. From the look in her eyes and her sly smile, I can tell that Ixchel feels that she wants to care for him, nurture him, but then to capture him... and capture his heart.

And that's exactly what she does.

Chapter 16

I stare intently at the mirror, at the dark, mysterious eyes of Ixchel who will some day become my grandmother. And then I gaze past them to the terrifying face of La Bruja. She's looking at me through the bars of my cage. And I realize that the witch has the same mysterious eyes... the same smile as Ixchel, though La Bruja's smile is cruel, evil, twisted... the smile of a *thing* that wants to destroy me.

"Magic time," she cackles, and she swoops down to the floor, picks up a handful of those bloody fingers and tosses them into the pot. The potion explodes as she does it, sending a foul smelling, gray-green mushroom cloud toward the ceiling of the cave. A lot of it pushes its way up the chimney with a loud "whoosh." But there isn't enough room up there for all the smoke and mist to escape, so it thunders back into the cave, picks up speed, and begins to swirl around the place like some captured tornado. Lightning crackles. The witch's brew has turned into a fucking cyclone.

The snakes begin to writhe desperately as though someone's lit them on fire. The sound of their squirming is amplified somehow. It mixes with the swirl of the wind and builds into a maddening roar. I see Tiger's goons, now awake, trying to bury themselves in the sand as the windstorm tears at their hair and clothing. I see the flames that burn before all those religious statues, fanned by the storm, beginning to rage like wildfire. I see La Bruja grab her cat and scuttle back into the depths of the cave cackling as she goes. "What fun... what fun." And, through all this madness, in the mirror whose frame is once again alive with slithering serpents, I see sweet Ixchel crawling into Conrad's bed, kneeling up above him, untying the simple cotton shirt she wears, lifting it above her head, shaking free her hair, pulling his hands up onto her youthful breasts, climbing onto him, seducing him into the very act that creates my father.

La Bruja is screaming above the wind.

"Run free, my beauty," she cries, as though her magic has taken on a life of its own. The cauldron now jerks back and forth. A chain breaks sending the huge black pot crashing to the floor of the cave where its stinking, molten slime spills everywhere. The burning muck spreads over the pond of serpents boiling them alive. It swallows up the goons who are too dazed to escape it. It floods toward my cage and in the process melts the bars that block my escape. I jump back, catch the bars at the back of the cage and lift myself above the molten slime.

The mirror suddenly falls backward, landing face up. I can jump onto it, run across it to safety, I think. It almost seems to be inviting me. Its surface sparkles with bright beach sand. For a second my mind warns me of danger, that perhaps I might fall into it, fall into the past, becoming captured in some nightmare of the witch's making. Is that what this is about? I can't wait for more than a second, and so I dare to dive onto the mirror, to begin charging across it, but as I do gnarled twisted old witch hands, dozens of them, fly up through the sand, reach for me, scratch at my feet and legs with long jagged nails. One green old hand grabs me around the ankle and holds me fast. A set of knife-sharp nails rakes across my inner thigh, down the back of my calf. They draw blood which immediately begins to fester and ooze.

The slime from the cauldron rushes up over the edge of the mirror scalding the serpents in the frame. They fall away at once. I push myself up off the mirror's sandy surface with my one free foot and kick hard at the twisted hand that holds me. It lets go as another set of claws gouges into my foot. But I land cleanly on the sand, and then I bound across the beach full of grasping clawing witch hands, somehow able to use the mirror as a bridge to get me out of the cage. I hurl myself over the pit of vipers, and dive into passageways that I can't even remember.

I'm breathing too heavily now, I know it. The air's putrid, nauseating. I begin coughing terribly. Still, I have no choice but to suck down great swallows of the witch-cauldron's airborne brew.

Blood and green pus ooze from the deep scratches all across my legs. But I run until my legs are screaming, then stop for just a second, fall back against the side of the cave, and try to gather myself, but the putrid air is strangling me. I'm feeling weak from the loss of blood, but I know that if I don't start moving again I'll probably suffocate on the spot. My only hope is to try and outrun the witch's whirlwind.

I turn back in the direction I was running (I hope) and notice that there's a faint spark of light up ahead. I charge toward it. The light holds steady, growing brighter as I come. It has to be *daylight*, I realize. If I can only get there (get out of this fucking deathtrap of a cave) I'll be okay. I'll find my way through the jungle somehow.

As the light grows brighter, glittering off the slimy cave walls and the crazy stalagmites that march like droopy goblins alongside of me, I charge headlong into a wall of jagged rocks. The light is above it all, brighter still, at the very top of the rubble.

I'm choking on air that is still so thick I can almost chew it. It smells like rotting snake meat and vomit, and it's calling up every meal I've had in the last month, trying to force them to jump up my throat and pour out of my mouth.

I stop, bury my face in my hands, tighten every muscle in my body, say a quick prayer, "Santa María por favor, sálvame!" And I start to climb.

The rocks fight me. My legs want to surrender. The witch owns them now. They don't want me to get out. For every step I manage upward, the rocks trip me, cut my hands, and threaten to send a whole avalanche down on top of me. But I keep climbing... and praying. And finally, calling up strength I was sure I'd lost in La Bruja's mirror, I make it to the top.

The light is nearly blinding, and the way out of the cave is terribly narrow. My head is swimming, my stomach has launched its own cyclone, and seems to want to tear itself apart. The air seems just as thick as it was at the base of the rock pile. But I know that the light blasting through the opening has to be daylight.

I grab hold of the narrow sides of the passage, and somehow manage to pull myself through.

And then I nearly fall over in shock!

I'm not outside. I'm at the shore of some vast underground lake. The dome above it is bright, as though the stalactites that hang from the ceiling are really crystal chandeliers that give off their own incredible brightness.

I'm still choking on the dust from the windstorm, still sweating from the heat of the cauldron, and still dizzy from the loss of blood to that witch-fingered mirror. I stagger to the edge of the water. It looks so cool and so deceptively inviting.

Knowing the power of my enemies makes me realize that drinking from this beautiful lake could kill me. But hell, at this moment I'm ready to take that chance.

I fall to my knees, push my face into the cooling water and drink deeply. It's delicious: sweet, clean, and incredibly refreshing.

I wash my face in the water's sparkling softness. I drag myself out into the cool and do everything I can to wash away the blood and pus that still fester from the wounds on my legs. The wounds tighten in the water, seem to twist themselves unnaturally into ropelike cords that wrap themselves around my legs then run up over my chest and on toward my face.

I drag myself out of the water feeling my whole body tightening as I do. Then I drop down onto the shoreline and drink some more. I suck in the pure sweetness of the water... gulp it down until my thirst is quenched. I push myself up on my forearms, my burning ravaged legs stretched out behind me. I watch as the ripples in the lake calm, and a clear reflection forms in front of me.

And then I scream in mortal terror.

3
Alicia

Chapter 17

My good friend Miguel is acting as a chauffeur today. We ride in his long sexy car... up the tree-lined road that leads to Señor Popcorn's hacienda in Cancun. As we go I am amazed to see that there are giggly, happy, soggy children everywhere. They are in swimsuits diving into the great pool in the center of the front lawn. One round little niño of maybe three is stomping around in a puddle along the side of the road. His sister – a girl of six – runs up to him to save him from our speeding car. But we are nowhere near them, really. And as we pass, she sees this, and so she joins her brother in the puddle splashing water at him as he kicks it back at her.

I see older kids, teenagers mostly, running back and forth along the rooftops engaged in a full-on water fight. It is the boys against the girls, and shapely Latinas, not too far above our heads, grab buckets of water and throw them high in the air. They drench their boyfriends who stick out their buffed chests and welcome the great splashes as though they were lovers' kisses. Then the boys answer with squirt guns to the squeals and joy of the girls.

Further up the drive, little kids climb brightly colored plastic stairs and then slide down great water slides that have been put together all across the whole front lawn. One ten year old has loaded an inner tube with his amigos and they spin down the slide only to be thrown high in the air at the end of the ride and splash down into a deep pool, to the cheers of everyone.

The smaller niños are all naked, running around and squealing like fat happy puppies. Anyone over the age of four has some kind of swimsuit on... mostly.

A well-developed, pre-teen girl is wearing nothing but a water soaked t-shirt. She's marching around showing off her sexy new body... until mamacita comes running down from the porch, grabs the girl by the arm, and leads her away to the cat-calls of the crowd and the wails of her skinny boyfriend.

"Don't do this to us, mama," he cries as he falls to his knees. "¡Por favor, no! ¡Estás rompiendo nuestros corazones!" You're breaking our hearts!

The fashion models, who still live in Señor Popcorn's guest com-pound, are all out in their bikinis, looking as beautiful as I once looked before I was murdered. But today the girls have no time to pose. They are busy running everywhere, sometimes sliding and tripping in the wetness, looking awkward as they reach down to grab a little guy, tuck him under one arm and then snatch up another. They're trying to keep the children from drowning while the kids splash and throw water at everyone in sight.

Miguel's car circles the driveway, and he lets me out in front of a huge sculpture that has been built by the front porch. I think it is a statue of a saint... made entirely of ice. And now I see Fernando de Cervantes himself, Señor Popcorn, dressed in baggy shorts and an orange silk shirt covered with paintings of bright red and yellow sombreros. His huge feet squish over the sides of tiny flip-flops. He's chipping ice from the statue and using the ice to fill trays full of snow cones. These he hands to his beautiful wife Eva who then pours mango or berry syrup over the cones and carries them out to the pool and los niños.

Today, I have made myself visible, even though I know that my reflection will not be seen in the water. Ghosts have no reflection, but who will notice when there is so much splashing going on.

Water fights are everywhere. Right across from the sculpture and directly behind me, young teenage boys are preparing a water cannon that they hope to turn on the teenage girls. I know that their evil goal is to blast the girls out of their swimwear. These are the sons and daughters of the families who work on Señor Popcorn's vast estate, and the girls may be wearing bikinis for the first times in their lives. The local padre is standing by of course, ready to give a benediction when it is time for supper. But in the mean time he stares with growing concern at the powerful weapon the boys are preparing... a great hose leading into a spiral housing with a huge dripping nozzle on the front of it. The padre suddenly drops his prayer book and charges at the contraption, hoping to use his own body to save the virtue of all these innocent young women. A smiling boy, who stands directly behind the water cannon, shrugs.

"No, Carlitos," his mother calls to him. I like that name. But this Carlitos is far more of a devil than my husband, because to spite his mama, he points the cannon directly at the priest and twists the great dripping spigot that should blast a ton of water at el padre. But the cannon is better behaved than the boy, because it does not blast. Instead, it gives a noisy hiccup, launches a quick burp of water, and is silent. Carlitos looks disappointed, the padre relieved. The grownups laugh. Several of them point to a great kink in the hose leading up to the nozzle. The girls giggle and strut off across the lawn never knowing how close they came to having their new bikinis stripped away from them by this mechanical monster. Carlitos notices the kink in the hose. There's still time he thinks, but within seconds el padre has the boy in a headlock.

"Alicia, mi ángel," Señor Popcorn calls when he sees me. He hands the ice pick and the tray full of cones to one of the bikini girls who is helping him, and then he comes rushing up to me. He is soaking wet, and suddenly so am I... wet from the great big hug that he and his soggy clothes are giving me.

"Alicia," Eva calls as she comes running. More wet hugs.

"¿Qué es eso?" I call. What is all this?

"It's June 24th," Eva tells me.

"Oh, of course," I answer. "So?"

"So it's el día de San Juan," Señor Popcorn says.

"Hay que celebrar," his wife adds.

I look around. Not only are there kids everywhere: swimming, having water fights, playing on the water slides, but there is also a mariachi band tuning up across the lawn, and a deliciously vast Mexican dinner being prepared. In the front corner of the lawn, a group of young men and women, dressed in white gowns and suits with bright yellow and red stripes on them, are setting up a maypole, preparing to do traditional Mexican spring dances.

"San Juan Baptista," my host says. "He baptized Jesus, remember? So, he is the patron saint of water. Yes?"

I shrug. I was never good at catechism.

"And much of Mexico is a desert. So, we gather every year on this day to ask the saint to help bring us the rain."

"I see."

"But not too much."

"No."

"No chubasco!"

"No monsoons."

"And while we pray, we do what Mexicans do best."

"And what is that?" I ask as if I did not already know.

"La fiesta!"

A new voice from behind me suddenly calls out the words, and I turn to see my best friend, Sylvia Morales, standing there. She is also a ghost, but she too has made herself visible and has donned a bikini so revealing that I'm sure that only supernatural forces are holding it in place.

She tosses a bucket of water all over me, and I allow myself to get even wetter. (Even though I could have disappeared and the water would have gone right through me and splashed onto Señor Popcorn, I decided not to disrespect my old friend and benefactor.)

"I am drenched," I cry.

"Like a soggy chihuahua," Sylvia laughs. "So, shake it off, chica. Let's see if you still look as good in a bikini as you did when we were shooting those commercials in Puerto Vallarta."

"But I am dead," I say.

"Well, duh! So am I! And you don't see me hiding in the shadows."

"I came to talk important business with Eva," I say becoming suddenly serious. The danger of my mission and the fact that Carlos is being held prisoner must be burning in my eyes.

Sylvia ignores the look; she grabs me and shakes me.

"No business on a saint's day," Sylvia says. "Only partying and laughter are allowed on the day of Saint John the Baptist. Seriousness can wait a few hours, girlfriend."

"I guess it can," I whisper, as I try to contain my suffering. Everyone else seems not to see it.

"We celebrate like this every June 24th," Eva says. "Isn't that right, Fernando?"

Señor Popcorn gives his wife a big grin and nods. But as soon as she turns away he looks at me, rolls his eyes, and shakes his head, and I know that making Señor Popcorn's home into a water park is a *new* idea, from his beautiful *new* wife.

"Wipe away that sadness, girl," Sylvia whispers to me. "We can solve your problems whatever they are. We are strong; we are invincible."

"We are dead," I remind her, but even as I say the words I begin to feel much better. I am with my friends, and they will help me save Carlitos as they have before.

Now, I see Eva's parents, Enrique and Yolanda Córdoba. They are making their way toward us from the porch. I am very happy to see them, because it is even better if I am able to talk to Eva and Yolanda together.

"It is such a wonderful celebration," Yolanda calls.

"Are you responsible for all this?" Enrique asks his daughter. He is still not sure of his son-in-law. He remembers all the years that he tried to have Señor Popcorn captured and executed as a drug kingpin. But that was before Eva fell in love with my benefactor, and Señor Popcorn turned from a life of crime to a life as El Rey del Maíz. The King of Corn. Now, I am told that he is the head of a great *empire,* selling corn for every purpose, almost singlehandedly saving the economy of Mexico.

"This festival?" Eva asks. "My doing?"

Enrique nods.

"Why, no, papa. It was all Fernando's idea wasn't it, querido?"

"Of course, it was," Señor Popcorn blusters as he winks at me.

Enrique misses the wink, smiles happily, and goes up to embrace Fernando.

"I continually misjudge you, my friend," he says as he hugs Señor Popcorn. Now Enrique is getting all wet from the great man's soggy clothes.

During the hug, Señor Popcorn's eyes roll from me (a look of acceptance) to Eva (a look of appreciation) to Yolanda, who once fancied herself as even a possible lover. This look especially interests me because it tells Yolanda more things than I can ever describe. At least it says, "Thank you for your daughter." But it also says, "I hope you are proud of me," and especially it says, "Be careful what you're thinking, Yolanda, because I'm your son-in-law now."

And then suddenly, that chesty pre-teen chica with still nothing on but a wet t-shirt comes zigzagging through the crowd holding desperately onto her grinning boyfriend and being chased by chubby mama who is waving a one-piece bathing suit over her head and calling "¡Ven aquí, Verónica! ¡ Ven aquí!" "COME BACK HERE, VERONICA!"

The old lady lunges forward to grab Veronica, and as she does she runs right into me, tossing me backwards into the pond in front of the statue of San Juan. My high heels flip up into the air, and I land on my backside.

Everyone is laughing except me. I am thrashing around and choking, which is hard for a ghost to do. Miguel arrives just in time to wade in and lift me from the pond. He is laughing maybe loudest of all as he slings me over his shoulder and carries me to the bath house where he puts me down and stands there grinning while I continue to cough and snarl and try to straighten my hair.

Sylvia comes running up to me. "Bikini time!" she cheers. And I guess it is. In spite of the sadness and importance of my mission, it is time to relax with my friends for a little bit.

After all, who can resist el día de San Juan?

Chapter 18

"This is very serious business, mija," my friend Señor Popcorn says.

I nod. "Rescuing my husband is the most serious thing I can think of."

"So, how will you do it without the help of a man... of *many men,* in fact?"

We are sitting in El Señor's conference room: he, his wife Eva, her parents Enrique and Yolanda Córdoba, my ghost friend Sylvia Morales, and me.

Eva takes her husband's hand. "This is women's business," she says as she raises his thick fingers to her lips and kisses them. Señor Popcorn's eyes sparkle, and then he realizes what is happening, and he pulls his hand away and frowns.

"*Rescuing* is man's work!" he says. "Let me at least have Miguel accompany you into the jungle."

"He would only slow us down," Yolanda says. "I know the way. I know the woman involved."

"A witch," Enrique grumbles shaking his head. "Getting rid of her will require a posse."

"A mob, you mean," Yolanda says. "And you're wrong."

"Please, Señores," I beg the men. "This is my husband. Dealing with witches is something only *women* understand."

"So, you hope to *nag* her into releasing Carlos?" Enrique grumbles.

Now I am growing impatient. It must show in my eyes.

"Please leave us, gentlemen," I say.

The two men look at each other for a moment, then at me, and then they both rise and leave.

"We'll be nearby if you need us," the popcorn man adds as he and Enrique walk out the door.

"Por favor, no," I whisper to the others.

"Señor Popcorn can be such a macho shithead," Sylvia says as she crosses her eyes and sticks out her tongue.

"And such a truly wonderful man at the same time," Yolanda adds batting her eyes.

We all look at her, wondering once again about this attraction she shows for her daughter's husband.

"*Both* of them can be wonderful men," she adds hurriedly.

"Yes, Mother."

And just then the ghost of Carlyle August pops into Señor Popcorn's chair at the head of the table.

"You're exceptionally hard to keep up with, Alicia," he says in that Cary Grant voice of his.

"Maybe I don't want you to keep up."

"Now, why would you say that?"

"Women's work," Sylvia says. She has met Carlyle and understands him. But the others are stunned. They've never seen him before or been exposed to his charm and good looks.

"Well, if it's women's work," Carlyle says, "don't let me interrupt. I'll just sit here quietly in the corner and admire your efforts... and maybe take some notes. Do you need a stenographer?"

"Okay," I answer getting more and more impatient with all these delays. "Take your pinchi notes."

Carlyle pulls a pad and pen from his jacket, flips up the first page, and prepares to write.

"Ectoplasm," he says pointing to the pad.

"CAN WE START, PLEASE?" I shout. "Carlitos is in great danger."

Everyone quiets for a moment. And then Yolanda Cordoba begins: "So, this Tiger Joy person has told you that she's had your Carlos taken to the cave of the meanest witch in Quintana Roo?"

I nod.

"That has to be La Bruja. I know exactly where she lives, in that maze of caves a few miles outside of Tizimin."

"We can find it," I say. "But do you think we can talk La Bruja into giving my husband back to me?"

Yolanda lowers her eyes. "She never gives back anything. Period!"

"That's why Doña Cuca is the answer," Eva says. "She's my friend, and she knows how to deal with the witch."

I remember Doña Cuca from the last time I was in the Yucatan. She's the curandera who saved Señor Popcorn's life.

"But why would a healer know how to deal with a witch?" I ask.

"Very simple," Yolanda answers. "Because they are sisters."

Carlyle is deeply involved in taking notes. He seems to be trying to write down everything we say. But when he hears the word "sisters," he stops and stares... the way all of us do.

"A medicine woman and a witch... are *sisters*?" I ask.

"And they hate each other," Yolanda adds.

"Yes, there's hatred there," Eva says, "but also understanding. La Doña knows how to handle La Bruja, if she wants to."

"So, if we can get Doña Cuca to help us," I say, "I can get my husband back."

"But that's a big 'if'," Eva responds. "A *very* big if. She will only do it if she really wants to."

"And if she's in the mood," Señora Yolanda adds.

Whatever the chances, this is still the first real hope I've had in weeks.

"What can we use to bargain with Doña Cuca?" I ask.

There's silence.

Finally Eva mumbles, "She never really asks for much, just a few coins. I often help her with her healing when I can. You know... my work in trade for hers."

"But that's hardly enough to pay for a confrontation between sisters who have hated each other for centuries."

"Centuries," Carlyle mumbles and makes a note.

"What we give her has got to be incredibly valuable," Sylvia says. "But what?"

Suddenly, Carlyle smiles.

"Come now, ladies. You're not using your heads. What is it that no woman can resist?"

We all look at him like he is loco.

He just responds with that cute smile and closes his note pad. "Let me put it another way. How old is La Doña?"

"No one knows," Eva answers. "She could be a thousand years old for all we know."

"Really?" Carlyle asks. "And she lives alone?"

"In the middle of the jungle."

"With a television?"

"Of course not."

"Even better. What is it that older women want... really crave, especially the ones who live alone?"

"Male companionship," Eva says.

"A lover," her mother answers.

Carlyle shakes his head. "More important than even that."

"Beauty," I say.

"Not really."

"Youth?" Sylvia tries.

"Maybe," Carlyle says. "But I think an old woman who lives alone would want one thing more than anything."

"Is this some kind of quiz?" I ask as I pull Carlyle's note pad away from him and throw it at his head. He ducks, and its pages crumple against the wall and then fall flat onto the floor.

"Carlitos has asked me these kinds of silly questions all my life. They drive me crazy. We don't have time for logic puzzles."

"Of course not, dear lady. I just thought the answer would be obvious."

"Well, it is not."

"Of course it is," Carlyle says. "Some nice, juicy...."

"Telenovelas," Yolanda answers.

"You're very close, lovely Miss," Carlyle says. "But the real answer is GOSSIP!"

"You're kidding?" Sylvia says.

"You know it's true."

He is right, of course, but what kind of gossip do we have that would interest an old curandera? Señor Popcorn turning into El Rey de Maize? Not good enough. But then Eva speaks up very softly and slowly.

"We have the *perfect* story, don't we, Mama?"

"I don't know what you mean," Yolanda answers.

"I think you do."

"Well, what the hell is it?" Carlyle grumbles, and I'm glad he does it for me. This meeting has been maddening.

Eva and Yolanda eye each other as though they were bitter rivals. Then they compose themselves.

"We will do it to save Carlos," Eva tells her mother. Yolanda bites her lip and thinks. It appears that there are tears in her eyes.

"Sí," she says at last. Then she leans into the table, and everyone leans in toward her. "Just between us girls," she says eyeing Carlyle, who nods and smiles too as though he is really one of us.

"A mother and daughter in love with the same man."

"Bitterly in love," Eva adds.

"Painfully, heartbreakingly in love," Yolanda answers.

Both women sigh and slouch back into their chairs as though in agony.

"That will definitely do it," Carlyle says as he nods his head.

And he's right.

#

The following morning is cool and misty, but we are dressed for the ride: Eva, Yolanda, and I. Each of us has chosen to wear our best riding outfit: boots, plaid shirts, kerchiefs, tight jeans and buckskin vests. I am amazed how Eva's mother looks so slim and fit.

We lead our horses out of the stables. My ghost horse, a monster called Espanto Negro (black ghost), is enormous and obedient and only seems to appear out of the nothingness when I need him. I have heard that no rider has been able to tame him, and yet he makes himself tame for me.

Today, Eva has chosen to ride a palomino; Yolanda, a mare so snow white and well groomed that she looks like something out of a fantasy movie. As we walk into the morning mists, we may all look like we are about to enter such a film. And then the feeling becomes even more real as we hear a rider approaching.

First there are only hoof beats, and then suddenly he bolts out of the mist and is right on top of us. He reigns in his horse and rears up as he pulls off his hat and salutes. The horse is huge and black, and the rider is dressed in black as well. I think I am looking at Zorro (the Antonio Banderas version). But this man is even handsomer than that... if it is possible. And he looks so familiar.

"Good morning, ladies, you're looking quite sporting," he says, and I recognize that Cary Grant voice at once. It's Carlyle.

"All present and accounted for, are we?" he asks.

"Macho shithead," I hear someone whisper. I can't see her. But this is a voice I know too well... Sylvia.

"I'm sorry, Carlyle," I say, "but we are off to do important *woman's* work."

"Won't these stupid men ever get that into their thick heads?" Sylvia asks invisibly.

"Come now, sweetheart," Carlyle says, "I vowed to be your knight in shining armor and protect you." His smile is almost blinding, and I think he may have done something to make himself look even more handsome than he is... or is it just those black jeans, form-fitting shirt, tight bandana, and that black hat which he again pulls from his head as he gets down from his horse and bows to us.

"We don't need this stupidity," Sylvia curses secretly. She has still not shown herself. "And look at that one," she continues, and I turn to see Yolanda growing dizzy at the sight of this beautiful vaquero.

"How can La Señora concentrate on our business when she is almost fainting from desire?" Sylvia moans.

"Carlyle," I say, "you are very gallant, but we must do this on our own."

"Now, now, Alicia, I can be silent and stay out of the way until there's trouble. And then, and only then, will I jump in and save you all."

He jerks his gun from his holster. Yes. He is also wearing a black gun and gun-belt, which somehow has gotten lost in all the other blackness. He points the gun over here, over there, back behind his shoulder. It would be comical were things not so desperate.

"I've had enough of this," the invisible Sylvia tells me, and I sense that suddenly she is gone. And then I see her off in the distance running toward us through the mists. But she is not dressed for the ride now; she is in a great white gown... the kind worn by the rich ladies who lived on the Ranchos of Old California. A thousand petticoats foam around her legs like the mists through which she runs.

"Oh, ¡gracias a dios!" she cries as she runs right up to Carlyle. "I thought you had gone."

"Not yet," he answers, catching her in his arms as she stumbles forward (on purpose). She is making sure that her fabulous cleavage reveals itself in all its splendor. As Carlyle stands there, holding Sylvia, they look like a couple from the cover of a romance novel.

"What do you need, glorious lady?" he sighs. Sylvia too has cranked up her beauty.

"Stay with me... protect me."

"Why... what's wrong?"

"It's the library."

"Señor Popcorn's magnificent library?"

"Sí. It is haunted!" Sylvia pulls away from Carlyle, bends forward to dust off her gown, and reveals even more spectacular vistas of her bosom.

"The library is haunted?"

"By two ghosts who make love all day and all night. It's driving me mad with desire."

Sylvia is a very clever girl, is she not? You'd think Carlyle would recognize what she is doing, but I don't think he does... okay, maybe.

"The sound of their passion might shake the whole building down," she says.

Carlyle looks at me, looks at Sylvia with her bodice so ready to be ripped. He himself is torn.

"We don't need you this badly," I tell him. "Help the poor girl."

"Por favor, Señor," Sylvia begs, eyes calling, gown shimmering, breasts heaving.

"I see my duty!" Carlyle shouts at last as he mounts his horse and lets it rear high on its hind legs. Then he sweeps Sylvia up onto the saddle behind him and charges off into the mists, turning to me only at the last moment and *winking* wickedly.

He knows exactly what has happened.

I sigh.

Eva smiles. "I hope that haunted library will still be standing after this is over."

"We may be able to hear their orgasms all the way to Doña Cuca's," I add.

"Oh, I hope so," Yolanda sighs.

And then we all burst out laughing.

After no more than another moment, the three of us are on our horses, charging along the beaches that lead to the jungle home of Doña Cuca. We know that there is no more time for humor. We must save my husband now.

Chapter 19

The route we take to Doña Cuca's home is very direct and much simpler than the jungle path we followed when we visited her a year ago. Now we ride our horses along the beach for several sweet, cool hours even as the heat of the day builds just beyond the tree line. Finally, Eva leads us to a small lean-to at the head of a very rough trail. A tiny man is sitting there; he is as brown as the vines that surround him. He smokes a pipe, seems to be humming to himself, and nods as we approach.

"¿Viene a visitar Doña Cuca?" he asks.

"Sí." Eva answers.

"Eva de Cervantes?"

"Sí, yo soy."

Eva smiles as she dismounts and walks up to the lean-to.

"¡Hola! Señora," the little man says, and then he turns to Yolanda. "¡Hola! Señoras!"

The two women nod back at him and then the little man hops out of the lean-to and takes the reigns of their horses. Yolanda has dismounted by the time he reaches her. I am invisible, and my ghost horse needs no attention. So there is no need to appear, which I think would only startle and confuse him.

"¿Cuántos dias se quedan?" he asks.

"How long will we stay?" Yolanda repeats with a shrug. "As long as it takes."

The little man seems to understand this, and he nods as he leads the horses back to the lean-to.

"No importa," he mumbles. It doesn't matter. And I know that he will take care of our horses for as long as is necessary.

We are feeling fresh from the ride on the beach, and so, when Eva pulls a backpack full of personal things down from her horse and hoists it up over her shoulders, it is no trouble at all, and soon we find ourselves in the thick of the jungle.

The heat builds, but the going is easy for me. I pass through trees and glide over swampy marshes as though they are not even there. More honestly, it is *I* who am not here, not of this world, anyway.

Señora Yolanda has little problem either, fit as she is. A less healthy woman would easily be overcome by the heat, and the dank jungle air, and the millions of bugs that swarm around our faces, and the frightening chatter of the monkeys, and the squeal of wild pigs, and the snakes I see gliding along tree branches that I don't want to touch even though I am invisible. Crocodiles swim under the swampy water; I see their huge tails moving, but their great jaws will not open to bite the feet of ghosts... (I hope).

Whatever. We finally make it to the door of Doña Cuca's little home, and then I begin to feel that maybe all will be well very soon.

Doña Cuca lives in a strange old building, and she herself is a strange, short, tough-looking person who comes rushing out of the front door as soon as we are in sight of her.

"Eva and Mama," she calls. "Eva and Mama." And then she sees me even though I am invisible. Curanderas have that power.

"Welcome, Alicia," she says. And then to Eva, "How can I help all of you?"

"It's a very long story," Eva answers.

"Oh good. I love long stories. Tell me. But first come inside."

We follow Doña Cuca into the old building, which is very oddly shaped for the jungle. There are two thick columns holding up the corners of a front porch that should not be standing there at all. Dozens of ugly colors stain the stucco walls, but mostly they are dirty orange. The floor is covered with pink and white tiles that have been laid in a dizzying pattern. But the ceiling!

"Ah, the ceiling," Yolanda sighs in gratitude, because it is made of wooden beams, and – in spite of the creatures who are hiding up there and scurry away as we enter – it keeps the place magically cool.

"I think mother and daughter can sleep in here," Doña Cuca says showing Eva the very bedroom where she and Señor Popcorn first made love. Eva nods gratefully, but looks questioningly at her mother.

"Don't worry, mama doesn't have to know," I whisper. And I remember how, at the height of their first lovemaking, Eva, a curandera herself, saw me standing in the corner of the room watching them. She winked and smiled at me without shame.

"Put away your things," Doña Cuca tells the two women although she must realize that all they have is the contents of one small backpack between them.

"You," she says turning to me, "this way," and she leads me into the kitchen. "We'll make some coffee."

I wish ghosts had a better sense of smell, because I know that Doña Cuca's kitchen contains so many wonderful smells: spices and tea and coffee and chocolate and all kinds of magical herbs.

Doña Cuca stands on her tiptoes and pulls down a battered old pot that she pours water into. Then she adds portions of hand ground coffee and other ingredients and starts the pot boiling.

"And now," she says, "Here's a special treat for you, Alicia's ghost."

I look on in fascination as the little woman gets down on her hands and knees and crawls through a small door in the floor. She disappears completely. There is a rattling and banging around, but soon she emerges again with a big jar so cold that it is sweating.

"Ghost tea," she says. "Cold ghost tea. I'll bet you never thought you'd be tasting this."

"No, never," I say with a smile.

Her stumpy fingers pry the lid off the jar, and I can feel the sweetness of the tea calling out to me.

"Ghosts don't need tea," I say, not really believing it at all.

"Of course they do, mija," she answers. And she pours a great splash of tea into a big glass and hands it to me. I taste the tea and feel tears form in my eyes. I can't help it. I am taken back to my childhood when my mother made such treats for me... whenever she liked me that is, which was not very often.

"Mmmmm, smell the coffee," says Yolanda as she enters the kitchen. She takes a seat at the wide table in the corner of the room. Eva slides in right beside her.

"Chocolate?" La Doña offers as she serves up a big plate of dark powdery chunks.

"Mmmmm," Yolanda repeats.

The old curandera digs out three large pottery mugs and places them on the table. Then she pours coffee in all of them, returns the pot to the stove, and comes back to take her seat at the table. Everyone has avoided the one chair that must be hers. It has a high back and is painted in thick lacquers of orange, yellow, red, and dark blue.

We sip, we chew, we sigh, we laugh, and we feel very, very good. And then Doña Cuca says, "Okay, so tell me what you came to tell?"

And, like some ancient old mariner I read about when I was in high school and so madly in love with Carlitos that I don't really remember very much about the old sailor but I do know that he had to tell his tale, I begin mine. You already know it.

#

It is now much later, the dark of night, and I have told Doña Cuca of my entire life and death and after-life. I've told her about Sigmund Freud and of my love for Señor Carlos Mankowski. I've also told how Tiger Joy sent Carlitos to La Bruja for punishment.

"I see," Doña Cuca says with what seems like growing anger. "And so you want me to face my evil sister and save your husband for you?"

My eyes flit to Eva's, but we say nothing.

"There's no way that I will do it," the curandera tells us bitterly, and then she gets to her feet and begins to clear the table.

"But we don't want you to confront your sister," Eva says. "That's not really why we came here at all."

"Yes," Señora Yolanda adds. "We just thought you liked gossip, and so we brought a ghostly little story for you."

"Not interested," Doña Cuca says as she clatters the plates together.

"What we really want," Eva says as her eyes widen with excitement, "is your opinion on a matter of great importance between a mother and her daughter."

Doña Cuca's anger seems to fade at once. "Oh, I see," she says. She actually begins to smile, and she returns the cups to the table, pours more hot coffee, and settles in. "Better tell me *that* story then."

"It is the story of two women in love with the same man," Eva begins.

"And what a handsome hombre," Yolanda adds. "Not a really *young* man of course, but one whose gaze contains so much power and majesty that it just makes a woman's heart begin to...."

"STOP IT, MOTHER!" Eva calls. "You're talking about my *husband*."

Yolanda Córdoba pulls back as though she's been struck. "I know," she says as she turns to the curandera. "You see, Doña, Eva and I are in love with the same man."

"Fernando de Cervantes?"

"Sí."

"Fickle woman," La Doña says. "You went to my sister, La Bruja, and allowed her to cut off your finger so that she could make a potion that would make Enrique Córdoba fall in love with you."

107

"I know."

"Then you went back to her to so that she would make another potion that would allow your husband to track down Señor de Cervantes and kill him."

Yolanda stiffens. "I wanted him for myself, and when I couldn't have him... I... I wanted him dead."

Eva gasps.

"Even though you would be taking him away from your daughter?"

"Sí." Yolanda whispers the word; her eyes are downcast. She is red with shame.

"And now you see your daughter happily married to him, and you understand just how wonderful a husband Señor de Cervantes is, and so you change your mind again. You want him even more. And now you come to me and ask that I resolve this triangle that is forming between your daughter, her husband, and you."

Yolanda shudders, draws in a deep breath, and then nods.

"¿Valgame Dios, Mujer, estas loca?" Doña Cuca asks. "I would rather fight my sister to save this Carlitos Mancowski hombre, than help *you*."

"But I love him," Yolanda squeals.

At those words I see tears forming in the eyes of Eva even though she is a very proud woman. Doña Cuca ignores her.

"Does Señor de Cervantes love you, Yolanda?"

Eva's head jerks sharply to her mother as though the answer to this question will determine the fate of their relationship.

"I don't know," she says.

"Has he ever called on you?"

"He offered to take me to the opera once," Yolanda says. "Though maybe he did it so he could be near my daughter."

"Has he sent you secret love letters?"

"I don't..." Yolanda sighs dramatically, "I don't think so."

"Has he ever made love to you?"

"Of course not."

"Has he, in fact, encouraged you in any way?"

Now it is Yolanda whose eyes fill with tears while Eva's face softens into a gentle smile of relief.

Doña Cuca stands, walks right up to Yolanda and (as they say on television) gets right in her face.

"Do you know what happens to a woman who secretly lusts after another woman's husband?"

"I can imagine," Yolanda whispers.

"I can more than imagine," Doña Cuca says loudly. "I saw it happen. I was part of it." She turns and begins pacing back and forth across the kitchen floor like some angry leopard in the moonlight. She is thinking, perhaps arguing with herself. Then she turns back to Eva's mother.

"What would you have me do, Yolanda?"

Yolanda cannot look anywhere but at the floor. But her eyes are bulging now, and her breath is ragged as though she has transformed into some rutting animal.

"Tell me," Doña Cuca, demands.

"Deliver her husband to me," Yolanda growls.

"Mother!" Eva cannot believe what she hears. But La Doña is not surprised.

"I thought so!" She says the words as though she were condemning Yolanda Cordoba to death. Then she shuffles back into her seat; she waits till everyone calms, until all our eyes focus on her, until there is absolute silence.

"Now," she says at last, "Let me tell *you* a story."

Chapter 20

"I can still feel the excitement in the air," La Doña, begins. "Two teams of fine muscular young boys stand on the ballcourt, ready to play, to settle an argument between two families over the ownership of several chinampas (floating gardens) just outside the city. Using a ballgame to settle a dispute is a longstanding practice of our peoples in all the Maya city-states.

"The boys are in their late teens. They wear the classic gear of the ballgame: a loincloth, hip and thigh pads, and, before the ballgame begins, huge headdresses made of bird feathers and silver. These great displays are too heavy to wear during the game, but perfect to inspire the crowd before. And we are *so* inspired.

"We stand on one high wall of the long ballcourt like modern cheerleaders, my sister and I. That is almost what we are, wearing our red, blue, and orange huipil blouses. They are decorated with representations of the heavens and the gods. Our skirts are bright blue; our necklaces, bracelets, and rings sparkle in the hot sun as we cheer our team.

"On one side are our boys: Ichik and Ehahan, on the other, (I can still remember their names) Chac and Ikan. We think they are playing for control of the chinampas, but that is not the only reason for the game. My sister is secretly vying with me for the love of one of the players, Ichik, whose family claims the floating gardens.

"My sister's name is Akhushtal, and she has taken a great chance to win the love of Ichik. She has thrown her spirit to the dark side, made sacrifices to the evil ones, and conjured wicked

110

spells in order to gain control of the minds of the players. She has already given a secret potion to Ichik that will dull his reflexes and slow his play, though he does not know it. Akhushtal also intends to distract the players during the game; this *I* will soon learn to my horror. What *Akhushtal* will learn to *her* horror is that Ichik and I are already lovers. In fact, I am carrying his child and doing my best to hide it from everyone.

"This is my memory of our lives five hundred years ago. We live in a great Maya city-state, my sister and I. It is built amid hundreds of caves, near a deep underground lake that provides water for us all. The city is vast, with royal palaces, high pyramids, marketplaces, and ballcourts for playing our ancient game.

"Our father is a scribe who writes books for the Ahau, our king. We believe the king of our city-state is a descendant of the gods. His blood is sacred, and his word is final. But times are good. Farms encircle our city and provide plenty of food. We never go hungry.

"The world is so very sweet, I think as I stand on the high wall looking into the ballcourt. My sister, Akhushtal, is already La Bruja, though I am not yet aware of it. I eye my man, my Ichik. He smiles up at me, taps his heart, and points to me as the opening ceremonies begin. I cheer, I turn to my sister and smile, and her eyes are so narrow, so sinister. 'What could that be about?' I ask myself. If I had only known.

"I am too happy to pay attention to Akhushtal. Our team will win, Ichik's family will gain undisputed possession of the chinampas, and we will be married within days, and then I will have my *son* (I hope). Little do I know that these few moments I am experiencing on top of this wall before the ballgame begins are the closest I will ever come to true happiness.

"A heavy three-pound ball is centered in the ballcourt, and play begins. Chac (our rival) launches the ball from his side of the court, and my Ichik returns it with a swift butt of his hip. The ball flies back and hits the wall at the end of the court: points for our side.

"Another exchange begins, this one longer; Chac drives the ball at Ichik who returns it, this time with a slam of his upper thigh. The ball volleys back and forth and now, with a sudden hit, Chac drives the ball into the air, and it passes through a small stone hoop that sticks out from the wall on one side of the court.

"The crowd cheers excitedly, but not me... not my friends... not my family. This nearly impossible shot has given a great advantage to the opposing side, and now only another such shot will allow Ichik and his partner to win the game.

"This event is more dangerous than it seems. Although it is about the ownership of the chinampas, if the king wishes, the losers can be executed right there on the floor of the ballcourt. Of course, none of us believe this will happen. Executions are usually reserved for our enemies who are captured and often made to reenact the final battle of some war as part of a well-planned ballgame. And, of course, at the end, the players on the enemy side lose and all of them become human sacrifices.

"But these are local boys, well liked by the whole community, and this game is being played to settle a domestic dispute. What king would want to kill the loser of this game?

"Play is intense. Chac is inspired; he drives the ball with a hip-butt so hard that it flies against the leg of Ehahan. Three pounds of flying hardball leaves a terrible bruise, but if it hit him in the chest, it would have killed him.

"Ehahan goes down with a cry of pain. I put my hands over my eyes. This is more than I can bear to watch. I turn away, but once again I am shocked to see that my sister is doing everything she can to hide a smile of happiness.

"What is she thinking, I ask myself. She is my sister, I thought she loved me, I thought she loved Ichik too....

"Oh!" I suddenly say out loud as I cover my mouth with my hand, and then, "Oh, no!"

"I hear the cheers; I have to keep watching. Another volley. Ichik is playing better than ever; he scores more and more points, though he can never win unless he or his partner can drive the ball through the hoop above the floor of the ballcourt. But then, all at once, his actions slow. He cannot even get to the ball to return it as it flies by him. He stands, bending over, hands on his knees. Akhushtal's spell is starting to work. Beside Ichik, his partner Ehahan is hobbled by the wound he received.

"Now, Chac drives the ball from his side of the court, and this time, by luck or the grace of the goddess, Ehahan blocks the ball and sends it skyward, toward the hoop, toward a win for our side. But suddenly – and I see this only out of the corner of my eye – my sister waves her hand, and a thousand bats swirl up out of the caves beside the ballcourt. They fly madly into the court, disrupting play, making it impossible to see if the ball actually goes through the hoop. They descend on the players, attacking them, ripping at their flesh; the game is stopped. The players run for cover and in that instant, the bats draw together and fly into the crowd. They attack everyone. I smash many of them away with my own hands and see that several other bats have landed on the rest of my family and are gouging great bites out of their flesh. Several bats even dare to menace the king and his court. Meanwhile, my sister is waving her arms frantically trying to send the bats back into their caves, realizing that spell casting is a dangerous weapon in the hands of a novice witch.

"Finally, the bats swirl up over the ballcourt and dive back into the caves.

"There is a long, stunned silence. Finally, the players make their way back out onto the court, and the king slowly approaches the forward edge of the wall.

"'The chinampas go to the winners,' he proclaims when he gets there, 'the families of Chac and Ikan.'

"There is bitter disappointment on our side, because Ichik's family has lost property. But we know we cannot dispute this decision.

"'And to Ichik and Ehahan...' the king says as the crowd leans forward anxiously awaiting some kind of compensation for the losers....

"'DEATH!' he says.

"'What?' My sister runs wildly across the top of the wall. She pulls as close to the king as she can get. 'I was promised!' she shouts. 'I was promised that if they lost, Ehahan would die, but Ichik would be given to *me*!'

"Guards move in on my sister to silence her. But the king comes to her, pushes past his own guards, and looks at her. She is so pathetic, a young girl who has sold her soul and gotten less than nothing in return.

"'Did *I* promise this?' he asks.

"Akhushtal does not answer. She only looks at Ichik as tears roll down her face. The misery in her eyes has never really left them, I don't think, nor has the anger and shame.

"'Did *I* promise this?' the king asks again.

"Finally Akhushtal whispers, 'No.'

"'Who then?' the king asks.

"Akhushtal does not answer for a very long time, and then her wail rings out all across the ballcourt, all across the city, I think: 'NOOOOOO!!'

"'You will tell me by the end of the day, in secret, or you will die,' the king says. "'And...' he stops and thinks for a moment... 'I must tell you that you are a very incompetent witch.'

"Akhushtal's body is now a sad twisted form.

"'You endangered the people,' the king continues, 'you endangered the royal family, and as punishment the boy you love *will* die. It's as simple as that.'

"'YOU CAN'T!!!!' My sister cries. The king's guards move up to protect him. He motions them away.

"'The king does what he chooses, witch,' he says. 'Now, silence, or I will sacrifice *you* alongside your sister's lover.'

"Akhushtal slumps onto the floor. I stare at her in disbelief.

And how does our divine king know so much about our lives, about Ichik's lovemaking? It's his job, I guess. And then I turn my eyes back to the ballcourt.

"Ichik looks up at me. The guards already surround him. The high priest is already approaching him, walking slowly, drawing his dagger. Ichik locks his eyes on mine as he is forced to his knees. He smiles with love and never looks away from me, even as the cut is made and his heart is ripped from his chest."

#

"Did your sister tell the king who made those promises to her?" Yolanda asks Doña Cuca.

"Who offered to give Ichik to her if she made him lose the ballgame?" Eva asks.

"I don't know who it was," La Doña answers. "But Akhushtal must have told the king everything he wanted to know. After all, she's still alive. It's five hundred years later, and she's still alive."

Doña Cuca gets up from her chair, stretches, and yawns. "The dishes will keep," she says. And then to Yolanda: "As for you, you sorry old woman, I think you need the cure, don't you?"

"The cure for...?"

"Stupidity," La Doña answers. "But also for misdirected lust. You want your daughter's husband? Go home and fuck your own man, please him, and I think you'll find pleasure for yourself."

"But I want Señor Cervantes so badly...."

"You can't have him," La Doña answers. "I will give you teas that will tame your heart, and you will wear the leaves of the gray plant below your waist to draw out the ill humors."

"How long will it take?" Eva asks. Now that her mother is no longer a threat to her marriage, she looks on her with sympathy.

"Only one long hard day, I think. So we'd best get some rest. I will be up early to make preparations."

I look at Eva, asking her with my eyes how we can bring up the subject of Carlitos's rescue. But Eva's look tells me to be nice to the old curandera for now. Before we leave, we will speak again of Carlitos and his rescue.

"I can clean up the room," I say to La Doña.

"A ghost housekeeper," she mumbles with a smile. "That will be most unusual, and very nice. Thank you."

And so everyone but me heads off to their beds. Yolanda will not know that she is lying side by side with her daughter in the same bed where Eva and Señor Popcorn first made love.

Chapter 21

It is the darkest part of the night, and I am going crazy with anger. Dr. Freud would *not* be proud of me.

I *have* washed and stored all of Doña Cuca's dishes and cups without breaking a single one. But now I feel that I should gather them up, head into her bedroom, and throw every cup and every plate right in her face. I want to shatter them against her boney old head, not stop until she lies half-dead in a bed full of shattered pottery.

I am sure Dr. Freud would tell me not to do this, to think of my mother and all the evil her temper caused. That would make me calm again, he would say.

Okay, maybe I can become calm.

"Yes," I whisper, as I shake out my ghost arms and feel myself calming. I can slip into La Doña's room and watch her while she sleeps. I may be able to enter her dreams, understand more about her, and use her dreams to give her an important message about saving Carlitos.

I like the idea. Who says psychoanalysis does not work? And so I glide into the curandera's bedroom.

She lies on a simple wooden slab. ¡Gracias a dios! She is fast asleep or she would see me no matter how invisible I make myself. Curanderas can do that. The sound of her snoring is like the engine of some speedboat out on the gulf. It winds and winds, making me nervous as it grows louder.

I give Doña Cuca a ghostly touch on the face and she stops snoring. Her mouth searches for a more comfortable shape and then her lips twitch and she starts to speak.

"Mancowski," she says in her sleep.

This greatly surprises me.

Across the bedroom I see herbs and leaves spread out on her night table. I don't know what they are, but I can tell that they give deep sleep and maybe amazing dreams. Do I want to invade such dreams? The drugs may make the dreams as scary for me as I would make them for Doña Cuca.

"Mancowski," she says again without ever opening her eyes. "Carlitos Mancowski."

She smiles and smacks her lips. Her breath smells full of twigs and swampy things. Still, I draw closer. She turns toward me and slides her hands under her head, palms together, like a small child.

"Mmmmm," she sighs.

I find this all interesting but frustrating. I just want to jump into this old woman's five-hundred-year-old brain and bang around inside her head. She smacks her lips some more. I poise to dive, but then she says, "*Conrad* Mancowski."

"¿Qué?"

I have never heard of this Conrad person.

"Conrad Mancowski," she repeats. "Éra un buen hombre."

I want to ask her how she knows he's a very good man, but all I say is, "Sí."

"Mancowski," she repeats as she flips onto her back.

I stare at her, frustrated again, ready to dive into her dreams.

And then she jumps full upright in bed, and her eyes fly wide open. She is staring at me.

"Ixchel Mancowski," she whispers.

"Sí?" I don't know what else to say. I've never heard this name either.

"She was my great, great granddaughter, Alicia."

"Sí?"

"That makes *your* Carlitos...." her eyes are wide now, like headlights shining on the center of my heart.

"BLOOD!"

"Carlos's blood?"

"*My* blood, Niña. Carlitos has to be my great, great, great, great grandson."

I stop and think on this for a moment. Is there any logic to it?

"Does that makes him blood of La Bruja as well?"

Her answer comes very slowly. "Yes, it does."

"Will that not matter to her?"

"It will only make her hate him even more, because he comes from my union with her lost love, *my lover*, Ichik."

There is long silence in the room as we stare at each other. And yet, we are not really thinking of us. We are thinking of Carlitos and his ancestry.

"WE HAVE TO SAVE HIM!"

The old woman and I say the words together, like a promise.

#

Doña Cuca gets up from the bed and walks into the center of the room. Her eyes are wild.

"Watch me," she hisses. And how can I not.

Suddenly, as though she has been punched in the stomach, she doubles over with a cry of pain. Her knees buckle; she lets out a terrible scream. I have never heard such a scream before, except maybe from a great cat in a jungle movie.

Her arms jump forward of their own will and then her elbows bend backward. It looks like all her bones are breaking inside of her.

Her head turns toward me; her jaw pulls forward and animal fangs grow out of it, right in front of my eyes. Doña Cuca's head begins to jerk back and forth. She growls in pain from all that is happening.

"¡Que Dios me ayude!" God help me! It is the last human phrase she is able to say. And then, in one quick move, she rips off her nightshirt.

I expect to be horrified by the sight of this ancient body, but it is already turning young. Her skin is tightening; her muscles grow from deep inside. Claws jump from her fingertips. Short, coarse hair spreads from her ankles and quickly up her legs, over her thighs, across her back and chest and finally over her face. It pushes out any human hair that might be left.

Doña Cuca falls forward on all fours now, and comes toward me. I jump into invisibility, but she still sees me. Even in the form of a jaguar, she is still a curandera.

"Aliciiiiiaaaaaaa..." she purrs, and her animal tongue licks those jagged teeth.

I tremble even though I am a ghost.

She snarls.

"Alicia... *this* is how it's done," she says. It is the voice of an old woman that still comes from a jungle cat. And then Doña Cuca, this curandera who has become a wild animal, leaps silently onto the bed, through the window, and she's gone.

At that moment, Eva de Cervantes, and her mother run into the room. They almost trip over each other as I shift back into visible form. I want them to know that I am all right.

"We heard a jaguar!" Yolanda says. She is white with fear.

"Was it really in here?" Eva asks. "Did it take Doña Cuca?"

I shake my head. No. "Doña Cuca *became* a jaguar," I say. "And she has gone to save Carlitos from the witch."

4
Carlos

Chapter 22

I look at my reflection in the waters of an underground lake. Quasimodo seems to be staring back at me. (Make that Quasimodo after someone spent half an hour pounding his face with a baseball bat.)

My skin is now dead green, my face battered. The biggest bulge, at my temple, has a jagged cut across it that still oozes blood mixed with watery pus. Nice.

My forehead looks cockeyed... like someone took my skull and jerked it into the shape of a half-inflated soccer ball. My mouth's a gash that can't begin to hide teeth that are impossibly crooked. Nasty sores fester on the edges of my lips and down into my throat.

I run my tongue over the inside of my cheeks and gums. I can feel scabs and sores everywhere. They taste like rotting meat.

My head feels the way a punching bag must after a two-hour session with Macho Camacho... or even me at my best, which is hardly what I am now.

I pull my hands up in front of my face and see that they're changed too. My fingers are now thick stubs with swollen knuckles. I try to bend my fingers; I can't. My knees can't straighten either. My back's got a nasty hump on it, as though someone grafted a huge sack of shit onto my shoulders and I'm stooped over from the weight of it. I *am* the fucking Hunchback of Notre Dame... only worse. I make that guy look as handsome as Carlyle August.

To top it all off, my smell is disgusting... as much from that sack-of-shit hump and festering sores as from the fact that, thanks to my recent girlfriends – La Bruja and Tiger – I haven't bathed in weeks.

"JESUSSSSSSS!" I shout across the cavern, and even the sound of my voice is ugly.

So, I get it. This is what she's done to me. This is my torture: being turned into a monster. She still hasn't even let me out of the damn cave. I'll probably die in here.

I look around; let my eyes search the high limestone walls. And suddenly, in spite of everything I've been through, I realize that the place is beautiful. The stalagmites growing up from the floor look like frozen fountains. The orange and yellow dome of the ceiling arches overhead like the great cathedral in Mexico City. An opening at the very top sends a shaft of sunlight down to the sparkling waters. The roots of ancient trees extend down through the cave and into the floor below. They look like the massive pillars in some holy place.

I can't remember how I got to this lake, but I have to admit that I like it here maybe just a little too much. It would be easy just to die here. I search the walls but there's no sign of an entrance. I may not be able to find my way out again, nor back to the witch's cave with all her snakes and blood and hacked off fingers. Not that I would want that anyway.

As I turn and try to stagger away from the lake, I suddenly realize that I can barely move. My legs are twisted with what seem to be ropes of swollen, festering flesh. They seem to bind my legs and make it difficult to walk or even stand. Pain chokes them and won't let go. Christ, I've never felt anything like this... not even after my toughest prizefights in Mexico.

Somewhere, not too far away, I hear the screech of a wild animal.

Some jungle cat must live in here and will probably be tracking me down soon so that she can have me for supper. I wonder how she'll feel though when she gets a closer look at me... probably lose her appetite.

Out of the corner of my eye, I catch some movement along the far wall. A huge jaguar moves along the edge of the lake. She isn't even trying to hide from me. It's almost as though she wants me to see her.

Suddenly, a fight to the death with a jaguar seems damn inviting: two monsters going at it. I'm so fucked up that I really want to strangle *something*. I've got enough hatred in me to crush a tiger. In fact that's exactly what I'd like to do. Get my hands on Tiger, and squeeze the life out of her!

But what I'm facing is Central America's native cat, el jaguar.

"Come on, gato," I shout across the lake. "Come and get me... let's dance. If one of us dies, so what?"

"SO WHAT?" I scream out loud, and then I know.

So Alicia!

Thoughts of Alicia sweep over me: Alicia dancing along beside me as we walk the beaches of San Lucero, Angry little Alicia beating up her bicycle, Jealous Alicia throwing books all across my living room, Sexy Alicia reenacting her world famous *Playboy* photo spread, Loving Alicia saying her vows in the Hapsburg Chapel when we became man and ghost, Alicia nearly burned at the stake by the Inquisition.

"The dead shall not marry the living!" They kept shouting, I remember. But she *did* marry me anyway, in spite of them, in spite of everything. And we're *still* married... so I can't die on her now.

"Stay alive for her," I tell myself. But she's never seen me as I am now: a monster.

Will she be able to look past this Quasimodo face and see her husband? Will she be able to see my soul?

I actually laugh out loud at that thought. Right now, my soul looks worse than my face. It's the soul of a would-be murderer. That's why I can't die. If I do, I'll go straight to hell and never see Alicia again.

I drag my aching body to the far side of the cave, where an outcropping of rock might protect me if the jaguar decides to attack.

And suddenly the cat is right in front of me! She screams into my face. (I thought *my* breath was bad.)

I wanted to take the first punch at the cat, pound my fist right into her face, but now she's too damn close. So, I lunge forward, pull the huge cat off her feet, and I heave her across the floor of the cave. I feel a moment of elation, and then the pain returns. So, I fall into a boxer's crouch, fists raised, as the jaguar comes toward me again.

I figure that I must look like some great ugly troll even to this big cat... one beast fighting another.

I circle, but the jaguar does not, she pads slowly up toward me instead, insistently, head-on. I back away, guard still up, ready to pound my fist into her face.

She flashes her claws as if to drive me back. And I *do* fall backward, and my left hand slams against the cave wall. When I touch the wall of the cave, I hear it speak to me. No shit! Unbelievable!

"DON'T DO THIS," it rumbles.

But the wall isn't exactly talking; it's more sending a loud message right through me. I forget about the jaguar for a moment, and touch the wall again.

"WAIT! LISTEN!" it says.

"For what?" I ask as I turn back to the jaguar. And she's standing there just a few feet from my face certainly able to dive for my throat, rip it open, and kill me in an instant. But she doesn't. Instead, the *jaguar* speaks to me... in the voice of an old woman.

"Vengo a salvarte, Carlitos."

What?

She licks her great teeth and sits back down on her haunches. "I have come to save you," she purrs.

"Your wife sent me."

And then she moves slowly toward me and begins to lick the corded wounds on my legs.

Chapter 23

I'm following the jaguar through a narrow passage at the back of the cave. Somehow, she's restored the power of my legs. A jaguar that is also a curandera? I wonder... impossible.

The light drops dramatically. It's not quite pitch black now, but it's close. My grotesque form hobbles along behind the cat. She moves fast and expects me to keep up. I only wish I could see where the hell I'm going.

As my eyes get used to the darkness, I find that we're on a narrow ledge high above the floor of the cave. One false step and I'll fall several hundred feet, probably bouncing off several limestone projections on the way down. That'd put an end to this nightmare, I decide... and to me.

"Hang on," I call to the cat, but she doesn't stop, doesn't even look back, just keeps moving. The big ugly lump on my back is weighing me down, but I have to keep up. So, I decide that the best thing to do is just focus on her, don't look down, don't slow down, don't worry about my monstrous shape, just go with the spiritual connection between me and the cat and let it drag me along. It seems to work, at least until we come to a sharp switchback in the trail. It's almost 180-degrees. I close my eyes for a second, lug my ugly form around the turn, and when I do, I hear voices.

There, far below us, is a small group of men, marching across the floor of the cave. Two of them are pulling a wagon covered with a blanket. They're following a woman who's strutting along like a majorette, moving so quickly in fact that they can barely keep up with her.

I gasp as they draw closer. It's fucking Tiger Joy and some of her bodyguards. The guys are dressed in those black martial arts outfits. She wears black too, latex or leather... I can hear it squeak as she moves.

The jaguar watches them parade by.

"Keep up, damn you," Tiger calls to her boys. As usual they're tall, lean, perfect physical specimens, and yet every now and then they have to break into a run to catch up with her.

"I'm not slowing down for any of you," Tiger growls. "And, if someone falls behind, I'll see that he never walks again."

That's my girl.

Suddenly the boys are right up with her, grunting and sighing, but staying with the twisted bitch. Even the damn wagon is moving quickly enough.

"We need to follow them," I whisper to the jaguar. She seems to smile. Then, in three quick leaps, she bounds down onto a lower trail that heads off in the same direction as Tiger and her boys.

I close my eyes, think about rolling over on my stomach, dropping down from the ledge, hanging by my fingertips, and falling to the first of three great boulders that form the oversized steps to the trail below.

"Fuck it," I say instead and throw my ugly bulk down after the jaguar trusting to some unknown laws of physics and balance to get me there safely. I make it... in a quick, death-defying plunge.

The new trail is still above the floor of the cave, and we stay just far enough behind Tiger so that she won't notice us.

Soon, the gang is marching back through the wash of cauldron blast, dead snakes, and severed fingers that leads into the witch's cave.

"La Bruja!" Tiger calls in that *bitch-from-hell* voice of hers. "Get out here, you piece of shit!"

The jaguar and I duck into the shadows as La Bruja comes scuttling out of the far corner of the cave. She's looking in our direction, and she can't see us.

"Where the hell's Carlitos?" Tiger hisses.

La Bruja steps back nervously.

"We had a deal."

La Bruja plays with her fingers like a high school kid who's caught reading a dirty book in the back of math class.

"He's here," the witch mumbles.

"Yeah? Like where?"

"In another part of the cave."

"Well, bring him to me."

La Bruja steps forward, looking like she's trying to ingratiate herself to Tiger.

"The mirror worked well," she says with a toothless smile. "You'll be pleased. When he tried to escape, witch hands reached out and cut him. They infected his legs, then his brain. He's transformed himself into a monster."

That's a new idea I think. Transformed *myself?* What the hell does that mean?

"Good!" Tiger smirks. "I want to see him so I can spit in his hideous face."

"Oh, you will," La Bruja answers. But then she looks down at her fingers again. "Only...."

"Only you don't know where he is, do you, Witch?"

La Bruja starts trembling, and I have to ask myself why this powerful witch is so damn intimidated by this slight Chinese girl. What's Tiger holding over her? I find out soon enough.

"We brought you such wonderful treats too." Tiger says.

"Treats?" La Bruja's eyes flare hungrily.

"That's right, two."

"Let me see them?"

"Why not? Look, but don't touch."

Tiger's boys pull a thick blanket from the small cart that they've been dragging along. There are two small children under it, a boy and a girl, both about six years old. They're dressed in simple clothes, pastel t-shirts, shorts.

"Hansel and Gretel," the witch sighs as she hobbles up to them, inspects each one, and then gives the little girl a tight pinch on the cheek.

"I haven't tasted children this tender in a very long time."

The witch actually starts drooling.

"Tastes like chicken, I suppose," Tiger says.

"Much sweeter than that."

Tiger puts her hands on her hips. Her expression is cruel. "You don't get either one of them if you can't produce Carlitos."

"No!"

"In fact, I'll cut off all of your future deliveries."

"But I paid you for those deliveries in advance."

Tiger sneers. "Who gives a shit? No more Carlos, no more children for supper."

La Bruja looks panicky.

"Don't stop my deliveries," she begs.

She takes the little girl's arm and sizes it up, the way a butcher might inspect the foreleg of a lamb before slapping it under the meat cleaver.

"Mmmmm. You'd be a tasty one, princess," she coos to the girl. Then, before anyone can say anything to stop her, the witch pulls the little girl's forearm to her mouth, bites it and begins to suck her blood. "Mmmmm!"

"GET YOUR HANDS OFF OF HER!" Tiger shouts, and the witch obeys at once.

"No Carlos! No treats!"

The little girl is so shaken that she can barely stand. She reels as though she is going to pass out.

The little boy's pale blue shorts blossom a dark stain as he wets his pants.

"Please save us," he says to one of Tiger's men. The guy gives him a funny look, then stiffens and pulls back his fist as if to punch the kid right in the face.

"DON'T DAMAGE THE MERCHANDISE!" Tiger screams. And the guy backs away immediately.

"How long before you can find Carlitos?" Tiger asks as she steps up, takes the children away from La Bruja, and sends them back toward the cart. One of her boys lifts the kids onto it and then wraps that dark robe over them again.

"I'll have Dr. Carlos *Mancowski* in a few days."

La Bruja says my name with disgust.

"A few days?"

"It's a big cave."

"Bullshit!"

Tiger turns quickly to her men and urges them toward the witch. Five guys charge forward, but this time the witch only smiles. With a simple flick of her wrists and a twist of her fingers, she freezes the men in place.

On the ledge beside me, the jaguar starts growling almost silently. She's seen this kind of thing before. She knows exactly what La Bruja can do. But personally, I'm amazed. The men now begin to turn to stone. Their eyes gleam with panic for a second, and then go dull and cold.

The men's color fades to the shade of the cave walls. Then, they begin to erode like rock formations. Cracks ripple through their bodies. Little pieces break off and tumble to the ground as the men become stalagmites right there in front of me.

"Nice trick" Tiger says indifferently as she walks up and rests her hand on the top of one of her former warriors. "But you still don't get the kids."

The witch jerks toward her. She must be weighing the possibility of turning Tiger and what's left of her guards into stone as well.

"Hurt me and you lose your supply of kiddy-treats. Do you want that, old woman?"

The witch heaves a heavy sigh. "Just give me the girl, and I promise you'll have Carlitos within two days."

"You think I want to wait around that long?" Tiger asks. "You'll have to bring him to me in San Francisco. Then you can feast on all the baked, boiled, and sautéed children you could ever want. Hell, I'll cook up a nice kiddy stew for you myself."

"The girl, please, now," the witch pleads. "Just the little girl... for supper?"

Tiger shakes her head in disgust.

"NO WAY!" she says as she turns and stalks out of the cave.

Her two remaining soldiers follow dragging the cart and the doomed children with them.

Chapter 24

I'm out of the cave, running hard to keep up with the jaguar as she heads into the jungle. My body's still not right. I can feel it. I'm limping along and that sack-of-shit hump on my back is heavier than ever. I call to the jaguar, but she doesn't turn, doesn't answer, doesn't even slow down.

My limping run seems to go on forever. But, in spite of it, in some ways I do feel better, because I'm out of the cave, away from the painful images of the past, away from the smell of blood and rotting flesh.

I feel safer too. Who's going to mess with this cat? Okay, maybe some of the poisonous snakes that zigzag though the waist-deep bogs we have to splash through... but the snakes all seem to turn away at the last minute, afraid to take on a magical jaguar who's leading a hobbling, hideous monster through the heart of the jungle.

It's almost nightfall when I finally stumble forward between two huge jacaranda trees and into a clearing beside a small lake. All around it, jungle vines twine their way toward the shore; caves look like black pits in the nearby limestone cliffs. But there's a little bit of a beach that's clear and sandy.

I move toward the water, thirsty as hell, hoping to see if everything I've been through has somehow worked a cure... a small one anyway. Has part of my monster-face faded? Can people stand to look at me now? Can I stand to look at myself? I shake my head. I don't think so.

I run my tongue over the inside of my mouth. The sores are still there, I can feel them; I can *taste* them too.

I take a quick look back over my shoulder for the jaguar. I want to thank her at least for getting me out of that damn cave and curing my wounded legs... but she's gone. I spin around completely, searching the jungle, looking at the long tree branches and the openings of caves. She's nowhere. I'm alone, in the middle of the jungle, and night is coming fast.

Maybe I'm too hideous for anything to attack, I decide. If so, it ain't worth it. I'd rather get out of this monster shape than be grateful for my ugliness.

I turn back to the lake, lean over the water and groan. I still see the face of that ugly *thing* looking back at me: bleeding sores, twisted forehead, festering mouth. I look at my hands; my fingers are stubby and swollen; I'm barely able to bend them. The ugly hump still sits on my back.

I run my hands over my face, and I can *feel* the ugliness.
'FUCK!"

I pound my fist into the shallow water and cut it on the sharp rocks below the surface. Bright red blood pools up immediately. I don't give a damn. I'm so frustrated that I slam my fist down again... and again and again.

I scream in some wild voice that probably invites half a dozen predators to drop by and have me for supper. But I'm so fucking angry that I don't care. I keep slamming my fists into the water and onto those rocks. The water boils with blood. I'm beating my hands into mush, and I'm so fucked-up that I start thinking that maybe I'll get lucky and bleed to death.

Finally, when there's maybe nothing left of my hands but broken bones and torn flesh, I stop. The surface of the lake ripples for a while... I stare some more. It finally clears. The blood is gone. My reflection reappears.

I'm still a monster!

I close my eyes.

"Christ, Jesus, help me," I pray. And when I open my eyes again, beside the face of that hideous *thing* staring back at me... I see Alicia.

#

My wife's image smiles.

"Que tengas paz, mi amor," she whispers. Be at peace.

I'm so happy to see her that I want to reach for her and pull her into my arms, but I'm too damn ashamed. I cover my face with my hands. I can't stand to have her look at me like this.

Alicia floats in front of me, out over the water; she reaches to me and pushes my hands away. Then she lifts my face by my chin so that she's staring directly into my eyes.

"Eres hermoso," she sighs. You're beautiful.

"My face is a garbage pit."

"I see no garbage there," she answers with a slight smile.

I point to the gash on my temple.

She reaches up and begins kissing the spot.

I flinch, but in a moment she pulls back to look at me... she's smiling broadly now. "All better." Then she leans in as though hungry for more.

Her warm lips begin kissing me all over my face, over all the other scars and bruises. Sometimes she even licks them. I would find it disgusting if it weren't so damn *healing*.

But still I stand and wrestle away from her.

"Can't you see what happened to me?"

"Nothing, my love."

"I almost committed murder."

"I don't see that." And now her lips move to mine. Her tongue flicks over sores so nasty I don't even want to think about them... let alone touch them... let alone *taste* them.

Alicia reads the horror in my eyes. "You are delicious, Carlitos."

How the hell can she stand it? I step backward, away from her.

"There's nothing good about me, babe."

Alicia shakes her head impatiently. She's breathing more heavily now. Her words come quickly, almost breathlessly.

"Oh no, Carlitos, you *are* good. Tiger is the murderer. She deserved to die. Besides, you didn't kill her. And anyway, now she is trying to kill you."

Alicia smiles confidently. "But I won't let her!" Her look turns goddamn hot. "I have better uses for you, mi amor."

She leads me away from the lake, over to the mossy earth farther up the bank.

"No more sadness, Carlitos. Let's have some fun."

She's actually laughing when she pulls me to her and kisses me again. Her sweet tongue reaches into my mouth and swirls over the sores and wounds.

Is she nuts? I wonder, but I know she's curing me just the same.

"Didn't that feel good, Carlitos?" She asks breathlessly.

What can I say? I nod.

"Muy bueno," she giggles, and suddenly, her clothes disappear. She's naked, smiling, happy, but so damn sensuous. She cocks her hip, looking like some feral jungle animal. She's muscular; her flesh is smooth, dark, and *real*. She laughs when she sees the shock on my face.

"What did you expect, Carlitos. I did not come here to show you my clothing. I came to the jungle to *mate* with you."

WOW!

She stalks toward me as though I were her prey. She reaches forward and tears off my shirt in one harsh motion.

"Mmmm, no monster here."

She steps up, licks my chest, then reaches behind my shoulders and pulls me to her. She presses her breasts into me, squeezes me tight against her, healing me with her touch. But I still can't relax.

"Stop thinking, Carlitos. Forget about your mind and listen to your body. I like what it's saying. And I like what it makes me feel."

I don't think I have to tell you what she's talking about.

She pushes me down, wrestles off my pants, and climbs on top of me.

"This is what we were made for, my love." And then she takes me inside her.

She's all over me, making love, *really* making love there on top of me in the grass. What the hell can I do but surrender. We thought we might never see each other again. And now we're together as man and ghost, and it's more than great.

"Oh, yes," is all I can sigh. But that's enough for Alicia.

She goes wild, bucks on top of me screaming with pleasure. She raises her arms and tangles her fingers in her hair. Her breasts pull upwards and bounce up and down above me. The view is magnificent. The sky darkens, and she keeps going. And now it starts to rain, and we still don't stop. The wind picks up. Lightning flashes over the roof of the jungle. There must be a thousand explosions. And still we're making love.

The rain is thick and hard. It washes over both of us, and our marathon love gets even wilder. Alicia leans forward over me, digging her fingernails into my chest, staring into my eyes, screaming wildly; I'm afraid that she's going to explode. She does. But magically I don't. We're drenched... still clutching each other as though we don't *dare* stop. And maybe we don't ... so we keep it up...

FOR HOURS!

#

It's morning. I open my eyes, and see Alicia lying there beside me...still naked, still horny as hell. I can tell by the shape of her nostrils if nothing else. Okay, she's glowing bright red and her nipples are hard and pointed.

"You're still hot for me, huh?"

"Sí, Carlitos." She smiles, bites her lip, and then she gives me that sexy giggle as she lowers her face into my lap and opens her lips.

"My treat," she whispers as she swallows me, and, in a second, I'm done... probably for the next month. Well, maybe not. Not with Alicia around.

I fall asleep again and when I awake this time, she's standing there looking down at me.

"Come on," she giggles. "I want to show you something."

She takes my hand, leads me to the edge of the water, pulls me down onto my knees in the soft wet sand, and whispers, "See, my love, you're beautiful."

I look. And I am. I'm fucking beautiful.

I have a glow from a night of endless sex. But far more importantly, the scars are gone, the hump is gone, and my twisted limbs are straight. Hell, I look better than ever.

"It was all in your mind, mi amor."

"And you cured me."

"Lovemaking can sometimes screw your head right back on straight, Carlitos," she giggles.

"Is that what you were screwing?"

She swats me playfully.

"Maybe the most important part of it, though."

"If you say so."

I kiss her quickly, and I'm so damn happy that I run right into the lake, bound out past the sharp stones, and into the soft muck beyond. I launch myself and swim out to the very center.

Are their crocodiles in here? Who gives a shit? I'll kiss the first crock that comes up to me. That should keep the rest of the bastards away.

But no crocodile comes by. And when I turn back toward the shore again I see Alicia mounted on an enormous black horse.

"My ghost horse, Espanto Negro," she calls to me. "He will carry us to Señor Popcorn's hacienda. There we can make much more love if you want to. Are you ready for that?"

I'm not sure I'm capable of any more lovemaking in the near future, but hell, maybe I am, and suddenly I feel so damn ready that I can't help but shout, "Ole!"

I swim, then run toward her through the waves. I vault up onto the horse and land right behind my wife, ready to ride.

The horse rears, and we charge off into the jungle, eager for civilization, showers, clean clothing, food, drink, and who knows what else.

Chapter 25

"It will only be a little party, mi amor," Alicia says.

"Sounds good to me," I answer. And the truth is, it does.

We arrived late last night after a wild horseback ride through the jungle and along the beaches. Espanto Negro moved slowly and carefully through the swampy water and tangled vines, then bolted into the open and galloped all-out along the edge of the shore... all the way to Cancun.

We arrived so late that the master of the house and his wife (Señor and Señora Popcorn – Fernando and Eva de Cervantes) had already retired. So, Señor Popcorn's right-hand man Miguel welcomed us. He showed us a little bungalow at the edge of the estate and made sure that we had a hearty dinner delivered to our room. Alicia and I spent a good hour and a half bathing each other in the enormous Jacuzzi. Later, after I'd had enough to eat, I climbed onto the big soft bed and fell immediately into a dreamless sleep that lasted for more than 24 hours.

But now I'm wide-awake.

"A *breakfast* party?" I ask.

"Why not. It is a tradition on the great rancheros... breakfast complete with Bloody Marys, mimosas, margaritas, fizzy gin drinks, mangos, papayas, huevos, bacon, breakfast rolls, coffees. It will be wonderful."

"Can't wait."

"So then put on the sexy new clothes Señora Popcorn bought for you," Alicia says, "and let's go."

I slide into a neat light blue polo shirt, some linen slacks, a brand new pair of loafers, and we head out the door.

Across the lawn I spot tables full of goodies. I also see many very close friends. The first to come running up to me is the great man himself, Señor Popcorn. He hugs me, then goes to Alicia and gives her a hug too.

"Come, have something to get started," he says. "And you have to meet the people who've come to welcome you home."

Señor Popcorn's wife, Eva, glides up to the great man's side and takes his arm. "We tried to keep it small, just a very few friends," she says. "But we *did* want to have Assad and his family here."

"You brought them all the way from San Francisco?"

"Of course. Why not? You're safe, everyone's happy. We have to celebrate."

I spot Assad and his beautiful wife Veronica standing at one of the tables. A chef is whipping up some made-to-order waffles. Their little son Carlitos, standing beside his mother, is excited about the Mickey Mouse waffle that the guy has just pulled off the grill. As I march toward them Assad turns, then breaks into a run, charges toward me, catches me around the waist, lifts me off the ground, staggers around, almost falls over backward in the process, but manages to put me back onto my feet while still giving me a great hug. He has tears in his eyes.

"So glad to see you, bro," he says in his thick Persian accent. The "bro" doesn't quite fit, but Assad has always wanted to be cool, which I think he is, in spite of the fact that we disagree so violently on how to organize the records in his store.

Veronica comes running up to me too. She's tall, gorgeous. She gives me a hell of a hug, then nuzzles a kiss into my neck.

"You might not be here if it wasn't for these two," Alicia says. "They helped me bribe the ghosts at the women's correctional facility."

"It was nothing," Assad says quickly. And he blushes.

"Come, amigos," I hear Señor Popcorn calling. "Let's feed this young man before he dies of starvation."

"You *are* quite thin," I hear a honey voice add, and I turn to see Amy Joy smiling at me. She runs up to me and gives me a bigger hug than her sister did. Over her shoulder, I see Alicia bristle. She's glowering at Señor Popcorn.

"Why is *she* here," my wife whispers too loudly for anyone to ignore. They all look away.

"Veronica insisted," he answers. "Said she helped you figure out how to save your husband."

"Well, that is true," Alicia admits.

"So forget your jealousy for a few hours, Niña, and just enjoy the celebration."

"Sí," Alicia answers, but she steps forcefully between Amy and me, takes my arm with both hands, and leads me toward the bar.

"Thank you for your help, chica," she calls over her shoulder to Amy, then under her breath she adds, "Now get away from my man."

Amy puts her hands on her hips disapprovingly. But she doesn't try to interfere as my ghost-wife and I head up to the bar where margaritas, mimosas, and other drinks are being served. I take a Bloody Mary for myself, pick out a ghost mimosa for Alicia, hand it to her, and then raise my glass. "Saludos, mi amor."

She bats those big eyes at me and says, with a perfectly American accent, "Saludos yourself, *handsome.*"

WOW! That's new.

The other guests now descend on us. Señora Popcorn's father-in-law, Enrique Córdoba, the ghosts of Alicia's fellow models, Chula Contreras and Sylvia Morales, they all want to wish us well. We chat while handsome hombres in starched white uniforms serve up plates full of breakfast hors d'oeuvres. Baby Carlitos munches away on his Mickey Mouse waffle. I recount my adventures with the snakes in the cave. And then I see Señor Popcorn's mother-in-law, Yolanda Córdoba, making her way through the crowd arm in arm with a very old woman. The other guests step back and make way for her. Alicia smiles when they finally come up to us.

"Carlitos," she says, "Please allow me to introduce la curandera, Doña Cuca."

"¡Buenos dias, Carlitos!" she says.

It can't be. But, as I stare into the old woman's eyes, I know at once that it's true.

"You're the jaguar."

She smiles and purrs.

Holy shit!

I'm surprised enough, and then I am suddenly startled by the mariachi band as it blares out the first loud notes of the morning's entertainment. Fortunately, I don't spill Bloody Mary all over myself, and soon we are all following Señor Popcorn as he leads us to a great round table that has been set up on the far side of the lawn.

"Breakfast is served, my friends," he says.

We take our seats. And then another old ghost-friend fades into our presence, Padre Hidalgo.

Before anyone can greet him, he makes the sign of the cross and begins the benediction.

But just then a piercing scream cuts through the air, stopping everything.

We turn in the direction of the sound. It's come from the edge of the jungle behind us. The scream comes again, long, loud, and painful. I get from my chair and run in that direction. Alicia is right with me; so are Señor Popcorn and Doña Cuca.

I dive into the thickest part of the wild. I don't have to go far. A few yards from the edge of the property I see a young woman kneeling over a dying man. Scratches rake across his face, over his neck and his chest. His stomach is pulled open; guts spill from the wound. The man's eyes are wide with panic, and blood pours from his mouth. He gurgles as he tries to form words.

I recognize the young woman who is kneeling there. It's Marie Elena, wife of Señora Popcorn's right-hand man. The tattered body she's looking at belongs to her husband Miguel.

"Oh, Carlitos," Marie Elena sobs as she spins toward me and buries her face in my shoulder.

Doña Cuca rushes up to us. She kneels down beside Miguel, runs her hands slowly over his face; feels the blood pouring from his throat. I start to say something, and she just shakes her head.

"Carlitos," Alicia sobs as she reads the hopelessness in Doña Cuca's eyes.

Then both women are staring at me...

What?

Everyone is staring at me.

"Do it," La Doña says with a grunt that sounds like both a curse and a command. What the hell is she talking about?

Eva pulls up next to us now. She studies the situation for a moment, studies the other curandera.

"Yes," she sighs, and nods her head toward me.

"Carlos Mancowski," Doña Cuca calls, and this time she takes my hand and moves it slowly back and forth over the body of the dying man.

I don't know what to do. I close my eyes. I pray, hoping that it's what the women are asking of me.

And then, through my closed eyes I see myself as a very, very little boy, and my grandmother, Ixchel, is speaking to me as she guides my hand to a little bird that has carelessly flown headlong into a storefront window. It hit with such noisy force that it must be dead.

Ixchel still has the wide innocent eyes of the child I saw in the witch's mirror as she fell in love with my grandfather, and now she molds my fingers around the little head of the bird, and she forces me to squeeze.

"You are descendant from a long line of witches... you have the power," she tells me. "You can cure when no curandera can ever cure, even the most hopeless cases."

I squeeze the bird and feel it begin to stir under my fingers. It cheeps. I open my hand, and it hops up and flies away.

Ixchel kneels back and smiles at me. "You are such a good boy, Carlitos," she whispers. "But you must always use this power for good. Too many of our family have used it for evil."

I feel a stirring under my fingers now, and I open my eyes to see that the bleeding at Miguel's neck has stopped. He no longer spits up blood. His eyes have become clear. The great wounds in his chest and stomach are healed. He reaches up and takes me by the wrist and squeezes... powerfully.

"Thank you, my friend," he says.

Marie Elena grasps me even tighter, then spins from me to her husband and embraces him.

Doña Cuca is beaming at me, as are Eva and Alicia. "You have saved him," the old curandera whispers to me so that none of the others can hear. "You are true to your bloodline. You are a witch."

"Great!" I sigh. Only Alicia picks up the sarcasm in my voice.

Now Señor Popcorn blusters forward with half a dozen men behind him.

"Take Miguel back to the house," Doña Cuca commands. "Let Eva tend to his wounds."

"Your wife too is a curandera," she tells Señor Popcorn. "She can complete the cure."

Señor Popcorn nods. "But what or who the hell attacked Miguel?" he asks.

Doña Cuca shudders. "Yes, *what* is the right word for the monster, Señor. *She...* has joined us."

"She?"

La Doña doesn't look up but keeps talking, as though to herself.

"I have to face her. I have to deal with her right now."

"Deal with what? Who is she?"

"I have to do it alone this time. No one can come with me."

"I need to go with you," I say.

"No! Alone!"

"Let me send an army," Señor Popcorn shouts.

"It can only be me. No one must come."

Alicia begins to rise to her feet.

"Do you hear me, Alicia?" La Doña says to her. "No one must come."

Alicia nods as Doña Cuca continues.

"I have to face my sister alone!"

5
Alicia

Chapter 26

Doña Cuca moves swiftly through the jungle, and as she does, she transforms into the jaguar. I am right behind her... invisible. She can clearly see me though and, just before we break out onto the beach, she turns and growls at me. She does not want me with her.

"It is okay, Señora Jaguar," I say, "I have hidden successfully from your sister before."

The jaguar snarls again. Then she crouches as though she is going to pounce.

I stand my ground. She lunges. I close my eyes, and she passes right through me. I spin around as she comes back toward me again.

"Please, Doña. There is no time for this. I will keep my distance and only observe. I promise."

The big cat pulls her ears back, pulls her long whiskers down, and then *slinks* through me very slowly. I feel a terrible flowing shock like cruel electricity as she does this. It is a warning, I know. But I *have to* follow her, and she must know that too.

Now, we are on the beach, and as soon as we move away from the jungle we see La Bruja standing against the purple sky, which has now become stormy and full of fright. She wears her long, tattered, white gown. A double necklace of snow-white finger-bones falls down over her breasts. The thin fabric of her skirt flaps in the wind. Snakes twine around her feet. Doña Cuca does not change her jaguar shape. She merely pads up to her sister with an awful rumble coming from her throat.

La Bruja looks at her with some amount of fear, I think. And suddenly she becomes an animal too... a great pit viper nearly eight feet long, with a scaly body and a huge black head. She rears up above the cat revealing her bright yellow belly...

And then she lunges.

I want to gasp, but I know I should not. So, I stuff my fingers in my mouth and bite down hard. *Ouch!*

The jaguar swipes at the viper with her claws. The snake jerks back and then dives under the big cat and quickly whips around her middle. The jaguar swats at the viper and manages to knock its head close enough so that she can catch it in her mouth. Holding the snake's head between her jaws, La Señora twists wildly, throws herself up into the air, and lands on top of the monster. But the viper's coils tighten.

The two thrash there on the beach and the sky goes purple-black as smaller snakes squirm up out of the sea and move toward the big cat. They begin to slither up over her body. Still, she bites down harder and harder on the head of the viper and tears at it with long bloody claws.

There must be hundreds of snakes now, swarming up from the water to help their mistress. Soon, the jaguar's form is hidden under a mass of writhing serpents but she still thrashes around under them.

¡Dios mío! Things are getting desperate, I think. This is where I have to step in, I know. But I gave my promise.

I stop and wonder what to do. Should I let Doña Cuca die because I gave my word that I would not interfere? Would she want me to stand here and watch her suffocate under a pile of snakes? Is there any logic to that?

As Doña Cuca fights for her life under millions of squirmy snakes, I try to calm myself and think as Carlitos taught me:

If Doña Cuca's sister is killing her

But I gave my promise not to interfere with them

Then I *should not* interfere.

Therefore I should just watch Doña Cuca die because she would want me to.

QED

That makes no sense to me at all. Logical is just not the way my brain works. Besides the jaguar has begun a low mewing that sounds as though she is suffocating under the snakes and losing her battle for life. And so I decide to be most illogical and dishonorable and come to her aid. But before I can do anything, Carlitos comes rushing along the beach. Lightning ripples all around him... with the shape of his body, with each stride, and especially over his shoulders, down his arms, and into his hands. His fingers have lightning crawling all over them. He marches up to the tangle of snakes that form a slithery blanket over the body of the jaguar. Lightning flashes from his fingertips as he sends beams of laser light directly down the center of the snake blanket. The power from each hand pushes the smaller snakes apart. They split as though someone has driven a huge meat cleaver down between them. Fire crackles over their skin and they come loose from each other. Then they squirm away from the writhing bodies of the jaguar and the great viper and scurry back into the water making a strong sizzling sound as they enter the waves.

La Bruja, the great serpent, rears her head with the jaguar still draped over her. She studies Carlitos like the cold-blooded reptile that she is. She feints toward him. Carlitos stands his ground. His hands are pointed downward toward the beach, and lightning flows through his body, from his fingertips, and down into the sand, which melts into puddles of glass where the lightning strikes.

Witch fingers suddenly push up from the sand and grab at my husband while hands and arms appear. But just as quickly he stomps his foot on the nearest grabbing hands, crushing them like so many hungry spiders. SPLAT!

The grasping fingers quickly pull back below the sand and within seconds, La Bruja returns to her human form.

She stalks toward Carlitos for a few steps, then turns suddenly toward her sister, the jaguar.

"You just can't fight your own battles, can you?" she shouts above the wind.

"What about all the damn snakes you brought with you?" Doña Cuca responds as she too becomes human and points to the tangle of vipers that are once again slithering toward her out of the water.

"So, what about them?"

"Call them off."

La Bruja shrugs and shakes her head. But Carlitos points at the vipers once again and an arch of lightning flashes from his fingertips to the snakes on the beach. There's a zap and crackle and the snakes jangle nervously as a million billion watts of witchcraft (or something like that) pour into their bodies.

I smile in my invisibility. I like this.

"The boy learns fast," La Bruja says, as she shakes her head unhappily.

"What's to learn? He has the blood of witches," La Doña answers.

"Powerful witches," La Bruja agrees, and she almost smiles at her sister.

"Palaver?" La Doña asks after a long moment.

"Sí," La Bruja whispers. "Follow me." And she turns her back on us and walks into the wind, which is now whipping at her robes and her hair, making her look like some lost ship trying to fight her way back to the safety of the harbor. Doña Cuca struggles along after her. I turn to see that Carlitos is not coming. He simply smiles and shrugs as if to say, I've done my job, and I guess he has.

I watch as he turns and walks slowly down the beach and away from us. There's a happy bounce to his steps; he's almost dancing. Being a witch must be something he enjoys. And so I float after the sisters, smiling because of the happiness of my Carlitos, and the fact that I am not affected by winds at all. And that is why it is sometimes better to be a ghost than either a curandera or a witch.

At last we come to a small lean-to tucked up against a limestone cliff. In the center of the little shack, a black pot hangs over a circle of stones. Inside the circle is a fire that seems to have been out for some time. The sisters draw near the cauldron. I move slowly backward toward the surrounding woods, trying to be as invisible as their magical powers will allow me to be.

"Care for tea?" the witch asks her sister.

"Yes, but let me make it for you."

Doña Cuca pulls a small packet of dry leaves out of her pocket.

La Bruja does not like this, and she scowls for a very long time. Finally, she simply flashes her fingers at the fire, and it bursts into flame.

The water in the pot boils quickly and soon the witch sinks two cups into it and pulls them out full of boiling water. Her sleeves, arms, and hands are wet, but somehow they are not burned.

Doña Cuca must think this is normal because she does not even look up. She just continues to wrap the leaves in the thin cloth she brought with her, and she starts to hum.

"Stop that nonsense," La Bruja says. Doña Cuca ignores her as she ties a small string around the ends of the cloth and dunks it into La Bruja's cup.

"Teabags, teabags," Doña Cuca sings.

"I detest them."

"So very convenient."

La Bruja spits into both cups. "That's for convenience."

La Doña peers into her cup, makes a face but says nothing, just takes the teabag from the witch's cup and puts it in her own.

"Why are you always so hateful?" she asks.

"You know why." La Bruja's face grows darker than the stormy sky. She takes a sip of the tea, and within seconds she is smiling.

"Mmmmm, this *is* good tea. What's the flavor?"

"My own special blend."

"It's giving me a little buzz."

Doña Cuca smiles too, sips her tea, and waits a long while. Then she whispers something that only she and I can hear.

"A little buzz, yes. That's why you won't mind telling the truth, *Princesa*."

#

The two women settle into the back of the lean-to, sipping their tea and staring at each other, each waiting for her sister to say something. Finally, Doña Cuca mumbles, "You were always the pretty one."

Her sister's eyes light up. "Yes, I was."

"Everyone called you La Princesa."

"The Princess," the witch repeats, and she begins to fluff her tangled hair as though she were a great beauty.

"Papa was in love with you, you know."

As the witch remembers these things she actually seems to become younger and more beautiful.

"He gave you everything."

And now, even though I am a ghost, I realize that, growing up, I had a sister like La Bruja. *"She thought she was a princess too."* I almost say the words out loud, but I realize that I made a promise to be silent, and I know that I cannot break my promise.

"Back in the days of the empire," Doña Cuca continues, "Papa was always giving you gifts."

La Bruja beams. "My favorite was the monkey. Remember the little monkey figure? He had arms and legs that could move."

"I had nothing."

"You deserved nothing; you were such a nasty bitch."

Doña Cuca cackles. "I was, wasn't I?"

"You hated me, I could feel it," La Bruja says.

"It was just because Papa always liked you better."

"Did not!"

La Bruja actually sticks her tongue out at her sister. "I remember the time he gave *you* a wonderful little figure too," La Bruja says.

"The ballplayer?"

"I don't remember what it was; I just remember that it was brightly polished and very, very nice. Papa came home from his work, and we both ran up to hug him, but then he turned away from me and smiled at you. For that one moment, I hated *him*."

Doña Cuca rolls her eyes as though she were eight. "He only did it because Mama told him not to ignore me. She told him that he spent too much time with his *Princesa*." Doña Cuca says the last word in a nasty way that is full of anger and the need for revenge.

La Bruja smiles anyway; she likes hearing her nickname. Then she frowns.

"On that day he *was* nicer to you. He gave you the little statue, and I saw how your eyes lit up when you reached up on your tiptoes to take it from him."

"I was thrilled."

"And then you disappeared... took it back to your room to play with it, remember?"

Doña Cuca's eyes suddenly flame at her sister. Her smile disappears. "What I remember is that when I turned to say 'Thank you, Papa,' I saw that he was giving you a figure too."

"I don't think so. Are you sure he gave me something?"

"I saw him, and it wasn't a tiny sculpture of a ballplayer... it was a big jade figure of a GOD!"

The witch, who now looks even more young and beautiful, smiles at the memory. "We were so spoiled, weren't we?"

"*You* were so spoiled. By Papa! And that day he teased me with the name that the village children used to call me. Do you remember it?"

"I was La Princesa to everyone, even the other kids. And you were.... I guess I don't remember."

Doña Cuca now has tears in her eyes. "They called me Pulgita – little *flea*."

"That's right," La Bruja remembers. "I thought it was cute. Very... nice, anyway, I think."

"Then why did Mama get so mad the one time Papa called me that?"

"He was just teasing."

"Of course, he was. But to call his own daughter the same nasty name that the street kids called me... it just made me very sad, that's all. What kind of name is that for the sister of the Princess?"

"Papa never teased you that way again."

"Mama would have beaten him with her broom if he did, and he actually did use that name once more when we were alone, just before my Celebration."

"When Mama and Papa announced that you had become a woman and were eligible for marriage."

"Yes. I was sixteen and he did it then, at the worst of all possible times. 'You will make some man a very lovely bride,' he said to me, and then he added, 'you little flea.' It ruined everything."

"You were always too sensitive."

"Your Celebration was a year before, Princesa. Papa had arranged a wonderful union for you with Chac. And whenever Chac and the chaperones would come to the house to see you, Mama would call me to be with her when she greeted them.

"And I would stand there smiling at Chac, who was such a handsome boy, and Mama would beam at him. But as soon as her back was turned, Chac would begin teasing me and reciting that nasty rhyme that the street kids used when I was little:

Little flea, little flea,
Your sister has such beauty
So why are you so ugly
You scrawny little flea?

"And even the chaperone would laugh until Mama came back to the door, and when she did, Chac would give me a look that said, 'Don't you dare tell your Mama what I said,' and so I didn't."

La Bruja is smiling as though none of this is very important and does not matter to her at all.

"I remember when we were in the market," she says. "Mama was getting bananas for the evening supper. And Chac came up to us with his friends."

"Not to us, to *you*, they clustered around *you* with their backs to me, and I was so sad that I just stood there staring at the ground. I was on the outside, but still it was better than having them start chanting that stupid rhyme."

"I thought it was a wonderful moment," La Bruja says. She is not even aware of her sister's sorrow. "All their attention was focused on me."

"But then I felt a hand touch my arm," Doña Cuca says and her eyes brighten. "And then it touched my face."

"I don't remember that."

"It lifted my chin so that I was looking into *his* eyes, which were so dark and brown and beautiful."

"I don't remember that either."

"It was Ichik."

As I sit in the shadows looking at these sisters, I am amazed. At the mention of the boy's name, Doña Cuca is suddenly as beautiful as her sister.

"He asked me to walk with him. I did. I had experienced my Celebration; I was of marriageable age. Papa had not yet committed my life to anyone. I thought I could convince him that Ichik was the one."

La Bruja's beauty does not fade, but a jealous look comes into her eyes.

"Ichik was really just trying to get close to me, you know," she says. "He knew he could not have me because I had been promised to Chac. But I fell in love with him anyway."

"Papa did not give me to Ichik immediately," La Doña continues as though lost in her own thoughts, "even though we were both of marriage age, and of the same level of society. Everything was right for our union. He would have made a great addition to our family. But Papa said he had to think about it. Why was that?"

"I don't know," La Bruja answers, but her eyes tell me that she is lying.

"Papa *did* allow Ichik to call on me, and to try and convince him of the goodness of our marriage. He came to see me every day with a chaperone, and we walked together... and we talked... sometimes about *you, Princesa*."

"What did he say about me?"

"Oh, I shouldn't tell you."

"Please."

"You might not like it."

"Of course I'll like it."

Doña Cuca shrugs and looks past her sister to me. She winks, and then says the next words very quickly, just to get them out of her mouth, before she can change her mind.

"He said you were too full of yourself to be really beautiful and that he felt sorry for Chac, who didn't understand that."

La Bruja's eyes narrow. Doubt fills them and her beauty begins to fade. Her eyes shift across to the distant sea, searching for something, some idea that might suggest that she is better than her sister in spite of this criticism. And then she smiles.

"Here's something you didn't know, Pulgita. Ichik tried to force himself on me one day. I was just standing with some other girls near the marketplace, and he grabbed me and pulled me into the shadows. He had his hands all over me, on my breasts, up under my dress, I was saving myself for Chac, and yet he came after me. I said 'no,' but he insisted. He was kissing me when I broke away and ran all the way home. He almost raped me."

Doña Cuca laughs. Her smile is bright. Now she is more youthful and beautiful than her sister.

"I was there," she says. "You didn't see me, but I was coming up the path in back of the market. I saw what happened. *You* threw yourself at Ichik, and he pushed you away. When you grabbed him down there, he slapped you."

La Bruja's appearance returns to that of an evil witch. She stares angrily at her sister.

"I know the day you are talking about, and it wasn't that day; it was a different day. And he did throw himself at me."

"You threw yourself at him," Doña Cuca repeats as she stands.

"And when he didn't give in, you killed him."

Everyone gasps, even the snakes that have once again begun gliding toward Doña Cuca.

"The king killed him," La Bruja answers.

"But you set it up, didn't you? For the first time in your life *you* were jealous of *me,* and you couldn't stand it. La Princesa actually lost the very best of all the boys to the little flea."

Irony is something Mexican women understand very well, I think. And Doña Cuca seems to understand it better than any of us.

La Bruja shakes her head sadly. "It doesn't matter what you think or what you say."

"You took my husband from me."

La Bruja sighs. "It still doesn't matter," she says, "because of Ixchel."

Chapter 27

Doña Cuca stares into the fire, and then speaks slowly, as though she has been taken back to the very city where she grew up... to maybe the most important day of her life.

"I met Ichik in the square on the day that a young warrior was to have his heart torn out. He had been captured in a recent war, which was only fought to gather victims for human sacrifice.

"Ichik and I stood near the temple, watching and listening to the doomed boy. He was covered with flowers, and the sweet smell was overpowering even from as far away as we were. He knew he was going to die that day, and yet he was trying hard to hold fast to the images that the high priests had given him... beautiful young women would meet him in paradise after he gave his life for the good of the city.

"We watched as the high priest came up to him and gave him a drink. It was some kind of drug that would excite him and almost make him look forward to the moment of death.

"The warrior smiled as the priest approached. Maybe he knew of the drug. He almost seemed to be resigned, and he kept repeating the sacred poems that they had taught him.

"'Are you ready to be sent to the heavens?' the holy man asked.

"'I am.' The young warrior's voice was strong and confident.

"'You know that your blood will feed the Gods, and they will bless our fields with great harvests.'

"'I do.'

"The priest held the cup to the warrior and whispered, 'Drink this, and you will feel absolute joy.'

"The warrior stared into the eyes of the priest for a moment. I thought I saw him fight back the beginnings of terrible fear, and then he regained his confidence and drank, and as he did, wild music began to sound from the group on the steps of the pyramid. Then, throngs of girls came running out from behind it. They began dancing... first away from him and then back again. They swayed wickedly. Young men joined them as they wove back and forth in a dance that was meant to please the Gods and encourage them to accept the warrior and his sacrifice.

"You were there, Princesa," Doña Cuca tells her sister as they stare at each other. "I saw you dancing, and I know that the warrior could not take his eyes from you. You were flirting with him, and, as the drugs began to take control of him, I knew that he was picturing you as his lover in paradise.

"The royal family came and sat in their box to watch the ceremony. Other important families also took their seats. The artisans came, including Papa and Mama, and others too who stood behind the royal box according to their rank. Even the slaves were allowed to watch.

"The high priests came forward. Many of them had hair that was thick, matted, and smelly. Their faces were caked with blood from so many human sacrifices.

"They snaked their way through the dancers. By now the warrior was caught up in the dance. His eyes were wild, and he even tried to dance along with the others as he stood there tied to the stake. He was even smiling into the faces of his executioners.

"'Now!' Ichik called to me, and we ran from the center of our great city and down into the jungle.

"We reached a huge tree whose branches extended out over a clearing. Beneath it there was fresh new grass.

"'I may die very soon just like the warrior,' Ichik whispered to me, 'a human sacrifice... only this time it will be on the ballcourt.'

"I looked at him in horror. I could already hear cheering and I knew that the high priests were preparing the dagger that would cut into the young warrior's chest.

"But you're only playing a game," I said to Ichik. "It may be deadly for our enemies, but not for the local boys who play it."

"'Sweet girl,' Ichik answered, 'I have so many enemies, so many people hating me... because they want me.'

"I didn't understand this. So, all I could think to say was, 'I want you too.'

"'And I want you... only you,' he answered. 'And now I have something to give you that can be with you even if I am taken away.'

"I threw myself at him then, and we made love, and the passionate music of the dance made our lovemaking even more exciting. It went on endlessly it seemed, until the poor doomed warrior let out a great cry of pain. And then he called out a single word, and I recognized the word even though we were now so far away from him. He called out your name, sister. He shouted, 'Princesa!'

"I ignored it, even though I knew what was happening. The high priest was cutting open the warrior's chest, reaching inside of it, and pulling out his living heart. I knew a bowl would be brought forward to hold the heart. Other bowls would catch the warrior's blood, which poured from his body just as Ichik's love poured into me.

"Your lovemaking was a sin against everyone..." La Bruja interrupted. "Even before the coming of the Christians, it was a sin."

"It was a miracle that saved my life and bound me to Ichik through eternity. Everyone knew of my love for him, but not that I had become pregnant. At least no one knew for a little while."

"Papa went nuts when he found out. He would have killed Ichik if the king hadn't already done it."

"I don't think so. Everything would have been perfect. Ichik would have made a great member of our family. But you became so jealous that you went to the king and asked that Ichik be sacrificed at the end of the ballgame."

La Bruja smiles. "That is why I became a witch, after all: to punish him for not choosing me. But, anyway, magic is in our blood. We both have it; it's just how we choose to use it."

"And La Princesa could not stand by and watch her sister marry the most beautiful boy in the city," Doña Cuca says bitterly. "She had to stop it, even though she already had a husband chosen for her."

La Bruja looks at her sister with both hatred and contempt.

"The king didn't like Ichik either, you know. He wanted him dead."

Doña Cuca's eyes grow wide. "I don't believe that."

"Think about it. I was not the only person in our city who *wanted* Ichik. Someone much more powerful than I did as well."

"The king's daughter? His wife?"

La Bruja looks at her sister and shakes her head.

"Even as an old woman you know so very little about the ways of the world, Pulgita. The king wanted the beautiful young boy to be *his* lover. But Ichik rebuffed him just as he had rebuffed everyone else... except you, little flea... except you. When you let him fall in love with you, you brought about his death as much as any of us."

Doña Cuca's face twists with terrible understanding.

"That's why father didn't want me to marry him. That's why, after his death, mother had me taken into the jungle to live with the curanderas, isn't it...to hide my daughter from the king."

"Oh no," La Bruja sneers. "The king wanted you to have your daughter. He wanted to watch her grow up and become the sweetest girl in the city. He wanted me to work spells to increase her beauty."

"I don't understand."

"Of course you do. What is the greatest human sacrifice there is?"

NICK IUPPA & JOHN P. MENDOZA

Doña Cuca looks suddenly terrified. She shakes her head. She does not answer, and after a moment La Bruja responds to the question herself.

"A young girl. A virgin. Tied to the stake in front of the temple. Covered with flowers. Fed the potions. Fed the dreams of heaven and lovers... those thoughts can even tempt a 12-year-old girl, you know."

"My God." Doña Cuca's hands are trembling now.

"Even God couldn't have saved her, Pulgita... or you. Once your daughter became a human sacrifice and had her heart ripped out, you would have been taken to the top of the great pyramid and thrown from it.... down onto the streets... while everyone watched and cheered."

Doña Cuca seems overwhelmed by these new ideas.

"So, mother saved me, and my daughter, Ixchel."

"Named after the moon goddess."

"Ixchel the first, I guess."

"There would be others... descendants... and they would all go on to become curanderas or witches, but all would have our magical gifts. And they would live alone in the jungle... and would take the lovers that the moon goddess sent them, and have more Ixchels... until one of their line would move into a small fishing village and fall in love with a stranger named Conrad Mancowski. And she would marry him, and pass on her magic to her children and her children's children."

As I sit invisibly and listen to this story, I am amazed and frightened. Two important questions jump into my mind. I studied a small amount of history in my school, and I know something about the Maya and their rulers. Finally, I can stand it no longer. I appear before the sisters and smile at them, anxiously.

"Forgive me," I say.

The two sisters only look at me. Their conversation has tired them so much that they have no energy to give me any trouble. Besides, I am even more *spiritual* than they are.

"The ghost of Alicia Maria Mejias Mancowski Mann, the wife of Carlitos," Doña Cuca says as an introduction.

"I would kill you," the witch grunts at me, "but I'm just too damn tired from all this storytelling."

"I am already dead," I remind her. "But thank you for sparing me anyway. Now please answer a question for me."

"Why not."

"What did the king do to your family? If your mother denied the sacrifice he planned to make of your sister and your niece, what did he do to them?"

La Bruja stands. She dumps the bucket into the fire and stirs the ashes to make sure they go out. A great cloud of steam and smoke puffs up from the dead fire and fills the little lean-to. Doña Cuca gets to her feet coughing, and then she hobbles out onto the beach to escape the evil cloud.

La Bruja doesn't seem to mind it. She tosses the cups inside the empty cauldron and comes out to join us.

"Time to go," she tells us.

"But my question?" I ask.

The witch wipes her hand across her grimy forehead and mumbles. I almost think she's praying, but I'm not sure witches are allowed to do that.

"I saved them," La Bruja says at last. "Maybe the only good deed I ever did in my life, and it cost me my city, my home, and the boy who planned to marry me.

"I took my mother, sister and niece to a distant village outside our city state, helped them fit in, worked magic to make it all happen. It took nearly a year, and the effort was so great that it drained away my beauty. When Chac saw me on my return, he would not even speak to me. No man wanted me after that, though I cast many spells to try and make it happen. There are so many tragic stories I could tell you about that time, Alicia. Just thinking of them fills my heart with sorrow."

She shakes her head in sadness. "I sincerely hope that I never see you again."

"I'm sorry," I say.

She walks slowly to Doña Cuca, looks her in the eyes for a long moment and sighs. I see the sadness and exhaustion on her face. I see that Doña Cuca has much the same expression. La Bruja kisses her sister on the cheek.

"Good bye, little flea," she says with more tenderness than I would have ever expected from the witch, and then she turns and walks slowly down the beach and out of my life.

Forever, I hope.

Chapter 28

An hour later I find my way into the great room of Señor Popcorn's estate. I try to assume the best human form I can think of: freshly washed hair, a summer dress that is purple/blue like the jacaranda trees that surround the hacienda. I have on high heels so that I am almost as tall as Carlitos.

"¡Hola!" I say wearily. Ghosts never get tired, so I don't know where this feeling comes from, but I am not full of excitement even though I am returning to the people I love.

Everyone in the room looks so sad: Carlitos, El Señor, and Miguel who is bandaged and still recovering from La Bruja's attack. Marie Elena has her hand on his shoulder trying to give him strength through her gentle touch, I guess.

Eva and her mother Yolanda stand by the fireplace, sharing glasses of brandy. Enrique is with them, as quiet as the others. I also spot Señor Marinara of the FBI sitting near the popcorn man. He looks worried.

Carlitos stands the moment he sees me and rushes up to me. He is my hero, is he not: mine and Miguel's and Marie Elena's and Doña Cuca's. I am sure that the ancient curandera is already on her way back to her home in the jungle where she will rest and remember with new understanding the events of her early life... and maybe for the first time in centuries she will begin to forgive her sister... at least a little.

So now I throw my arms around Carlitos, hold him to me and let him understand how good I feel about the fact that he is not *only* a master of the silly human art of logic, but also of the great supernatural art of witchcraft.

"I was worried about you," he says to me.

"But you left me of your own free will, mi amor."

"I know, but then I began to realize that you were out there alone with the sisters and all those snakes."

"Snakes do not frighten me," I say, "not very much anyway. After all, I am a dead person, no?"

"And I know no Dread Zone is nearby to destroy you."

Carlitos tries to smile, but he seems so worried.

"¿Que pasa?" I ask.

"New and bigger threats from Tiger Joy," he answers.

"Does that bitch never rest?"

Señor Marinara now comes up to us and adds to my husband's words.

"Tiger's out of prison," he says. "I'm afraid her hold on the guards is so strong that she comes and goes as she likes. She puts her twin sister Bunny in her place while she's away. The guards never say anything so we almost never know that it's happened."

"But I thought Bunny Joy was a sweet girl," I say realizing that none of the Joy sisters can ever really be sweet in my eyes, not when Amy Joy is after my husband's hand in marriage.

"Bunny's as kind and gentle as they come," Carlitos says. "She's a submissive... trained to be so innocent that the slightest cruelty makes her very upset."

"Sadists love that kind of girl," Marinara adds. "Her threshold of suffering is so low that it just heightens the pain that the bastards inflict."

I find this whole conversation disgusting. I mean, why are these men talking of things like this with so much understanding?

"Is it not your job to stamp out such injustice?" I growl at the FBI man.

"Believe me we're trying. That's why we're so worried about Tiger and her latest plans."

"The woman gave my husband to a witch who used her evil mirror to drive him loco with evil images of himself."

"But I think Tiger's moved on beyond witches now," Marinara says.

"Great." I roll my eyes. "My husband learns the art of witchcraft, and now his greatest enemy is beyond such things."

"You can help us, Alicia."

"I'm no witch."

"No, but ghosts have other kinds of knowledge that we can use to trap the bad guys."

"Or girls," I add. "But you did not always believe that, Señor."

"You convinced me," Marinara says with a smile of friendship, and I wonder what Carlitos would do if I explain how the FBI man was molesting me with his eyes when I came to ask him to help me get into Tiger's prison cell so that I could enter her dreams and find out where she had sent my husband.

But then I decide that agent Marinara really did help us, and so he is my friend after all. Therefore, I will not spill the beans about his lustful eyes. QED

Enrique Cordoba now joins us. His wife Yolanda is hanging tightly to his arm and I think perhaps she has begun to value the man who has taken such good care of her over the years.

"Tiger's consorting with spirits," Enrique says.

"She has always consorted with her dead uncle Lum," I answer. "We already know about that."

"But we hear that she's trying to learn how to summon up demons," Marinara adds. "Chinese demons... some of the worst kind."

"And how do you know all this?" I ask.

"There are a few prison guards who have not been completely corrupted by the bitch. Though we're starting to think that even they are playing both sides."

"They would have to, would they not... so as not to *blow their cover.*"

Carlitos eyes me as I say the words.

"Blow their cover?"

I shrug. "I am becoming an expert on the criminal element."

"The criminal element?

Now he laughs out loud. "You've been watching cop shows on TV."

"They are very instructive and informative, are they not, Señor FBI man?"

Agent Marinara makes a funny face. Apparently he does not agree. Others in the room are starting to giggle now. Perhaps I should not be testing my new TV vocabulary just yet... just because there is an FBI man with us.

"But there is some good news," says agent Marinara. "We've found Tiger's new lair."

"Where?"

"She's walled herself up in that little town she likes so much."

I bat my eyes intelligently. "San Francisco?"

There is a moment of silence. Even those people who had been talking to each other are now staring at me. Then there is a funny hissing sound, a titter of laughter, and Señor Popcorn explodes with silliness. He stands, falls back onto the big coffee table in the middle of the room, and has to hold his belly he is laughing so hard. Tears form in his eyes.

"The *little town* of San Francisco, Alicia?"

It is as though he has been so worried that my question finally gives him the excuse he needs to relax and laugh.

"Señor Popcorn, it was not that funny," I say.

"Maybe not," Carlitos answers. "But we have been sitting here for hours trying to figure out how to get to her before she gets to us."

"Where?" I ask again. And for some crazy reason, this starts everyone laughing even harder. Señor Popcorn is gasping for breath. Miguel is groaning. This angers me. I cross my arms and pull away from my husband.

"I did not come here to be laughed at," I say, and I look around for something to throw. I see a big Aztec vase on the mantelpiece, and I run over to it and lift it over my head, aiming it at the old man in the center of the room.

"I have been dealing with witches and snakes and jaguars all day and all night, Señors and Señoras," I say. "And I am in no mood to have anyone use their trifles with me."

This again strikes Señor Popcorn as funny, and he points at me and laughs some more. So, I *do* throw the vase at him, what else can I do. I know the meaning of this English word "trifling", and I also know that it is something I cannot accept.

Fortunately, Carlitos is one fast man, and he dives and catches the vase before it strikes either Señor Popcorn or the floor. In either case it probably would have broken into a million pieces.

Carlitos stands with the vase in his hands and stares at me. He is having a hard time holding back his own laughter. Señor Popcorn is not doing it very well either, though I can see that he is concerned about his Aztec vase.

"Lumling," Carlitos says.

"Who?" I ask.

Everyone laughs again.

That's it! I start marching out of the room deciding to be visible even as I pass through the wall.

"The town where Tiger is hiding," Carlitos calls after me. "Lumling, the little place in the Sacramento Delta where Tiger took Assad and me after she captured us on Mt. Shasta."

I turn, cross my arms, tap my foot, and growl at him. "I know nothing of this place."

Carlitos just stares at me. Then he turns to Señor Popcorn, and they study each other for a moment.

"Oh no," Carlitos says with sudden knowing. "Oh, Alicia, I'm so sorry. I forgot that you were in Arizona when it happened."

My husband comes up to me and hugs me. I turn myself into a statue when he does this. I want to feel as cold as stone to him. He hugs me anyway, and it is so nice that I cannot be a statue for very long, and so I melt into his arms, hug him back, kiss him, and he drops the vase.

It hits the ceramic tile floor and bounces without breaking.

Is this another sign of Carlos's magical powers, I wonder, or just a damn strong Aztec vase?

"What do you think, Niña?" Señor Popcorn asks as he pulls a silk handkerchief from his pocket, wipes his eyes, and blows his nose.

"About what?" I ask, and I look around daring anyone to start laughing again.

"About getting into Lumling so that we can finally put an end to Tiger Joy."

"Ghosts can let you in," I say.

"Carlyle August and the crew from the Purgatory Bookstore?"

"Better yet," I answer. "Mr. Foo, the Chinese ghost who has come to our aid so often."

"Great idea," Carlitos says, "I like it," and he grabs me and gives me big kisses.

I punch him in the ribs... very hard. That will teach him *not* to laugh at me just because I use words from famous TV cop shows.

Chapter 29

Two days later, Señor Popcorn, Agent Marty Marinara, and many armed men drive up to the Sacramento delta to capture Tiger Joy. They plan to enter the city of Lumling and go directly to the building that Carlitos remembers as the Joy Lum hideout. At the same time that they are driving into the town, Carlitos, his friend Assad, the handsome ghost of Carlyle August, the lovely spirit of Sylvia Morales, and I arrive at a spot just outside of Lumling. The FBI and Señor Popcorn will give us four hours to find a way to get inside the hideout and open the doors before they try to break in.

We are now standing in front of an old stone building, which has the words "Delta Water Station" set into the concrete above the doorway. The doors are unlocked and so Carlos and Assad walk right in. The rest of us become invisible.

At a small wooden table just inside the doorway, a fat guard in a blue uniform and policeman's hat reads a comic book. The pictures from the book reflect into his glasses and make him look silly. Superheroes are now covering his eyes.

"Help ya?" the guard asks.

Carlos nods and places a wallet with an identification card in front of the man.

"Ghostbusters," he says.

"Huh?"

"We're from the paranormal investigations unit of Homeland Security."

The guard picks up the wallet and looks at the identification card that the FBI has made for my husband. It has his name and the words:

Paranormal Investigations
• Homeland Security •
United States of America

in big letters everywhere. There is a picture of the capitol building behind the words.

"This some kind of a joke?"

"Guess they haven't told you about it, huh, Mac?" Assad growls in his best tough-guy voice. He presents his own Ghostbusters ID to the guard.

"Nope, guess they haven't."

"Then maybe we're not too late," Carlitos says.

"You got anything from an agency I've actually heard of?" The guard asks.

"Your boss ain't gonna like this, pal," Assad answers. He sounds like someone from those TV cop shows I have been watching. But then Assad pulls out a letter from Marty Marinara.

"And we do have this."

The guard takes the envelope.

"Let's just see here," he says as he scans the letter. "FBI... reports of paranormal activity at the station... sending his two best men....

"Highly irregular," he tells Carlitos and I can see that my friend Sylvia Morales has had enough of this guy.

She moves in next to the guard, and the smell of her sexy perfume catches his attention at once. He sniffs the air.

"What the..."

Sylvia reaches down and puts her hand on the guard's thigh. His eyes pop wide open. He looks down, sees the impression of fingers in his uniform, but there is no hand there to make them. And then Sylvia's hand *does* appear: nails painted red-black, long beautiful fingers, the tattoo of a spider web on the back of her hand, her delicate wrist. As Sylvia's arm appears, she also reveals her supermodel shoulders.

"Fuck me," the guard moans.

"Looks like there really *are* spooks in the place," Assad says.

Sylvia's entire beautiful body now comes into view. She is leaning over the guard, her low-cut camisole scoops down right in front of his nose. Most of her nicely rounded breasts fill his vision, and I can see them reflected in his glasses. Behind the lenses his eyes begin to smile. He licks his lips. Sylvia likes that, but I do not. I slap her on the behind and she squeals.

"Ándale, mujer," I say.

"Up here," she breathes to the guard, and he raises his eyes to her thick red lips, her sparkly eyes, her soft coffee-colored skin that now begins to rot right in front of him.

"I'm so hungry," she moans as her decaying flesh falls away from her skull. Her teeth chatter, and one eyeball rolls out of its socket and falls onto the fat belly of the guard.

"Fuuuccccckkkk meeeeeee! Ghosts!" he shouts as he jumps out of his chair, rushes to the front door and runs out into the night.

"We tried ta warn ya," Assad calls after him.

We move quickly into the heart of the water station, down a spiraling metal stairway and onto a black grating that forms a walkway between many large water pipes. Everything is crackling, bubbling, moaning, and seeming more alive than Sylvia, Carlyle, or I.

Carlitos and Assad run toward a big iron door at the far end of the grating. But just as they are about to reach it, we hear a roar, and a giant tiger comes out from behind one of the pipes. It sits down between the door and the men.

They stop at once, tripping over each other and almost falling onto the floor.

"Nice kitty," Assad whispers.

The tiger answers with another roar that echoes off the water pipes.

Carlos turns to me.

"Now what?"

He sounds like he thinks that I brought the tiger. I do not understand this at all, and so I shrug.

"This way," a new voice calls. It is our friend, Mr. Foo, who now fades into the end of another narrow walkway that runs off the one we are standing on. But it is still past the tiger.

"How the hell do we get around the big cat?" Assad asks. The tiger hears his voice and now slinks slowly toward him licking its lips.

"It thinks we're its next meal," Assad says as his face turns a very nervous shade of purple.

Mr. Foo cocks his head very much as the tiger is doing as it tries to decide which part of Assad to bite off first.

Carlitos pulls out his pistol and aims it directly into the eyes of the tiger.

"Don't do that," Mr. Foo calls and Carlitos lowers the gun.

The tiger lifts its great paw and places it gently on Assad's shoulder.

"Somebody better do *something*!" Assad sobs.

"Of course," Mr. Foo answers, and in one quick move he reaches down to his feet and pulls up a package as big as half of a horse. He tears off the wrapping paper and we see that it is a great hunk of horsemeat: big, black, raw, and bloody, with a scent so strong that it forces the tiger to jerk its head away from Assad just as it is about to rip off his shoulder.

The old Chinese gentleman heaves the bloody meat over the edge of the grating and it lands with a sickening sound on the cement floor of the station.

The tiger roars so loudly this time that the metal pipes vibrate in response. Then it leaps off the edge of the grating and lands smoothly right beside the bloody slab and roars again.

"Coulda been me," Assad sighs.

"Quickly, this way, Dr. Mann and Mr. Assad," Mr. Foo calls, and Carlitos and Assad break out running toward the old Chinese gentleman and the doorway he has opened in front of them.

#

Mr. Foo has let the five of us (two humans and three ghosts) into a great round tunnel that is really the inside of an enormous pipe. He holds an old lantern overhead and we can see that the tunnel's sides are slick black metal; there is a small stream of water flowing over its bottom, and – from this moisture – green slime grows up the sides of the pipe making it smell very nasty. The two men shuffle quickly over the damp floor. As they go, the water on the floor becomes more and more muddy as the pipe grows narrower and narrower and eventually feeds into a slimy tunnel dug directly into the earth under the town of Lumling.

"This is not good for me," I call to Sylvia as I float through the tunnel just above the muddy floor. I gag on the nasty smells coming from the slime. Carlitos's sloshy steps would be splashing mud all over me if I were not invisible. Even so, the experience is simply gross.

Sylvia says nothing. I can no longer sense her presence so I turn, look back for her, but I cannot see her.

"Hello, Sylvia," I say.

There is no response.

"Sylvia?"

"Carlyle?"

I hear no answer from either of my ghost friends, and think that this is a very bad time for them to give into the temptations of their ghost bodies, and begin having sex with each other right here in the mud.

"None of that now," I say, and then a creepy voice whispers out of the gloom, *"You're next, pretty girl."*

I feel something snatch at me, and I fly ahead, up to Mr. Foo and ask him, "What is in this tunnel that could threaten us?"

"Uncle Lum and his ghost traps?" he says.

So, the ancient founder of the Joy Lum Slave Trafficking Business has used his ghost traps once again to capture my friends.

"What do we do?" Carlitos asks as he catches up to us.

"They're *safe* in the traps... at least for now," Mr. Lum tells us. "It's just that they may never get out of them again."

"Great!" I roll my eyes yet again. "We cannot allow that!"

"Of course not. But we'd better deal with Tiger first and then worry about how to save our friends from her deadly uncle."

As he says this, we arrive at the base of a rickety wooden stairway that leads up into the darkness above.

"Right this way," Mr. Foo says as his spirit floats up the stairway and into the gloom. I follow, knowing that Uncle Lum has a ghost trap poised and ready for me too if I make the wrong move. Carlitos and Assad come after us.

#

We emerge at the back of an enormous room with high gray walls and dark draperies hanging everywhere. At the far end of the room, four of Tiger's men stand guard at the doorway to some inner chamber. Each man holds a machine gun. Mr. Foo and I hang back, but Carlitos strides right up to the guards.

"Miss Helen Joy, please," he says as if he's asking to see his local banker.

"That's *Mistress* Joy to you," we hear Tiger's harsh voice call from inside the chamber.

"Mistress Joy then, please," Carlitos says.

"Strip him of his weapons and send him in."

Carlitos throws down the pistol he has tucked into his shoulder holster, then he pulls up his pant leg and removes a knife he has strapped there. He tosses it at the foot of the guards. They smile and shake their heads as one of them, a handsome, smiling Chinese boy, steps up to my husband and does a pat down that is very complete.

This is not right, I realize. Carlitos is probably walking right into his death. Tiger will have him for supper... in very nasty little bites. I cannot let this happen. So I take on human form, a tough-girl-look with tight black jeans, high heel boots, and a black tank top. Across my breasts silk-screened letters tell everyone that I am "ONE MEAN MAMA!"

"Before you can see Carlitos," I call to Tiger, "you have to see me first."

There is a moment when nothing happens. Carlitos's eyes me with surprise but also affection.

"Careful, mi amor," he sighs.

"She can do nothing to me," I whisper, and we stare at each other for a long time... waiting for Tiger to respond.

"I'd rather see that Carlyle boy," Tiger calls at last.

I am getting ready to tell her that Carlyle is in one of her uncle's ghost traps when the handsome ghost suddenly pops into view right next to me. His suit is rumpled; his hair is mussed.

"Those ghost traps are terribly cramped," he says as he straightens his suit and tie. Then he pulls out a comb, goes over to one of the guards, and uses the reflection off his brightly polished rifle to comb his hair.

"You want to see *me*, Mistress Joy?" he calls into the chamber.

"I've been dreaming of you," she sighs.

"And I you."

I want to gag.

"She did look lovely in Paris, didn't she, Alicia?" Carlyle asks.

"In her dreams. All women look lovely in their dreams."

"Perhaps I simply bring out the best in her?"

I roll my eyes.

Carlyle winks at me. "Duty calls," he says, and then he walks up to Carlitos, pats him on the shoulder, and marches right into the chamber.

Carlitos and I stare at each other, both of us thinking that Carlyle has been led into a terrible trap. And at that very moment there is a loud zinging sound as though someone has been caught by his leg and lifted high in the air. There is also a harsh cry from Carlyle and then the slamming of a steel door.

After a moment the very satisfied voice of Tiger calls out from her chamber, "Won't you please come in now, Alicia?"

"What's happened?" I say to Carlitos, as I rush right past him. He follows me and grabs my arm. One of Tiger's guards pushes the butt end of his gun into my husband's side. But Carlitos is so full of concern for me that he is able to grab the gun and the man and throw them both far across the room. Then he takes my arm again and turns me around to face him. He puts his huge hands on either side of my head, pulls me right up to him so that we are nose to nose. His fingers suddenly begin fluttering over my cheeks. I close my eyes and hold them closed for a moment, and things suddenly become very peaceful.

I feel Carlitos's hands fall away from me. And then I slowly open my eyes.

I am in a great temple, it seems, with torches all around. Dancers in ancient costumes of feathers and gold sway in the background as a man in a high headdress moves toward me. His chest and abdomen are bare, sculptured beautifully as though he were some Maya god. Around his waist is a thin cotton wrap that falls to the middle of his thighs. His arms and legs are muscular and beautiful. Beside me is a great cauldron that sizzles and pops with a fiery liquid.

The man carefully removes the great headdress, and I see that he is my Carlitos. I smile. His eyes are full of worship for me.

I scream when Carlitos reaches into the cauldron, but he does not flinch from the heat. He does not cry out because his hand is burning. Instead he continues to stare at me as he pulls out a handful of foamy liquid. He flicks it at me and I feel it falling on my face, on my eyes, and onto my shoulders. It feels cool and peaceful. He holds out his hand to me. I want to reach for it, but I cannot move.

I am smiling. My eyes are bright with the sight of the dancers, the temple, and my handsome husband in his wonderful Maya costume. But I cannot move.

I cannot move at all.

6
Carlos

Chapter 30

I stare at my wife for a long moment, not at all sure what's happened. She's frozen as if bewitched. Did I do that? I want to stop and figure it out. And then I notice the wonderful tiles that are laid in such an orderly pattern on the floor of the outer chamber. They seem to be zigzagging out from Alicia as though she were the central point in some new kind of mystical star. There's nothing I'd rather do than count each tile.

"Alicia," Tiger calls again.

As much as I want to stay here beside my wife and count those tiles, I know that it's time to finally deal with the bitch. And so I spin away from my wife and the others and enter Tiger's chamber.

Tiger's curled up on her throne like a teenager, legs folded under her, leaning forward, staring at me. I look around the huge chamber. The ceiling is just as high as the outer room, with red and yellow draperies billowing down around stone-black walls. Suspended along the wall to my left is a massive cage with gleaming metal bars. Inside, Carlyle stands with his hands in his pockets, staring down... a look of embarrassment on his face. He shrugs by way of apology but doesn't say a word.

I check out the rest of chamber. In its very center is a deep circular pit, maybe twenty feet deep... maybe forty feet across.

The floor of the pit is painted with Chinese symbols, all red and gold and black. As I walk around the pit toward Tiger, I see her pet pacing down there. It looks up at me and snarls hungrily. Is this the same tiger that Foo bribed with horsemeat just a few minutes ago? Not sure. They look alike, but this beast doesn't seem the least bit calmed by having eaten half a horse. It definitely wants more. It definitely wants *me!*

"Mi Carlitos," Tiger giggles as she jumps down from her throne and marches up to me. She's wearing a black v-neck halter-top that shows off her muscular shoulders and lots of cleavage. She also wears a pair of hip-hugger leather leggings that squeak as she moves. Her heels are a mile high.

"It's time we settled this once and for all, don't you think, Carlitos?" she coos.

"Good idea."

"That's Courtney Love down there." Tiger points to the big cat. "She's hungry, poor thing. Hasn't eaten in days. I've kept her hungry for you, just like I've stayed hungry all these years... *for you*, mi Carlitos."

She pouts at the thought of her supposed abstinence. And then suddenly drops into a Kung fu stance. "Now's my time to take you," she growls.

"Hand to hand combat?"

Tiger smiles and purrs.

"Don't suppose Courtney Love would eat her mistress, would she?" I ask, as I get ready to defend myself.

Tiger doesn't answer; instead she does one of those dive kicks that you see in the martial arts movies, the ones that seem to be in slow motion as the warrior flies toward you. This one isn't in slow motion at all; it blasts me in the gut, and I stagger backwards. Tiger spins and gives me a shot with the back heel of her other foot... rams me dead center in my mid section again, and I fall on my ass. Before I can get up Tiger is there, raising her heel to pound it right into my face. I catch her foot in mid-air, spin her around and send her sprawling. It's a good thing it happens when it does, because just then Assad comes bursting through the door. He spins quickly and fastens the huge deadbolt behind him, locking the door closed. I can hear Tiger's guards begin pounding on the other side of the door, and then I feel a sharp chop come down on the back of my neck, and I know that Tiger's back in action.

The blow knocks me to the floor, and when I turn over Tiger's sharp, seven-inch heel comes flying down toward my face. Again, I grab and twist it, this time I also reach up, take hold of her thigh, jump up, and pitch her away from me. But she lands on her feet, turns, and comes rushing back toward me. She kicks me in the face, right above my eye, setting off an explosion of blood. I can barely see. She does a back flip away from me, then runs at me and launches another of those flying kicks. I'm thrown back against the wall. Tiger rushes toward me again; this time she clasps both her fists together and pounds me with a two-handed roundhouse that tears my lip and sends me sprawling.

Blood spills over my face. But Tiger isn't about to show any mercy. Instead, she charges at me again. This time she's slamming the tip of those steel-toed boots right into my ribs.

What the hell's going on? My head is getting too fuzzy to ever be able to figure it out.

I stagger to my feet, assume a weak, hunched-over version of my fighter's stance. I raise my guard as best I can, and Tiger flies into me with another of those kicks that sends me sprawling backward on my ass. Now, I'm at the very edge of the pit. She marches up to me, smiles cruelly, then falls to her knees, leans into my side, and just heaves me over the edge.

Just what I need, a twenty-foot drop after having the shit pounded out of me by a little Asian girl. I feel disgraced. Courtney Love comes running up to me, excited by the blood that's smeared all over my face. The big cat opens its huge jaws to growl at me, and I've had enough. I drive my fist right into its nose. The tiger recoils, turns toward me again. And I punch it again: this time right in the side of the head. The big cat roars loudly. So, I slam my fist into it again, and then again. I start using the tiger's head as a punching bag.

"What are you doing to my baby?" Tiger Joy cries from the rim of the pit, and I answer by hammering the big cat right in its ribs. It falls away sideways and whimpers.

Tiger jumps down into the pit and, for the first time in her life maybe, she's undone by her shoes. That's right, those god-blessed 7-inch high heels. She lands on them standing up. Her legs twist out from under her, and she falls in a heap.

I'm a fucking mess, I'll tell you that, but I have enough strength left in me to take a running jump up the side of the wall where a small grating covers the door to the tiger's cage. I catch onto the top of the grating, push myself up over the edge of the pit and roll onto my back. I lay there gasping for breath.

I look at Assad, and he runs over to me. He tears off his shirt and uses it to wipe the blood from my face. Meanwhile we hear the clamber of boots through what must be a door just behind Tiger's throne. Tiger's boys come charging into the room, guns ready to blast me away. But just before they get to the edge of the pit, we hear a blood-chilling scream.

Tiger's boys rush to the edge of the pit and look down. I turn and look as well.

Courtney Love is standing over Tiger. The girl's neck is in the cat's huge jaws; Tiger's body hangs lifelessly. The cat drops her, walks away, comes back, and takes a swipe across Tiger's chest, opening the halter, those magnificent store-bought boobs, and her entire midsection in the same horrific motion. Tiger's guts come pouring out. The cat leans down and laps them up.

Machine gun fire riddles the floor of the pit, tearing apart the tiger and her mistress in a series of huge, explosive blasts.

The boys lower their weapons.

"Cat never liked her," says one.

"Shit – fuck," whispers another.

I can see by the looks on their faces that every one of these boys was in love with their mistress.

"What about this guy?" one of them says as he gestures to me.

"Mine," answers another as he points his machine gun toward me. But before he can shoot, a red rose seems to blossom right in the middle of his forehead... make that a *blood*-red rose.

He falls to the floor, dead.

"Drop em!"

It's Marty Marinara, who walks slowly through the open front door of Tiger's chamber. He's carrying a set of ancient looking keys in one hand and a smoking gun in the other. There must be twenty men behind him.

"And don't try to run away either, amigos." This is Señor Popcorn who has come in behind them. His men are following him too.

I look at my rescuers and then up at Carlyle in the cage. His eyes are wide; he looks half dazed from the carnage he's just witnessed.

#

I'm dizzy with the realization that my great enemy, the woman who has made the last years of my life such hell, is dead. Tiger Joy is dead! The horror of the way she died gives way to an overwhelming feeling of relief.

Ding dong! The bitch is dead. The realization sweeps over me like a cool breeze after a month-long trek through the desert. I gather myself, breathe in deeply, and march out of the chamber, beaming up at Carlyle who waits in stunned silence while Marinara's minions try to figure out how to get him out of that cage.

Alicia is still standing frozen in the outer chamber. She has an excited smile on her face as though she's watching a Broadway musical. But there's a vacancy to her stare as well. Like the show may be good, but there's nothing going on in her mind.

"Who did this?" Marinara asks when he sees her. "It's like she's bewitched."

I look around at everyone else in attendance: Popcorn, the paid assassins, the Chinese boys who have survived the carnage, and Carlyle who simply dissolves his way out of captivity and lands coolly on the floor. I shake my head.

"*I* must have done it."

"What are you, some kind of sorcerer?"

"Witch, maybe?"

"Do you know how hard it is to bewitch a ghost?" Carlyle asks.

I shrug, sigh, and then head straight for my wife. I take her by the hand. Her fingers are ice cold. She doesn't move. Then, she blinks.

Her other hand rises and brushes her cheek absentmindedly as she begins tangling her fingers into her hair... almost in slow motion. She turns toward me and smiles like a lovestruck teenager.

"Mmmmm," she sighs. "Carlitos."

"You do have the power," Carlyle says as he pats me on the back. "Congratulations."

Then images of Grandma Ixchel flash through my mind. I'm by her side at the fireplace. She has a cauldron, and she's brewing up something. "For your grandpa," she sighs with a look that seems very much like the one I now see in Alicia's eyes.

"Take me home, Carlitos," she murmurs dreamily.

"Right away," I tell her. "Just let me finish up with Marinara and Popcorn."

"Mmmmm," is all that she can say. But she's still smiling.

I walk over to the FBI man and the largest grower of corn products in the western hemisphere.

"Is she really dead?" I ask.

Marinara answers. "Looks like you won't have to worry about Mistress Joy ever again. She's shredded... blasted... never to return."

"And she's going straight to hell," Señor Popcorn adds. "No need to worry about *her* ghost coming after you."

"No possible redemption," I say with a grin. Heartless as it sounds, I'm liking it. The wonder of Tiger's departure from this life suddenly thrills me. I puff up my chest. I'm feeling a little like a conquering hero.

From across the room I see Alicia up on her tiptoes waiving at me. She starts bouncing up and down like a cheerleader, and she doesn't even know that *"ding dong, the bitch is dead."* Wait till she finds out about that.

"Carlitos. Oh, Carlitos... time to go home... time to go to bed."

I turn and move toward her, but as I do, the ghost of Mr. Foo flits up next to me.

"There is one minor matter that needs your attention," he says.

Alicia looks all soft and gooey-eyed. "Carlitos, do you own a Maya headdress?" she calls.

I can't stop smiling. Still, I turn back to Mr. Foo. "What minor matter?"

"Sylvia," Foo says. "Uncle Lum still has her."

I shake my head. I'm feeling so damn macho, all I want to do is go home and have violent, victorious sex with my wife. But I force myself to concentrate.

"I thought you said she would be safe in the ghost trap... that her rescue could wait."

"Yes... for a little while anyway. I need to do some investigating... clarify a few things."

"Oh, Carlitos..." Alicia sings to me, "You must show me your love potions."

I pat Foo on the shoulder. "Call me as soon as you find something out," I say. "Any time... except tonight."

Foo responds with a knowing grin that fades a little too quickly for my tastes.

"Just remember that Uncle Lum has just lost his favorite niece," he says. "If we give him too much time, his revenge will be monstrous."

"How much time is too much?" I ask as I glance over at my hungry wife. She's leaning up against the far wall, tangling her fingers in her hair, smiling coquettishly... Jeeze. I wonder just what the hell went on in that bewitching trance.

"I'll give you tonight, my friend," Foo says. "It will take me that long to determine the exact whereabouts of Lum and his prisoner. But... first thing in the morning I'll be at your house, ready to start our rescue mission in earnest."

"I'll be ready in the morning," I say as I catch Alicia's infectious smile and start running toward her.

"Just be careful with those love potions," Foo calls. "And don't do too much celebrating over the death of your enemies... they have not all perished."

"Ding dong!" I shout back at the negative bastard, and then I finally fall into the arms of my lovestruck wife.

She kisses me passionately, then gives me an inquisitive smile.

"Carlitos, you look so excited. Did I miss something?"

"Some good news," I answer. "But it can wait."

"I'm glad," she sighs. "It's time to work our own magic."

Chapter 31

Alicia is all over me as we ride up in the elevator from the parking garage to our apartment. Her kisses are hot, hungry, and excited. In between kisses she keeps talking about ancient costumes and love potions.

I fumble for my keys at the door, and my wife just can't keep her hands to herself. When I finally turn the key she pushes the door open and rushes past me into the bedroom... into the bathroom... stripping out of her clothes as she goes. I follow her eagerly, and when I get inside the bathroom door, there, sitting on the counter top, is a great Maya headdress. Beside it is a ceramic pitcher of cool bubbling liquid. Embedded in the side of the pitcher are the words "Poción de amor".

"Love potion," Alicia giggles as she grabs the pitcher. "How did you get this here so quickly? This *is* witchcraft, my love." And then she takes the potion and steps into the shower.

I don't really know what she's talking about. I didn't put this stuff here... I don't think... or do I have powers that I don't even know I'm using?

Mist swirls out from the shower. Within a few seconds the place is like a tropical fogbank. I strip off my clothes and follow Alicia. Her arms are open wide, and she's holding that pitcher over our heads, about to pour it onto me. I can't wait. I spin her around, and press her against the glass doors of the shower. But when I do, I notice the headdress, moving, snaking across in front of the counter. There's someone in it.

I scream as a burning pain runs down the side of my arm.

"Love potion," Alicia giggles again. But it's not. There's some kind of acid in that pitcher. The thing probably holds enough to turn me into a human garbage dump.

I push Alicia behind me, wrench the pitcher out of her hand, jerk open the door, and toss the contents of the pitcher right into the face of a slight young kid who has come up to the door wearing the Maya headdress and brandishing a dagger.

He screams in agony as the acid melts his face right in front of me. I toss the pitcher past him, and it strikes the countertop and shatters. Within seconds the whole granite counter has dissolved.

I twist the shower off, grab Alicia, and carry her out of the bathroom, carefully stepping around the dead kid with the melted face, the headdress, and the counter that is no more. Halfway through the doorway to the bedroom Alicia disappears... only to re-appear across the room by the bed. She's wearing a beautiful silk wrap, but her eyes are wide with horror.

"They're coming after us, Carlitos," she says. "Why now?"

"It's Tiger," I answer.

"Has she no respect for our love?"

"You know she doesn't," I say with a grin I can no longer contain, in spite of the acid and the kid in the deadly headdress. And then I add, "Besides, Tiger's dead."

Alicia stumbles backward at the words, almost falling off of the glassy high heels she's wearing. (What's with these women and their shoes?)

"How can that be?" she asks. "Who killed her; what killed her? Did you?"

"Not I," I say. "Though I really wanted to."

"Who then?"

"Let's just say it was a deadly combination of very cruel shoes and a very hungry pet."

Alicia's eyes grow wide. She shakes her head as though it is all too impossible to believe.

"She is really dead?"

"Sí."

"And she must have gone straight to hell."

"Everyone seems to agree on that."

"Then we are free," Alicia shouts as she begins to jump up and down in spite of her high heels, in spite of the fact that her large beautiful breasts want to bounce out of that silk wrap and take on whole new gyrations of their own.

"Carlitos, we are safe at last... you must make love to me like a god, in the name of freedom... to celebrate our new-found safety."

I smile, but then, like an idiot, I remember that we aren't quite that safe.

"Except..." I begin.

"No, Carlitos, no excepts. Let us just celebrate with luscious, steamy sex."

"But there's still Uncle Lum...."

Alicia stops jumping; her body settles. She pouts.

"He is seeking his revenges, isn't he? That is what those evil things in the bathroom were all about."

Alicia crosses her arms and her eyes and looks as silly as she is beautiful.

"He will not get those revenges," she says. "I will sit up and guard you all night long if I have to. No more acid disguised as love potions."

"No more Maya headgear."

Alicia frowns and sits down onto the bed.

"Aw, Carlitos," she sighs, "but I was looking forward to it... you looked so sexy in my dreams... a great headdress, a skimpy little cloth around your hips, your great muscles bulging everywhere."

I walk up to my wife and sit down beside her. She's still damn turned on, still breathing heavily. Her nipples are so hard they're about to punch right through that silk wrap she's wearing.

"You really want all that, huh? The loincloth, the muscles, the love potion."

"Sí, mi amor. That dream got me sooo excited."

I stare at my beautiful Alicia, trying to figure out some way to make her wishes come true... without getting killed in the process.

"Okay, follow me," I say, and I lead my wife out into the living room. "Make yourself comfortable," I say pointing to the couch. She slides onto it and smiles.

I move on to the kitchen, yank open drawers and cupboards, and pull out the largest pot I can find. Then I spin to the pantry, "Help me, Ixchel," I pray to my long dead grandmother. I close my eyes and randomly grab ingredients from the shelves. I dump them into the pot without looking at what they are. I toss it on the burner, set the thing boiling, and stir it with a thick spoon.

"Are you brewing up a love potion for me?" Alicia calls from the other room.

"Sí, mi amor," I answer.

I taste the brew as I go... it's definitely tingly and pungent. Alicia won't be able to drink it, I don't think, but maybe *I* can. I rummage through the drawers and come up with a large napkin that will have to serve as a loincloth.

"What else, what else," I ask myself.

Oh yeah, the muscles. I drop to the floor and do about 100 push-ups as quickly as possible, then a couple hundred crunches. When I get to my feet I'm feeling buffed, and the brew is bubbling. I ladle some into a thick mug and feel the steam warm my face.

"Headdress?" I ask myself.

I consider going into the bathroom and grabbing the one off the rotting kid, but decide I can do without it. So, I tie on the loincloth, take the mug, and make my way back into the living room.

Alicia eyes me eagerly as I move up to her. "Is that our love potion?" she coos.

"Maybe."

"Flick it onto me."

"What?"

"The way you did in my dream. Touch your fingers in it, and flick it onto me."

Alicia stands. It's a hell of a robe she's wearing.

"I like your body," she says to me.

I tighten my muscles, and her eyes glow.

I reach into the mug, touch my fingers to the love potion, and it feels cool and tingly. This could work. I flick my fingers to her, and she sticks out her tongue to catch the potion.

"Mmmmm, delicious," she sighs.

She opens her robe and pulls it back behind her so that she's standing nearly naked in front of me.

"More potion please, all over me."

I reach into the mug and pull out a handful of the tingly stuff. I smear it across her cheeks.

"Ooohhhh," she breathes.

Then down over her chest.

"Sí, Señor!"

She drops the robe, and I slide the mug onto the coffee table as she jerks the loincloth from around my waist.

Chapter 32

The streets are awash with pulsing red lights. Sirens blare. Horns honk. Crowds of businessmen and women jam together forming a wall around a massive accident that blocks all of Stockton Avenue in San Francisco's Chinatown. I'm at the back of the crowd. I turn away in frustration, and just then I spot a small band of early-teen girls, about five of them, rocketing through the crowd in their school uniforms – plaid skirts, knee sox, sensible shoes, starched white shirts with blue school ties. The girl at the very front of the pack is maybe fourteen, and she looks so damn familiar.

I fall in behind the girls and shadow them into the thick crowd. Somehow they're breaking through, rushing up to the accident, giving me a chance to see it too... a smashed-in taxicab. Looks like it's plowed right into the side of the ornate Lum Family Building. A young woman in her mid-twenties is sprawled on the pavement close to death; inside the taxi a very young girl is somehow trapped in the back. The driver is panicking, pounding on the front window, shouting instructions to the girl in Chinese, even though the kid is clearly not from this part of town. The little girl is screaming hysterically; the engine compartment of the taxi is billowing dark smoke that threatens to burst into flames.

The gang of teens takes this in. They seem more interested in the panicked stupidity of the driver than the danger to the young woman or her daughter. The girls' faces turn into sarcastic grins. They roll their eyes.

"Really?" one giggles in response to something the taxi driver says.

"Duhh!"

The lead girl isn't talking... the one who looks so familiar. She's maybe the only one who is thinking clearly. She rushes up to the passenger side back door, jerks it open, reaches in, unhooks the seatbelt that's tangled all around the little girl, and pulls her out of the car.

The driver looks on in great relief and gratitude. He says something to her in Chinese. She doesn't respond, just jerks the little girl away from the car as the engine compartment erupts into flames.

Now, the teen is kneeling in front of the little girl, talking to her, soothing her.

The kid nods, and I get the feeling that she's hearing a lot more than a lesson in how to escape from a burning taxi cab. She casts a desperate glance at her mother's body lying twisted in the street, then she reaches up and takes the hand of the big girl and lets her lead her away. One more glance back, tears in her eyes, then she follows the bigger girl obediently.

I move toward the girls to learn more, but as I do a redheaded cop steps in front of me.

"Where do you think you're going, chico?" he demands.

I can't believe it. I know I'm not dressed up, but I'm still a college logic professor who also has the bearing of an ex-prizefighter.

I try to sidestep the cop, but he comes right with me. "Excuse me, but you can't pass." I feint to my right and move to my left as I used to do in the ring. The action confuses the redhead, so he takes out his billy club and clocks me right across the forehead. I fall forward toward the girls. As I look up at them, I hear the little girl tell the teen, "God bless you... you saved my life."

"For many reasons," the other girl says, "remember!" The little girl nods. And then the two push on into the crowd and are gone. I raise myself on my hands as I watch them go.

"Keep your eyes to yourself, you dirty spic," the cop says as he steps on me and pushes me down onto the pavement.

"What do you want?" I ask.

"That you keep your fucking eyes off of the young ladies," he says, and then he clobbers me again with his club.

"I was just trying to..." I begin, and then the pounding starts. "We don't want your kind around here, pendejo," he calls, and at that moment the siren of an approaching fire truck screams at me. So now I'm taking a beating and hearing the screaming sirens, and then the roar of tigers, but I sure don't know where the hell that's coming from... and now the pounding of the club is accompanied by the vicious swipe of claws that rake across my shoulders and chest drawing more and more blood.

I suddenly jump up in my bed, wide awake. I'm drenched in sweat. I turn to Alicia and she's there, standing in the corner, staring at me, her fingers curled into her mouth, a horrified expression on her face.

"Such terrible dreams, Carlitos," she says softly. "You began thrashing around and screaming just before you woke."

I'm stunned.

"Did I say anything?"

Alicia looks troubled, very troubled.

I'm too shaken to be patient with her. "DID I?"

"Sí."

"What was it... what did I say?"

"I don't know."

"You couldn't understand?"

"No, I could not."

"You couldn't hear me?"

"I could hear you, Carlitos...

"But you were speaking in *Chinese!*"

197

Chapter 33

Four hours later I find myself in our little kitchen. Alicia has cradled me through the early morning. She's held me closer than a ghost should be able to, caressed me with loving arms, sung to me, calmed me from the images of the tiger's claws, the bigoted cop, and those scary young teens.

"You cannot remember the words you were speaking, though?" asks Mr. Foo. He's in our kitchen cooking again, just as he did at the start of our very first adventure up the side of Mt. Shasta... when we tried to save Amy Joy.

"I can't remember what I said," I answer. "Didn't even know I was speaking. But what I really can't forget are those girls."

"A gang of teenage girls?"

"Young... thirteen and fourteen."

"And they were Chinese?"

"The girls who did the rescuing, yes. The girl they rescued was very blond."

"But she was in Chinatown?"

"Passing through, I guess."

Alicia flits into the kitchen and takes a seat across from me. Her smile is meant to be reassuring, but it's so full of concern. She tucks a strand of her hair behind her ear nervously.

"Are you sure you are able to help us rescue Sylvia?" she asks me.

I shrug, "Nightmares have never slowed me down before."

"That's because you have not had nightmares before."

"What about El Cojo?" I ask as I remind her of our reunion in the United States after our marriage in Mexico. I had nightmares that El Cojo... Luis... an old enemy from our hometown, was coming to kill Alicia.

And he was, and he did kill her.

"Well *this* nightmare is very different," Alicia says. "El Cojo was a real person that I left in the desert to die. Of course he was going to come back and try and kill me.

"But I was neither American nor blond, mi amor." She looks at me in exasperation, and then laughs softly. "You were my hero back then, Carlitos... and you still are."

She flutters her eyelashes at me, and suddenly I'm transported back to the moment I saw her getting off that plane. It had been so long since I had seen her that I had almost forgotten what she was really like. And then there she was. And somewhere between her walk, her talk, and her beautiful hair my whole being was stolen once again. As we talked, I found myself slowly drifting from her words to her pretty eyes to the shape of her lips, then finally to all of her beautiful face. I spoke just to spend more time looking at her, and it made me want her forever. I let my feelings carry the moment.

"Dr. Mann *must* come with us this time," Foo says.

Alicia shrugs. "I know," she says. "But the Joy Lums still want their revenges against him... even more so now. So we will have to work extra hard to keep him safe."

"As it should be," Foo adds.

"So, where are we going?" I ask.

"Mt. Shasta."

"Again? To the Dread Zone?"

"Unfortunately, yes," Foo says. "Uncle Lum is planning to have Sylvia taken there so that she will be reduced to nothingness."

Alicia shivers; she knows first hand about Dread Zones and their power to destroy ghosts. It squeezes them out of the afterlife and into nonexistence.

"What have you learned about Lum's plans?" I ask Mr. Foo.

"My friends in Chinatown were less than helpful," he answers. "Apparently Uncle Lum has grown in power and reputation in the last few years. But I did learn that he left for Mt. Shasta very early this morning. He plans to use some of Tiger's boys to take Sylvia in her ghost trap and deposit her in the heart of the Dread Zone, in the center of a vortex at the very end of the mountain highway."

"You must be speaking of Panther Meadow," a gentlemanly voice adds, and I recognize Carlyle August at once. How the hell did he get in here?

"There are few real barriers for ghosts," Mr. Foo says as though he had just read my mind. He smiles at Carlyle. "Welcome, sir."

"I would be grateful for the chance to help save a lovely damsel in distress."

"Sylvia is my friend," Alicia says. "And believe me, she is no damsel."

I just shake my head and marvel at the words my wife chooses to learn and the ones she misunderstands completely.

"She's also very dear to me," Carlyle adds. "We've had many magic moments together."

"In that library back in Cancun?" Alicia asks. "Making passionate ghostly noises?"

Carlyle just blushes.

Meanwhile, crazy or not, I'm feeling the need to start the adventure. So, I wolf down a couple of pork buns, some good strong oolong tea, and I stand up at the table.

"Let's go!" I say.

The others nod, and I lead the parade of ghosts out the door... one man and three ghosts entering a Dread Zone where the ghosts cannot survive. We're ready to face a gang of young Chinese toughs to rescue another ghost caught in a deadly trap. But the truth is: I must be nuts. We've already figured out that Lum's number one target is *me*. So why am I going up the mountain? Then I catch sight of those Alicia eyes, her lips, her smile, and I know that I'd take on the whole world to be able to save her friend and make her happy.

Chapter 34

The Everett Memorial Highway snakes up the side of Mt. Shasta to an altitude of nearly 8,000 feet. Almost at the very end of the road, Panther Meadow spreads out wide and wild and dark. The local mystics know the power of its vortex, as did the ancient Indian tribes that once came to this place for a spiritual communion. Legends say that visitors have encountered aliens here, creatures that have built a huge colony inside the Mountain... in fact, they say that Shasta itself is really a massive glass dome created to house their civilization.

We reach the meadow in the late afternoon when the alpenglow has already begun to turn the peaks a dusty pink. Even this close to the timberline, the vegetation is lush. A stream cuts through the meadow allowing grass and large trees to grow in spite of the altitude.

As we skirt the edge of the Dread Zone, Alicia and her fellow ghosts are already turning purple from its deadly effects.

"Carlyle," I say, "Remember how you saved Assad and me the last time we were here?"

He smiles and nods with some effort. The Dread Zone is taking all his strength.

"How did you manage to survive in the heart of a Dread Zone?"

"I inhabited the body of a bear," he answers with some effort, and I remember when the huge creature shambled out through the darkness to protect us and fight off an entire army of Tiger Joy's assassins.

"If a ghost can enter a living thing," Carlyle says, "the creature's body will absorb the ill effects of the vortex." He tells me this in spite of the purple blotches which are now spreading over his handsome face. "We're going to see if we can do something like that again."

Alicia and Mr. Foo are already so sick that their ability to help Sylvia seems very doubtful. I turn to my beautiful wife and see oozing sores breaking out on her skin. She gives me a desperate look, and I have to turn away.

"I'm going to handle this alone," I tell them as I pull my new/old Chrysler 300 over to the side of the road. I open the door and slide out from behind the steering wheel. "You guys head back to town and get inside the nearest church."

"To take advantage of its healing power," Mr. Foo sighs, but then manages to smile. "Excellent idea."

Alicia tries to shake her head. I know she wants to help save Sylvia, but she's too weak to put up much of a fight.

"Okay, but you have to take this, Dr. Mann," Foo says as his quivering hands pass me a sawed-off shotgun. "Sling it over your shoulder. Maybe the bad guys won't notice it until you're close enough to use it."

"Will do," I say taking the gun and doing as he suggests, not at all sure whether his advice will help me or get me killed.

"We'll be praying for you," Carlyle adds. Then he moves behind the wheel, does a raggedy u-turn right in the middle of the Everett Memorial Highway, and careens on down the road to the church at the base of the mountain.

So, now it's just me... alone with the high altitude, a wind that's starting to howl wickedly, and a damn vortex that I can already feel wrapping itself around me. It calls me to a distant clearing in the meadow where a group of young men have already gathered.

They're Tiger's boys – or at least those that are left of them. I adjust the shotgun and march in their direction.

As I get closer I can see that they're standing at the edge of a great stone spiral that someone has laid out in the middle of the clearing. It's made up of large rocks that mark the shape. There are five boys: all young, thin, handsome, somber, wearing sharkskin suits, Gucci shoes, and dark sunglasses. They shiver in the harsh wind and stare at the center of spiral. There they've placed a sturdy rosewood table with a little bamboo box on top of it. I can tell by the ornate pattern on the box that it's a ghost trap.

The tallest of Tiger's boys has a huge owl perched on his shoulder, and he seems to be talking to the bird even though I can see that its claws are digging into him and drawing blood.

"Come to witness the sacrifice, Dr. Mann?" the kid says as he turns to me. The owl lets out a sanctimonious, "Hoo!"

"Sacrifice?"

"A soul for a soul," the kid answers without even flinching as the bird adjusts its position on his shoulder. It's clawing out plenty of his blood in the process.

"You took Tiger from us; so we're gonna send this beautiful señorita into the nothingness." And with that he steps into the spiral, moves to the ghost trap, and grabs it off the table.

The owl immediately springs from the kid's shoulder, clasps the trap in his talons, and takes off into the air.

I pull up the shotgun, but the bird is well out of range. So I take off running after it. Breaking into a hard run at 8,000 feet can be a little challenging, so I'm really out of breath when I reach the huge pine where the owl's perched.

The tall kid apparently didn't have any trouble with the altitude. He's right with me.

"What the fuck's he doing?" I shout at anyone who'll listen.

"I have no idea, Dr. Mann," the kid answers without even breathing hard. "Why would he want to play hide and seek with you?"

"Is that what we're doing?"

"Sort of."

"What a waste of time."

"Exactly!"

Of course, the damn vortex probably works on Sylvia whether she's in the trap or out of it. But it does need a little time to work. So what the owl is doing is preventing me from rescuing Sylvia and saving her.

The realization pisses me off so much that I grab the shotgun and fire directly up into the tree. The owl gives a nasty hoot and tumbles toward the ground, dropping the ghost trap in the process.

The trap hits the ground, and Tiger's henchman picks it up and rushes back down the mountainside with it. He swings back toward the spiral and lowers it carefully onto the table. Then he springs the trap open.

Just like that, Sylvia shimmers into existence sitting on the cabinet. Her feet point inward; her head and shoulders dip almost down to her knees. She's already half dead from the power of the Panther Meadow vortex.

Finally, she looks up and sees me.

"Carlitos," she calls hopefully, as I race toward her. But in that instant the huge owl rears up in front of me, pounding its wings, threatening me with its talons.

"Stay back. Don't interfere," it hoots in a voice that sounds very much like Mr. Lum. I realize that the old man has joined the festivities by taking over the body of this enormous bird. Carlyle was right. He's protecting himself from the ghost-killing powers of the Dread Zone by inhabiting the body of a living thing.

I don't have time to aim and fire, so I just pull the shotgun from my shoulder, grab it by its barrel and use it like a baseball bat to drive the owl halfway across the field. The ghost/owl/monstrosity squawks and sails sideways falling at last in a clumsy tangle of feathers and claws. Then it pops up onto its feet, tries to fly, feels the effect of a broken wing, and just hobbles off toward the treeline.

When they see it happen, Tiger's boys rush me. But I spin the gun around and blast a round of buckshot directly into them.

The shot rips the two lead guys apart. Their blood and guts spray all over their comrades who are also torn by the scattering shot. They fall back giving me just enough time to slide the shotgun back onto my shoulder, scoop Sylvia up in my arms, and head off toward the road.

"No, Carlitos," she sighs, "Save yourself."

But, hell, I'm in no danger. Tiger's boys are staggering around the meadow with no sign that they want to follow me. The deadly owl is still hobbling toward the trees making nasty Chinese hooting sounds.

I smile down at Sylvia.

"We're gonna make it, beautiful," I say. But now I can see Sylvia beginning to disintegrate as I carry her. Her flesh turns orange. Purple blotches swarm all over her skin and begin eating her alive.

"Oh Carlitos, I'm dying again."

I hear the anguish in her voice, remember the suffering that Alicia had to endure in the Dread Zone of Sinaqua, Arizona. But I also remember that our ghost friend Chantel Nightingale did not finally succumb to the Sinaqua Dread Zone. She died, and yet she didn't fade into oblivion as all the legends said she would.

"Imagine my surprise," Chantel told me with her last breath, "When I realized that there is something even after this."

I'm running hard down the highway now, carrying the rotting ghost of this once beautiful woman, knowing that there are a full twelve miles to go to get to the church, wondering at what point the powers of the Dread Zone will begin to fade.

I hear Sylvia groan as I carry her onto the highway, and charge along the road. Is there anything else I can do?

Her body seems so heavy with the rot of death. I run onto the sandy shoulder as the highway begins to zigzag. I'm rushing around sharp turns in the road where the vastness of Shasta falls away quickly to reveal multicolored plains that fan out all around it. They're speckled in the growing twilight... like paints dabbled across a hundred-mile pallet. Other, so much smaller mountains in the distance are painted with the same warmth.

But all this beauty is lost on Sylvia Morales, who now gives me a last sorrowful "Adios," as her oozing ghost-flesh turns to sand that simply slides through my fingertips.

I stop and fall to my knees. "Sylvia! I couldn't get to you in time."

My fingers fumble in the soft earth at the side of the road, sifting it for some trace of Sylvia, something that I can hang onto, some piece that I might use to put her back together.

"Dust to dust," I sigh, and my tears spill onto the parched high mountain earth.

From out of the dense pine forest on the other side of the road, a great brown bear shambles up to me. I back away immediately and pull the shotgun from my shoulder. But the bear has no interest in my gun or me. Instead it stops and begins to sniff at the sandy remains of Sylvia's ghost. It groans in heavy anguish. Then it looks at me with such sadness that I know that I'm looking at an animal inhabited by the spirit of Carlyle August.

"Carlyle," I gasp. But the bear backs away from me, shaking its head as though to drive away the horrible realization of what has happened to his beautiful friend. Then it just turns and gallops off into the woods. I think of running after it, and realize that the effort would be useless, so I begin trudging down the road yet again. Meanwhile, the magnificence of the alpine sunset sings all around me, but I'm too heartbroken to listen.

#

An hour later I make my way up the small stairway and through the high white wooden door of the church at the base of the mountain. I don't know what to expect but I'm damn happy when I find Alicia now fully recovered from the effects of the Dread Zone.

"Sylvia?" Alicia asks as soon as she sees me.

I just shake my head. My wife takes the few steps between us, falls into my arms, and begins to sob.

"Carlyle?" Foo asks before Alicia and I even begin to draw apart. "He said he was going to find a bear to inhabit."

I saw him on the mountain," I answer. "The bear, that is, but I knew that Carlyle's ghost was in there, and I could see the heartbreak in his eyes."

"So, where is he now?" Alicia asks.

"Still up there."

"Still looking for someone who has fallen into nothingness," she sighs.

I start to remind her about Chantel, but her fingers slide up to my lips and press them shut.

"Not now, mi amor," she whispers.

Alicia takes my hand and leads me out of the church. My new/old Chrysler is parked out in front.

"You need some sleep," she tells me. "Carlyle will find us in the morning."

We drive toward the freeway and find a quaint old hotel which has a comfortable bed, a late hours restaurant, and a nice hot shower. I check in; the ghosts disappear.

A half hour later I've scrubbed down, put on the hotel's thick terrycloth bathrobe, and ordered a steak and a bottle of red wine from room service. When they come I just stare at them and at my plate. I don't even open the wine. I'm not hungry at all, just tired, and feeling very much like a failure. I let Uncle Lum's owl play keep away just long enough to cost Sylvia her afterlife.

So, I fall into bed knowing that the ghosts are out prowling the forests, hoping somehow to encounter Carlyle. I'd like to help them but I can't; what I need at the moment is sleep, the deeper the better.

For a time, visions of Sylvia Morales swirl through my head, and they are such sweet memories: Sylvia preparing a fiesta at the home of the curandera the first time I met her, Sylvia dancing at Señor Popcorn's wedding, Sylvia taming Crown Prince Rudolph after he tried to sell Alicia to the Gypsies. Sylvia racing from the great hacienda to greet me when I returned with all those business deals for El Patron. Eventually, these memories of Sylvia give way to sleep.

But the sleep is not sweet... the sleep is not restful. It's haunted with visions of another little girl smeared with grease from another terrible accident.

Lights swirl around her, tow trucks, and an ambulance are on the scene. Gawkers step between us once again... closing off whatever access I have to her. I'm pushed to my knees, and then the crowd parts again allowing the gangly legs and sensible shoes of the young teen girls to practically stride right over me.

"So necessary," one girl says.

"Ohmygod, yes!"

The lead girl isn't talking. But she does look my way and smiles. My heart nearly stops. She's so young, so pretty. There's nothing harsh or callous about her. She's sweet, innocent. Who the hell is she?

She passes me as the rest of her gang stride by. Then she looks back over her shoulder and giggles.

"He's coming," she says to me. "Best be careful."

Then the crowd stirs. Men curse, women scream. They begin struggling against each other trying to get out of the way. I'm still on my knees looking through the legs of the now charging crowd in front of me.

A woman dives to my right, and behind her I see the paws of a giant tiger bounding toward me. It lunges at me through the crowd, through the dream, finally waking me with a bloodthirsty, heart-stopping ROAR.

Chapter 35

The room is pitch black.

I roll over in my bed, tap the front of my iPhone, and the time illuminates. It's 2:13 AM.

I look and listen for ghosts... no sign of them, but through the window, a bright spark of light suddenly flashes. I struggle to my feet, still shaking off the dream-sight of the tiger.

"Too real," I think, "way too real."

I stagger to the window, brush aside the thick window curtains, and spot the light. It's burning like a beacon but so far off in the distance that I shouldn't be able to see it. Still, it's there. Then a high-pitched whistle cuts through the night, piercing my head like a pickaxe. I grab my head and almost fall to the floor from the pain of it. I look around wondering if anyone else can hear it... I duck out into the hallway... no one is stirring. Only me.

Somehow, I know the light and the whistle are calls that I'm supposed to answer. So, I pull on my jeans, slip a white Mt. Shasta hoodie over my head, slide into my shoes and run out into the night and my car. It welcomes me with warmth that hasn't yet faded with the mountain cold.

"Come on, baby," I whisper as I crank the engine. And I'm happy when it roars to life. I check the surroundings for signs of ghosts who might want to join me. I see none. "Alicia," I call into the darkness. No beautiful ghost comes gliding into my car with sweet words to comfort me. Of course, the damn whistle is just as intense. So I slam the big Chrysler into gear and roll out into the streets of Mt. Shasta City then up the Everett Memorial Highway.

I follow the pinpoint of light and the sharp call of the whistle that accompanies it. I understand their message completely. "Hurry up, asshole. You don't want to take too much time again."

A short way up the mountain I see that the light is now off to the left of me. It's glowing somewhere in the deserted campgrounds at McBride Springs. I pull into the barely-paved road, and my car jostles over the ruts and potholes until it reaches the back of the campground. It's a double-sized site with a huge fireplace set right in the middle of it. There's the fire burning with a single, constant flame. The call of the whistle is almost deafening as I step from the car. I see another little girl with a smudged face dart forward in front of the fire. She stops, eyes me uncertainly for a moment, toys with the edge of her dress, and then calls to me. With that call the whistle stops abruptly.

"Please help me, Dr. Mann," the little girl says. "They want to hurt me bad."

I hurry toward the kid, but she's gone by the time I get to the fire. I know she's the one who has called me here, and I can feel the power of the vortex moving all around me. Beyond the fire I see a huge tent. It looks more like something from a medieval encampment, with thick black canvas walls that almost seem to breathe.

As I take one more step toward it, the doorway suddenly opens and half a dozen ancient Chinese warriors spring out at me... or are they merely the Joy Lum killers dressed that way? Two of the warriors are on me at once knocking my legs out from under me, throwing me to the ground. I regain my feet quickly enough to flatten the next kid who comes at me. But then two more grab me around the waist and heave me down again. The others advance, fists cocked; one of them even draws a dagger. As two more of the gang grab my arms and hold me down, the kid with the dagger raises it above his head just over my throat in some kind of sacrificial pose. Looks like I'm what's for dinner.

Just as the kid lets out some ancient tone and brings the dagger down toward me... he's slammed across the campground by the paw of a huge bear. This is no cuddly cub from a Disney cartoon, no comic character from some beer commercial. This bear nearly tears the kid's head off with one swipe.

As the warrior struggles to regain his feet, three more jump from the tent and rush the bear, wrestling him to the ground. But the bear is enormous, kicking and growling like some locomotive. As the kid with the dagger makes his way back to me with his weapon raised, the others jump on my arms and legs and pin me to the ground.

"This is for our mistress," the kid hisses at me, "the beautiful Tiger Joy." He lifts the dagger above me a second time and starts his slow, studied motion downward toward my throat. This time I feel the blade touch my neck before a streak of yellow and black flashes across the campground and dives on top of him. It's a jaguar, coming somehow from a thousand miles and a half-dozen cultures away. The huge cat squirms all over the kid, tearing his insides out. Then, with the kid's blood and guts still splattered all over its face, the jaguar turns and advances on the other warriors surrounding me.

Like a team of suicidal daredevils they peel off of me one at a time and rush the jaguar who makes short work of them one after another, until all that is left is one kid who had managed to climb right on top of me. His knees are on my arms pressing them into the ground. His young handsome face stares down at me, and I recognize one of Tiger's most faithful guardians.

"You killed my lady," he suddenly sobs and falls forward on me, his teeth clamping down on my neck as though he intends to tear my throat out. But before he can bite too hard, the kid suddenly flies off of me and sails across the campground landing in the same disheveled pile where all the other Joy Lum assassins have been dumped.

The jaguar struggles to her feet and glides up to me. She's driven another warrior away. Now, she looks down at me with eyes that seem so caring. Then she purrs and begins to lick my neck, licking away the blood that the kid had only begun to unleash.

"Carlitos," the jaguar sighs.

"Alicia?"

"Who did you expect, my good man?" the bear suddenly asks in a decidedly aristocratic voice.

"Carlyle."

"We just couldn't let these guys do any more damage to you."

"Sssssooo, now, Dr. Mann," hisses a distinctly Asian sounding voice that must surely be coming from a large snake that's slithering toward me from behind the fire. "You see that we are all together again."

I nod as I get to my feet and pat the jaguar face of my beautiful wife.

"We're protected by the bodies of these living animals... last night as we hunted for any signs of Sylvia... and today as we overheard Uncle Lum's boys preparing to capture and kill you."

"Tiger may be gone but her uncle's vengeance is relentless," Carlyle tells me.

"You are no safer than when Tiger was alive."

"But what about the little girls?" I ask.

"I can't figure them out," Carlyle says. "The one tonight... she was with the boys today, and she seemed so terrified."

"She asked me to save her," I tell the animals... who are somehow also my friends.

"Strange happenings, mi amor," Alicia purrs. "It appears that we will still have to protect you."

I shrug.

"But without my further assistance," Carlyle adds. "I've put together a new plan to save Sylvia."

"She's gone, Señor," Alicia answers. "There will be no saving."

"She disintegrated in my arms on the mountain," I say.

"I don't buy that," Carlyle answers. "Disintegration is an old ghost trick, and besides, there are plenty of places where she can hide."

"Beyond our world?"

"Why not?"

"You are talking about trying to get into heaven to find her," Alicia says. "Then – if she is not there – visiting hell itself. I do not think we are allowed such entrances."

"There are those who say it's been done," Mr. Foo answers. "I'm not sure how; but if Sylvia's blinked out of existence...."

Carlyle the bear suddenly pounces on the old Chinese serpent, catching him in his paws and forcing him to listen.

"We won't be talking like that, my friend," Carlyle says. "When you're around me, you will only say that Sylvia is in a much better place."

"I see," sighs the serpent.

"I just have to go out there and figure out which place it is."

Alicia lets go of my hand and moves toward the handsome ghost.

"But it could be very dangerous for you, you know."

Carlyle gives her a very troubled smile. He looks past her to me and shrugs. "I leave you in good hands, Dr. Mann," he says. Then he turns back to Alicia. "Take care of your husband, okay? We need him. Hopefully I will see you all again very soon."

Then he growls and is suddenly *completely* a bear that lowers himself onto his forepaws and shambles off into the forest.

Chapter 36

We're halfway back to Los Altos, and we've stopped so that I can get a good night's sleep. We're leaving Carlyle to his own crazy plans... at least for now. Alicia and Foo have returned to their human forms, and once Foo departs Alicia shares more of her passionate ghost love, which now seems to have a terrible sense of desperation about it. Still, I go to bed happy. Except now I'm dreaming of little girls and Chinatown again.

I'm at the corner of Grant Avenue and Washington where the traffic is slow moving and heavy as always. It's a foggy night, and the glitter of Chinatown is even more mysterious in the soft focus of the heavy mist. The wind swirls casually through the place, mixing old newspapers and handbills, the smell of soy sauce and teak and bamboo and silk and oolong tea. The traffic light changes. Gridlock! The Grant traffic is strung across the intersection blocking cars on Washington that now have a green light. Little by little they clear just as the light turns red again. There's an eye-blink when there are actually no cars blocking the way. Then, a summery station wagon with a surfboard tied to the roof starts to move slowly through the light on Grant, but a frustrated teenage driver on Washington has had enough. He floors his big yellow Mustang and tries to power through the intersection against the red light. The station wagon is too far along to get out of his way; it's right in front of him and doesn't even see him.

Accelerating with all the power of a 1970s muscle car, the kid plows into the side of the wagon, driving it across the intersection and into a hydrant on the other side of the street. Pedestrians who still cram the Chinatown sidewalks scatter in all directions as the engine bursts into flames. The driver bolts from the wagon; his wife jumps out of the other side and runs around to his, but I can see a little girl trapped in the back seat. Her door is caved in. She's terrified. As flames flare up around the hood, she scrunches down behind the front seat. Her dad and mom are trying to reach her through the opposite rear door, but the kid is screaming... too terrified to move. Meanwhile the driver of the Mustang throws his car into reverse and jolts back away from the wagon. As he does he pulls the wagon's passenger side door back with him. He jerks his car around to flee, and the door of the wagon pulls away from his car. It's even more caved in now, but it's at least open.

All the onlookers stand back as flames spread over the hood of the car. Mom and dad keep shouting to their daughter, but they're on the wrong side, and their little girl is too terrified to crawl over to them.

Suddenly, the figure of a young teenager runs up to the car. She forces the girl's door open all the way... so that she can reach in and pull the kid out of the wreckage. The little girl hangs onto her for dear life, and when I see them clutching each other I realize again that the rescuer is very young, maybe only thirteen or fourteen years old. She and the little girl rush away from the blazing car, which suddenly explodes, taking the car, mom and dad, and quite a few onlookers with it into oblivion.

I'm on the far side of the street. The station wagon is now a mass of flames. Onlookers press themselves back from it... against Chinatown store windows, or they rush in thick crowds down the sidewalk leaving the accident behind them. A fire truck plows through the heavy traffic and onto the scene. I fight my way through the crowd, rush after the hero girl, try to grab her, spin her around, and see who she is.

She makes her way around the corner of an old souvenir shop, and I stop dead in my tracks. There in front of me are a very young version of Mother and Father Joy. They wait eagerly for the teenager to bring the girl to them, and as soon as she does, they grab the kid and shuffle her into the back of a large panel truck.

When the teenager suddenly turns and looks back toward me, I finally recognize her. She's a very young and innocent looking Tiger Joy. What's missing from her face is the cruelty that will so dominate it later in life. Without that harsh attitude the girl is absolutely beautiful.

"We have our half dozen," Mother says to Father.

"What do you mean, Mother?" Tiger asks.

"The half dozen girls we need to expand our offering."

"Your offering?" Tiger looks surprised and angry.

"Yes, it's time for us to expand the family trade, bring in a few very high-priced girls of European stock."

"European stock?" Tiger is astounded. "What for?"

"Come now, Helen," Father says to the girl as he moves closer to her. "Didn't I explain that you would learn all about our business when you were a little older?"

"Yes, Father."

"I still don't think you are quite old enough, dear. Do you?"

"No, Father."

"But you are old enough to understand the importance of obedience. Do you remember how we talked about that, Helen?"

"Yes, Father."

"All right then. I want you to show me what a good obedient girl you can be. Okay?"

"Yes, Father."

"It will be difficult, but you can do it, Helen."

"Yes, Father."

"A sign of your obedience?"

"Yes, Father."

Mother steps up to Tiger and draws a dagger from her purse. It's short but highly polished and across the blade I can make out the engraving of a great, stalking Tiger.

"What you have to do is simple, but important," Mother says.

"Yes, Mother."

"The girls we have saved are all inside the truck, dear."

"Yes, Mother."

"I simply want you to take this dagger, go into the truck, and kill one of them... as a demonstration of your obedience to your father and me."

Tiger has turned, and I'm looking her right in the face.

Her face twists in shock, but then she seems to catch herself. She lowers her eyes, shakes her head to clear her thoughts, and looks determined.

"You can kill any one of the girls you like, Helen," Father says. "You saved their lives so you have the right to kill them."

"Yes, Father."

"Anyone you like," Father repeats. "Now are you ready, my pretty little girl?"

Tiger looks at both her parents and nods.

"So then, beautiful, what do you say?" Father whispers.

Tiger turns to her father and smiles, and it's a different kind of smile than I've seen in all the rescues she's performed... there are the beginnings of cruelty in it.

"Give me the knife," she whispers joyfully.

Chapter 37

We're at the Purgatory Bookstore in Los Altos now. The crusty old woman who runs the place has just put the "closed" sign in the window and taken a last walk around the premises even though she hasn't locked the front door. Pretty strange behavior for a retailer, I'm thinking, but not as strange as the feelings I get when I duck inside the front door and make my way up the stairway to the attic.

"Something's very wrong here," I whisper to Alicia who has just materialized beside me. I can tell by the concerned look on her face that she notices it too.

"They are not just trying to scare us this time, mi amor," she says.

I nod, remembering the first time I came here... when the ghost of old man Friedman turned himself into a giant spider and stalked me from over by the window.

We make it up the stairway, and Alicia gasps. So do I. Beside the big window that overlooks University Avenue is a great wooden cross in the shape of the letter "X". And tied to it with bright blue cable ties is the miserable-looking ghost of Jenny Beck. She's wearing nothing but raggedy underwear and is as emaciated as ever. The Goth girl sees us ascending the stairs and calls out, "Chill, dudes, or she'll kill ya!"

I spin and see the ghost of Tiger Joy sitting far back from the stairs... on a throne that she must have shipped in from Chinatown (maybe Ghost Chinatown). It's carved with great dragons that snake their way over the back of the chair and out to form its arms. Tiger toys with the dragons' teeth as she gives me an evil leer.

She's dressed all in white, if you can believe that: a white latex mini skirt, white low-slung halter-top, and high white latex boots. Even her fishnet stockings are white. Around her neck she wears what must surely be a white-gold chain with a dragon pendant hanging from it. Her earrings are jade. Her smile is hungry.

Tiger's boys surround her. They're ghosts too, standing in a line like a street gang ready to rumble. They all wear white slacks and t-shirts.

"Wait – what?" Alicia gasps.

"How the hell did you get here?" I hiss at Tiger. "If anyone deserves to go straight to hell, it's you."

"Watch your mouth, Carlitos," Tiger snaps. "Turns out I did at least one good deed in my life... enough to get me a pass, anyway."

Suddenly it all makes sense... all those dreams. Somehow Tiger (in whatever kind of whacked-out assignment she was on) did pull those girls out of the burning cars, did save their lives, and in the process sidestepped the express elevator straight to damnation.

"But you slaughtered one of them, didn't you?"

Tiger gives me a sexy little giggle. "More than one. But you know, it's your intentions when you *do* the deed, that count. And when I saved all those girls my intentions were pure."

I shake my head. Who's coming up with this theology... there's certainly no logic to it.

"So, now I'm takin' over, you fucking prick," Tiger says. Over her shoulder I can see Friedman stretched out on a rack. In another corner Royce Brilliant has been stripped naked and stuffed into a tiny iron cage. Still, he can't help eyeing Tiger's boys, and I'm thinking he actually likes things the way they are.

"Built your own little torture chamber up here, huh?" I ask Tiger.

"Seems that way, doesn't it?"

Alicia turns to Jenny and yells, "Make yourself invisible, girl. Get out of here."

"It's not that easy," Jenny sobs. And for the first time ever I see real fear in her eyes. Her favorite word, "whatever," is probably the farthest thing from her mind.

"We've managed to put your ghosts in a lockdown," Tiger says.

"It's against the Geneva Convention," Friedman yells from the rack.

"There is no Geneva Convention for ghosts, you old fool," Tiger calls. Then she nods to one of her boys, and he goes, turns a big crank, and stretches Friedman a little bit tighter. We can hear his ghost bones crack and his desperate sighs of pain.

"How can this be happening?" Alicia screams. "Ghosts have no bodies if we don't want them... at least not outside of the Dread Zones. We are above physical pain."

"Not when you're caught in one of my ghost traps, chica," Tiger growls, and she sashays over and points to Jenny's leg. There's an intricate little golden lock binding her ankle to the cross. The fact that it merely touches her leg seems enough to prevent her from disappearing.

"Hi-tech?" I ask.

"Ancient Chinese," Tiger sneers.

I don't quite get how it works, and I'm not about to ask for an explanation, because just then Tiger's boys decide to rush me. They're swirling nunchucks over their heads, and I'm forced to duck under the attack. I upset the first guy who gets to me, and he falls back into his brothers, tangling himself and the others in a knotted mass of chains and wooden clubs.

"Those things were never very effective," I call as I watch the boys scramble to free themselves from each other. "Besides, they're Japanese, not Chinese."

"That's debatable, Dr, Mann," one of them shouts as he

breaks free from the bunch and slings the great wooden end of one of the nunchucks at me.

"Which part's debatable?"

"Both parts," he answers. I manage to duck the swinging weapon, and it nearly pulls the kid off his feet.

"They can be effective and there is some suggestion that their origin is in ancient China."

"Unlikely," I say as I dive forward and hit him below the knees. The kid flips up in the air, and all of his nunchucks come pounding down onto his head. That pretty much takes care of him, and – when his charging brothers trip over him and once again entangle themselves in their complex weaponry – the attack is pretty much over.

I stand facing Tiger. All of her gang is in various stages of disarray around me.

"So glad you're safe, Carlitos," Tiger purrs.

"Stop calling him by *my* pet name for him," Alicia calls. Tiger just ignores her.

"You see, Carlitos, I've had a revelation," Tiger says as she strides up to me. She brings a riding crop along and flicks it across the palm of her hand as she approaches.

"It's not good enough for me to see you dead... especially not following one or another of your heroic deeds."

"My husband is a good man," Alicia shouts.

"Yes, of course he is," Tiger says as she stands in front of me and begins to flick the tip of the riding crop gently over my chest. "That's the problem. I mean, what kind of revenge is it to send your victim straight to heaven."

"You would be taking away the time he has to spend with me," Alicia says.

"Well that might be a good thing for our Carlitos," Tiger laughs. "But the problem is that I should be sending him *straight to hell*... where he belongs.

"Anyway, I am *not* going to capture you this time, Carlitos," Tiger adds as she turns toward me and gives me a quick biting snap with the end of her riding crop.

"You're free to leave."

"What's the catch?"

"No catch," Tiger grins. "Except maybe the fact that my goal is to *catch* you in the act of sinning... *catch* you when you are not in good grace. Bump you off at just the best possible time... for me that is... when you'll be damned for eternity."

"Sounds fair," I say knowing that I have no plans of committing any of the kind of sins that will send me to hell. So I put my arm around Alicia and move toward the stairway.

"Just one more question?" Tiger purrs.

"I don't think so."

"Hey, help out a poor little girl here, won't you please?" Tiger pretends to pout.

"I WANT TO GAG," Jenny Beck shouts from across the room.

"Just tell me the whereabouts of that handsome ghost, Carlyle August."

"He is out trying to find Sylvia," Alicia answers before she realizes that she probably shouldn't say anything at all to Tiger.

"Uncle Lum turned Sylvia into nothingness," Tiger says.

"Except Carlyle doesn't believe it."

"Wonderful! Thank you. I'll be able to capture him and return him to my torture chamber." Tiger gives a witchy cackle, and then charges down the stairs and out into the night.

I look at my wife who shrugs guiltily.

"I told her too much, didn't I?"

"It's okay," I start to tell her, but Alicia has already left me, taking off after Tiger, and I'm left at the top of the stairs unable to catch up to them. I'm not even sure where the hell they're going. Anyway, I know that I should try and rescue Jenny, Freeman, and Royce from this torture chamber. All that's really standing in the way are Tiger's boys.

I hear the rattle of nunchucks behind me, and I know that they've managed to untangle themselves and are forming up for another attack.

I smile eagerly and turn to face them.

7
Alicia

Chapter 38

Tiger flies through the night like a witch on her broom... not an old wrinkled witch but just as evil and scary. I race to keep up with her. I know a few ghost tricks too, maybe more than she does, since she has only just become a ghost, and then only because she is so damn lucky.

There are pathways to the underworld even for ghosts. It has always been easy to enter hell, believe me. My hope is that Carlyle has chosen to go to heaven first and has found Sylvia and is coming back to make things right at the Purgatory Bookstore. But it is more probable that Sylvia is no more, not aware of all that is happening or will ever happen again. I hope not.

I have made myself as invisible as I can. I have limited the breath of my very soul in the hope that Tiger will not notice me as I trail behind her. If she finds Carlyle I must be there to stop her when she tries to capture him.

Tiger flies from Los Altos into the coast mountains of California, into a forest as dark and tangled as any I have ever seen. The trees are old oaks, twisted like the witches Tiger reminds me of. The branches want to reach out and grab me, and I am in great fear even though I fly past them, over them, even through them.

The mountains climb and Tiger flies up with them, stopping only for a moment when a black panther rushes out at her and flashes its great claws. It makes her backtrack a little and then she charges ahead again. She is shaking her head now, and I hope she wonders if this journey is worth it.

A lion rushes out of the woods and challenges her too. He

swats at her with his monster paws, and I wonder where such a lion could come from in the coast mountains of California, or a black panther either. There is the spirit of a ghost in the lion that causes Tiger once again to shake her head and change her path. She tries another direction... down and to the left, into a clearing, and then a great wolf suddenly springs out at her. It is a mother wolf huge with milk, but this does nothing to soften her; it makes her even wilder than the others, and, as she licks her terrible lips and thinks of eating Tiger, the evil girl turns around and blasts past me in the other direction. No more will she try to climb this mountain, I think; she is headed downward.

I spin and follow her, happy that she did not notice me as she hurried by, and I am just as glad to be leaving these woods and the wild things that guard it.

But we don't quite leave the woods. The downward path turns into them again, and I have to fly even faster to keep up with Tiger as she flits through the reaching branches of hungry trees. Finally, ahead I see the entrance to a great cave. A river rushes up to it, then drops down into the mouth of the cave, becoming a wide, churning waterfall that dives deep into the earth. I listen as it thunders into the distance, and it sounds like it drops all the way to the very gates of hell.

Carved in the rocks above the drop are words in some language I do not know... but I understand them. **Abandon All Hope You Who Enter Here.**

"¡Sin esperanza!" I call and pray that I never have to follow this path into the drop. But then I almost feel better, because sitting on the river's bank, head bowed in sadness, I see the ghost of Carlyle August.

Tiger suddenly flies up beside him. She caresses his face, draws his lips up to hers, and kisses him. It is an embarrassing kiss believe me, and I am blushing... but more with anger than with shame.

"Do not kiss this evil woman," I shout at Carlyle. "She killed Sylvia."

"You don't believe that," Tiger says. Her hands are still holding his face. Her lips are still close to his.

"If you love Sylvia," I say, "then get away from that witch."

Carlyle looks sad and confused.

"If you love *me*..." I begin.

That makes Tiger smile, and I know at once that I have said the wrong thing yet again. Carlyle looks at me, and then looks back at this witchy girl.

"*Can* he love you, Alicia?" she asks. "Will you give yourself to him?"

Carlyle's look is blank. I want to see the sparkle in his eyes, or at least the kindness that I know. But there is nothing there. I'm not even sure he is interested in this conversation, but I have to answer anyway.

"I am married to Carlitos," I say as I hang my head because I know where Tiger is going with her arguments.

Her smile is so evil. "Come on, Alicia, how about a little action on the side, a little fling while Carlos isn't looking. Now's your chance! I'll never tell."

Carlyle looks to me and then back to Tiger. His eyes are not filled with the goodness that is always there now, just emptiness. Perhaps it is caused by his failure to find Sylvia, by sadness, by hopelessness, I don't know, but it is most illogical, and it makes me very angry. I want to throw something, but instead, I cross my arms across my chest and stare at him.

"Carlyle!" I stomp my foot. "Remember your goodness."

"Goodness?" Tiger giggles. "Don't be silly, girl."

"Alicia," Carlyle begins. "I'm so lost...."

"No need for that," Tiger gushes. "Forget the bitch. Let's you and I have a little fun."

I've never seen the look that now comes to Carlyle's face. It is as though he just does not know what to do... as though he has never had to make a decision in his entire life. And then I realize that Carlyle never ever really had to choose between anything. He grew up with silver spoons all around him. There was the silver spoon of wealth, the silver spoon of being so smart, the silver spoon of good looks and that suave voice, the silver spoon of great ideas and great success. What kind of silver spoons did Carlitos and I have: the old tin spoon of poverty, the sticky old spoon of logics?

Carlyle smiles uncertainly at Tiger, and that's IT!

I've had enough of this.

I march up to Carlyle, push Tiger out of the way, grab his hand, and jerk him to his feet.

"You need someone to bring you back to the real world, mijo," I shout. "If ever there was a time for logics it is now. And I know a fine professor who will tell you exactly what you need to do. His name is Dr. Carlos Mancowski."

Chapter 39

Carlyle and Carlitos have been in our living room for hours... talking about so many things: about love and death, about Sylvia and me, about good and evil, and Tigers. I left the room in great sadness after hearing Carlyle confess that he was growing so fond of Sylvia that he actually thought of marrying her in the ghost life... which is even stranger than a dead person marrying a living one. Unless you are married in life, why would you want to be married in death? I wonder. And then I know... because of love, estúpido.

The two are still talking. Their voices are low. I cannot even tell if they are friendly any more. But Carlyle's is – as always – polite, and Carlitos's is – as always – logical. Finally Carlyle glides into the kitchen and smiles at me.

"Thank you, beautiful lady," he says.

"Are you all right, Carlyle?"

"No, not really."

"Well, did talking to Carlitos help you, at least?"

"I'm not sure."

"But you are never going to see that Tiger person again, right?"

"Sorry."

"*Sorry* you are never going to see her again, or *sorry* you are going to see her?"

Carlyle smiles his sweet gentleman's smile, "I have to see her again, Alicia."

My heart sinks. Was all of Carlitos's logical talk for nothing?

"But why?"

Carlyle's smile is still sweet, but there is the gleam of uncertainty in his eyes. It is starting to resemble lust I think.

"Adios," he sighs, and then, bowing, he turns, glides through the closed door of our little apartment, and heads out into the night.

#

Moments later I walk into our living room and find that Carlitos has pulled all the books off the bookshelves and is rearranging them. He is so intent in his work that he does not even look at me.

"Carlitos," I call. "Did things go okay with Carlyle?"

He does not answer. He merely rearranges some more books.

"I always thought that books should be arranged by topic," he tells me.

"Okay."

"But now I see that I was wrong."

"Good."

"I'm going to rearrange them by author."

"Okay, but what about Carlyle?"

"Would you hand me that copy of *The Rise and Fall of The Roman Empire*?"

"Where is it?"

"Over there by the door."

"I will get it for you if you tell me about Carlyle."

"Just pick it up and hand it to me."

"Is Carlyle all right?"

Carlitos looks at me in confusion. And finally he just says, "No."

"What do you mean "No?""

"He's not all right."

"But he will be soon, sí?"

"I don't know... I don't think so."

"But what about all your logics?"

"Please, Alicia, just hand me the book and go to bed."

"Ghosts don't sleep," I say. "What's wrong with Carlyle?"

"He's going back to Tiger."

"What? To lead her into a Dread Zone?"

"Alicia, he's not all right, and he's not going to lead Tiger into a Dread Zone. NOW WILL YOU PLEASE, GIVE ME THE GODDAMN BOOK?"

My husband is yelling at me, and I don't even care that when Carlyle and I came back to the apartment, we found him badly beaten but victorious. Apparently he defeated Tiger's boys, rescued their prisoners (Freedman, Jenny, and Royce), and moved them into a peaceful new living space in the attic of the La Meremma Restaurante next door.

So, maybe it is a good thing that my aim is not as good when I throw a book as when I kick a soccer ball, because I throw the big book at Carlitos very hard. It misses him but hits the shelf and breaks it, sending all the books he has already put in place down on top of him.

Carlitos crawls out from under the pile of books, gives me a terrible look, and walks past me into the bedroom locking the door behind him. I, of course, can just fly through the closed door and he knows it. Still I can tell how angry he is... probably with himself for not being able to restore Carlyle to his goodness. So, I just let my husband go to sleep while I try to figure out if there is any way that I can use my ghost powers to fix a broken shelf.

Now, it is much later that same night. I have not been able to fix the shelf. And so I have gone into the bedroom to watch my husband sleep. I hear a rattling in the kitchen. Someone is in there, someone who wants to talk to me but is too polite to enter our bedroom.

I fly through walls and into the kitchen.

"Carlyle," I call, hoping that the handsome ghost has repented and come back to join us. But it is not Carlyle who stands there rattling pots and pans; it is Mr. Foo.

"We must stop them," he tells me. "They are planning something awful."

"Tiger! And Carlyle?" I ask hoping that I am wrong.

"I'm afraid so. They are in San Francisco, in Noe Valley, outside the home of one of the policemen who helped capture Tiger and throw her in jail. He's there with his young wife and little daughter."

"And what does Tiger plan to do?" I ask.

Mr. Foo turns pale with horror.

"Scare them to death!"

· · · · ·

Within minutes Mr. Foo and I are at the home of Officer Patrick O'Riley, and what a light show is going on inside. Colors of red and yellow and orange are flashing wildly in all the windows, tigers are roaring, banshees are screaming, and Tiger Joy cackles above it all like the Queen of the Damned. Only, she is NOT damned. (Though I still do not understand why.)

Mr. Foo wastes no time in flying into the house and up to the bedroom where Officer O'Riley, his wife, and their little daughter Peggy are huddled together in a corner while the great ghost of a tiger stalks them. The big cat growls as it paces; then it screams at them and flashes its huge claws right in their eyes.

Little Peggy is wailing without control. She is turned away from the beast. The officer has his arm raised trying to deflect the ghost scratches that cannot really hurt him, except through fear.

Suddenly, in the opposite corner where little Peggy has fixed her eyes, a demon rises up. Monstrous ram's horns curl out of his head; his face is blood red; fangs stick up over his lips. His chest is bare but scarred as though barbed wire has been wrapped around him and then pulled tight.

"You're mine, little girl," he growls as his big hands and long black fingernails reach for her.

The little girl hugs her father even tighter. "Daddy!" she screams. And now Officer O'Riley turns as he holds her. He has his other arm wrapped around his wife, and he begins to back away from the devil and the tiger as they move toward him. Devil fingers twitch as they grab for the little girl. The tiger pauses again and again to reach out trying to scratch out the eyes of the officer and his family.

A closet stands behind Officer O'Riley. He glimpses it over his shoulder and backs slowly toward it.

The devil and the tiger move forward. They drive the young family back toward the closet door, which, in the middle of one of the tiger's most vicious attacks, the officer jerks open. There is a scream of absolute terror as they step into the closet, which now seems to have no floor. It feels like a deep well into which they are falling.

The family screams as they fall. Dragons swim up around them, blasting them with fire breath.

Officer O'Riley is sweating and sobbing. His daughter has her little face buried in his neck. She dare not look anywhere, and she can hardly breathe. His wife is clutching him tightly.

"No, no, no!"

Suddenly, the floor rises up and crashes into them, as though they have hit the bottom of the imaginary well they have been falling into. And then the tiger, the dragons, and the devil all jump wildly at the young family about to close their fangs on them and eat them alive.

In that moment of fear, the family screams horribly and then...

Carlitos steps in front of them. In his hand he holds out a great crystal ball that swallows up the flow of all those monsters.

"Where did my husband come from?" I ask Mr. Foo. But he does not know, or is not prepared to answer anyway.

Carlitos raises the crystal ball in front of his eyes. It now sparkles with the faces and bodies of the demons he has captured.

He twists his fingers mysteriously over the ball until the monster-contents spin rapidly and then suddenly flash out of existence.

"You'll be okay now," Carlitos tells Señor and Señora O'Riley.

"But what about the monsters?" little Peggy sobs.

"Captured in this ball," Carlitos says as he holds it out in front of her. It is now nothing but a soft glowing round thing. He bounces it. It's turned to rubber. The little girl giggles nervously.

"But who are you?" Officer O'Riley asks.

"A local professor," Carlitos answers with a reassuring smile. "Believe me, I'm on your side."

"*Professor*," Mrs. O'Riley answers with glowing eyes that say she thinks my husband must work at Hogwarts.

"And how do I repay you?" the cop asks as he reaches for his wallet.

"Just keep an eye on your family. Oh, and hang onto the ball. I'm sure none of these monsters will ever dare haunt you again... but if they do, just hold up the ball, and it will suck them right back into it."

Carlitos turns to the little girl and in his eyes I see the look of the little boy who saved me from the bullies when I was only six.

"You okay, sweetheart?"

"I was very scared."

"Just spooky dream stuff," Carlitos says with a smile. "You'll be fine. Besides, it's okay to be scared. Sometimes it's the right way to feel. But now you're safe."

"But what if they come back?"

Carlitos smiles and points to the ball. "You've got the ball, right?"

The little girl nods and closes her eyes as tears of hopefulness squeeze out of them.

Carlitos looks into the corner and sees me. He moves toward me, reaches for me, spins around, and takes control of me. We begin to turn quickly, and as we do we catch a glimpse of a very angry pair of ghosts, Tiger and Carlyle, huddled together in the corner. They are cursing us.

Then we are back in our apartment, spinning into the living room, where the bookshelf is repaired and all the books are put neatly away.

"How did you do that?" I ask my husband.

"Witchcraft," he answers proudly.

"And will you work a little magic on me, please?" I ask.

"Most definitely, Mrs. Mancowski," Carlitos answers. "I love bewitching you."

Chapter 40

The tromping begins. Tiger pounds her way up the stairs to the attic of the Purgatory Bookstore in those high heel boots of hers, making as much noise as she possibly can.... almost as if she were alive. Carlyle follows, floating up the stairs as a ghost should float. The fat old shape of Uncle Lum comes tumbling after them.

"So, we didn't kill them," Tiger says. "So what?"

"Sloppy work," Uncle Lum answers.

"When a tidal wave begins to hit the shore," Tiger says as she reaches the top step, "it's always a little messy. And I'm launching a tidal wave of revenge. With Mr. Handsome here to help me, I can't miss."

She turns, wraps Carlyle in her arms and gives him a very dirty kiss.

"So, what next, goddess?" Carlyle asks as he staggers backward from the power of the kiss.

"Carlos Mann and that bitch wife of his?" Uncle Lum wonders.

"Pretty little Alicia," Carlyle sighs. He still has hot ideas about my body, I think.

Carlitos stiffens. We are hiding in the corner of the attic. Mr. Foo and I have cloaked my husband in shadows. Still, I fear that he wants to rush out there and pound on the handsome ghost who has always had a crush on me. I make my nails hard and sink them into my husband's flesh so that he will know that he must remain silent if we are to learn what we came here to learn: What will Tiger do next?

"You're still crazy about the bitch, hmm?" Tiger teases Carlyle.

He blushes.

"Tell me. What's she have that I don't?"

She pushes out her breasts so that her thin white t-shirt can barely hold them in, then she begins to slide them over Carlyle's chest. He turns almost purple as she does this.

"Not a damn thing, beautiful," Carlyle whispers in his Cary Grant voice. "There's *nothing* she has that you don't."

"Of course not," Tiger coos. "Good. Because there are a few enemies that are more important than Dr. & Mrs. Mann."

"Like?"

"Maclovio Renta," Uncle Lum says.

"Down in Mexico?" Carlyle asks. "I thought he was your partner."

"Some partner."

Uncle Lum shakes his head causing his fat ghost body to jiggle all over.

"Señor Renta is getting a little too big for his britches," Tiger growls as she grabs Carlyle by his shoulders and rakes her claws down his back. He smiles even though I can see ghost-blood oozing out from under his shirt. She's teaching him to enjoy the sexy pain she causes.

"The naughty boy is skimming off our profits," Tiger says, "taking some of our best looking prospects for his own, not showing us the respect we deserve."

She leans her lips into Carlyle's ear and whispers hotly, "Wouldn't you like to execute him for me?"

Carlyle swallows very hard. His eyes are wide with either fear or excitement, or both.

"I'm sure it can be arranged, goddess."

"I'm glad," Tiger growls. "So, a little trip down Mexico way, guys? What do you say?"

Carlyle nods.

Her boys smile.

"What about the prisoners?" one of them asks. "The old

Jew, the Goth slut, the queer?"

"Where are they?" Tiger wants to know. "Mancowski actually saved them?"

"Yeah," the boy answers. "He beat us down, undid their locks, and gave the trio new digs in the attic of a nearby restaurant."

"YOU INCOMPETENT ASSHOLES!" Tiger suddenly shouts, and she charges forward. From out of nowhere she finds a riding crop in her hand and she begins pounding on the boy who dared to talk. He falls to his knees. She beats on him and beats on him. Finally, as his whole body slouches to the floor, she raises one high heel boot and brings it down on his neck, pinning his face to the floor, forcing him to lay helplessly as the crop tears his flesh with bloody wounds.

After too long a time, I think, Carlyle steps forward, catches Tiger's hand in mid-air, and pulls her off the boy who is already unconscious.

"Save your energy, pretty lady," Carlyle whispers.

Tiger actually fights him for a moment, tries to wrestle herself free. She wants to go back and beat the poor boy to death. But Carlyle's hand is around her neck, his cheek is pressed up against hers, his other hand holds her arm down at her side, and his leg has trapped hers so that she really can't move. I'm impressed.

"These fools aren't worth your efforts," Carlyle says. "Let's go to Mexico, let's unleash the demons, let's get our revenge against Renta, and then let's capture Carlos Mann in some deadly sin, murder him, and send him down where he belongs."

"Yessss," Tiger purrs as she relaxes at last. "Thank you, lover."

But I can't believe what I have heard. Carlyle has become such a traitor. His mind is so captured by Tiger's white latex mini-skirts and high heels and bloody whip and evil mind that he is starting to think like her. He is truly our enemy now. I am sure of it.

We watch as Tiger leads her evil band down the stairs and out of the Purgatory Bookstore.

Finally I turn to Mr. Foo and whisper, "Bastardos!"

"How could he have turned so completely against us?" the old man asks.

Carlitos does not say a word. He just moves on down the stairs and out the door. And I am sure that he feels the pain of failure. What good did all his talk and all his logics do? I want to ask him. But I don't have to. I know.

Nada!

Chapter 41

So, now we are at Señor Popcorn's vast estate outside of Mexico City. He has rebuilt it from the ashes that Maclovio Renta left there.

We are gathered around the big table in the dining room: Mr. Foo; Carlitos; Miguel Carillo (Senior Popcorn's right-hand man); Marie Elena (Miguel's wife); Victor Estephan (one of Senor Popcorn's lieutenants); the great popcorn man himself; his wife, Señora Eva Córdoba de Cervantes; and I.

The living are sharing a great banquet, which is heavy with corn of all kinds: tacos and enchiladas made with corn tortillas, corn tamales, corn chips and salsa, creamed corn, rice and beans and corn, corn soup. There is even something I have never heard of before in my life... corn bread. Carlitos tells me that it tastes delicious with the rich butter that is also produced on the estate. The cows and chickens are happy. Mostly, they eat corn... like everyone else.

I am *sullen*, whatever that means. Carlitos tells me I am so because I want to do something to stop Tiger and Carlyle from destroying Maclovio Renta who is also called El Mago, the Wizard.

Part of me feels very angry with Carlitos for his failure to win back my friend (now enemy) Carlyle August. But part of me also feels pity for Maclovio and his people. Some of his men are fathers, I tell Carlitos, or lovers, or both. They will be killed as part of Tiger's evil plans, I am sure of it. But Carlitos doesn't care. He says Tiger is doing all of us a favor by ridding the world of El Mago and his men. And, even though Señor Popcorn is out of the drug trade, Renta still plans to do him harm.

"We can't just sit here and allow a massacre to happen," I say.

Mr. Foo nods. "Besides, there are always dire consequences when you stand back and let evil take place."

"So you just want to go in there and warn our enemy?" Señor Popcorn asks.

"Well, not exactly," I answer.

"What then, battle Tiger ourselves?" Carlitos says. "I've had enough of that."

"Me too," I sigh as I slump back into the corner. Mr. Foo looks angrily at me. I shrug. We have no support from the living persons in the room.

"Have a drink, my friends," Señor Popcorn calls, and he gestures for one of his servants to bring up several bottles of wine.

"*Ghost* wine too," the popcorn man adds.

"Oh?" Mr. Foo perks up. He hasn't had ghost wine in many years.

"I'm feeling quite thirsty myself," I say. "I'll have a glass too," and the drinks are quickly served.

It is now past midnight, and we are all drunk... except for Eva de Cervantes, that is. She is a good hostess and wife, and somebody needs to take care of all these men who are getting drunker and drunker and sleepier and sleepier. And then suddenly, out of nowhere, Señor Popcorn – El Patron that he is – staggers to his feet, raises his glass above his head, and announces, "To Sylvia Morales, one of the sweetest women to ever grace my hacienda."

We all raise our glasses in a toast; we clink, we sip.

"A true and dear friend," I add.

"A beautiful, beautiful woman," Miguel says.

"Hell of a body," Victor whispers. The men all nod in solemn agreement. And suddenly we are all crying. The popcorn man is sobbing.

"It is really my fault," Carlitos mourns.

"No, mi amor," I answer. "It was my mistakes that lost Sylvia." Ghosts tears are pouring from my eyes.

"On the contrary, I should have known better," Mr. Foo sighs.

And so it goes round and round, with everyone taking a turn blaming himself or herself until we are all blubbering like babies.

Señora Eva quietly goes from man to man squeezing the empty wine glasses from their hands. Marie Elena helps her. I am no use. I have slumped onto the floor myself and am now clutching the bottle of ghost wine between my breasts. Señora Eva pries it away from me.

"Time to let everyone sleep, sweetheart," she tells me.

"Ghosts do not sleep."

"We usually don't get drunk either," Mr. Foo slurs as he finally allows Marie Elena to slip the bottle away from him. Then he starts snoring like an old man who has yet to finally die. I close my eyes too. I don't know if I will sleep. But maybe I will dream of Sylvia: the day that Señor Popcorn asked me to move into his home where he would offer me protection and even help pay for Carlitos's schooling. I remember Sylvia shouting: "You got the invitation! Señor de Cervantes wants you to become one of his girls? Sweet!"

"Are *you* one of his girls?" I ask her.

"And proud of it," Sylvia answers, "Those invitations are hard to come by."

I am so happy that I accepted.

This is a very nice memory, I decide, a very nice dream... and it goes on and on.

• • • • •

Birds are out there on their branches, singing their hearts out, praising God, as Sister Maria Consuela used to tell us in grade school. Fortunately, ghosts do not get headaches, even from ghost wine. Otherwise I think the singing of the birds would not be a very welcome sound, and my face would be twisting in pain, as are the faces of Carlitos, and Señor Popcorn, and Miguel and Victor this morning. They are waking up slowly to the painful singing of the birds. And even the arrival of Señora Eva with a great pot of coffee and lots of cups and sugar and milk and corn muffins does not make anyone feel any better.

Mr. Foo fades into sight yawning and stretching. He is like the rest of them, but without the headache or the need for coffee. He looks out at the bright morning sunlight. And then his face fills with panic. He glances from one man to another, then at Eva with all her coffee, and then at me.

"It's happened!" he says.

"What has?"

"The slaughter! The annihilation!"

"Renta!" Señor Popcorn says almost victoriously, even though he has a monster hangover that seems to be bleeding out of his eyes.

"Let us go to their headquarters, Alicia," Mr. Foo says. "Let us see if anyone has survived."

"Wait, I'll come with you," Carlitos calls, and this makes me very angry. I fly up into his face and growl at him.

"Yes, come with us. *You* would not let us warn them. *You* deserve to see the damage you have caused."

Carlitos sits back down again and runs his hand through his hair. "No, it's all right," he sighs. "I can't bear to see any more of... the damage... that I've caused."

My heart melts. I move toward my husband and give him the strongest hug that I can.

"I'm sorry, mi amor."

"So am I," he says. "So am I."

"Alicia!" Mr. Foo calls as he floats in the direction of the doorway. "Time to go, time to see Tiger's latest abomination."

"Yes," I answer sadly, "time to see."

Chapter 42

It is not too great a distance from Señor Popcorn's wonderfully rebuilt hacienda to the desolation that exists in Maclovio Renta's estate. We must fly through the wide adobe walls that surround his courtyard, but within them there are immediate signs of Tiger's work. Dozens of men and women have stampeded up against the far gate, and they are all dead, their mouths open in eternal screams of horror. Some of them look like their very souls have been sucked from their bodies leaving them looking like deflated mannequins, hollow, without the stuff of life.

Something has stalked them, driven them up against the gate, and terrified them so greatly that they died on the spot. Then, whatever it was went to each of them, drew out their souls, and feasted. Handsome but hollow-cheeked young men wearing gunbelts and still holding six shooters in their hands could have blown open the walls of the great house with their guns or killed the biggest jungle cat. But no, they have fallen back in death... some of them with their sombreros still on their heads, some with their pistolas still cocked, still left unfired.

Young and old girlfriends and mistresses are now curled up in the arms of the men they loved, or they lie separate and apart, dead, alone, in the dirt. Some of them have their hands covering their eyes as if to shield themselves from the sight of something so horrible that even when they could not see it, the sound and smell of whatever it was still took their lives.

"Ghost demons," Mr. Foo tells me, "ancestral monsters from the family haunts, called upon to destroy the Wizard's soldiers."

"And to destroy *her*," I say pointing to one innocent looking young woman. "And them," I point to others, a very young girl no more than a teenager huddled together with an older woman in the terror of death.

"Camp followers," Foo sighs. "They chase young soldiers and often die by their sides."

I do not see the bodies of mothers and children scattered across the courtyard.

"Were there not families living with Renta's men?" I ask.

"Sí," says my husband who now makes his way through the doorway; his tear-filled eyes are instantly overcome by the horror he sees.

"You did this!" I shout at him. "It is a great, great sin you have committed."

Carlitos lowers his eyes and nods his head. "Mea culpa," he sighs. But the realization of what both of us have spoken dawns on us at once, and I scream.

"Oh, no! You have done it, Carlitos, you have committed a sin so great that now Tiger's murderers can send you straight to hell!"

Carlitos's eyes go far away, and he seems to be doing nothing. But then I realize that he is doing something; he is counting, counting the number of dead soldiers, counting the number of dead ladies and lovers. Dios mio, this is the worst thing he can be doing at this moment: counting.

"You must go to confession at once," I shout. "We must call up the ghost of Padre Hidalgo and have him hear your great sin."

Carlitos shakes his head, does not even look at me. He merely continues his counting.

"But there could be spies still here," Mr. Foo adds. "Even the animals could be Tiger's minions, seeking to ingratiate themselves to her by bringing her information."

I spot birds flitting down among the corpses; a few small snakes weave through the cactus gardens; rats scurrying along the bougainvillea vines that climb up and over the wall. One of the rats turns and chatters at me almost as though he knows too much, and I think this may be the very one who will tell Tiger all about Carlitos and his sin.

I rush toward the vines as the rat dives down on the other side of the wall.

"No," Señor Popcorn calls as he steps in front of me and catches me in his arms. Even though I am very much a ghost, he holds me until I materialize fully before I melt into tears and allow him to pass me to my husband who finally stops counting. He squeezes me tightly as we cry together over his fate and this horrible act of slaughter.

"I'll find a local priest," Carlitos whispers to me as he pulls me tighter to him. "In the meantime, we need to sort this all out."

"Make an act of contrition now!" I say stomping my foot and pushing Carlitos away from me. "Go over in the corner there and say your prayers."

And my husband does. He walks away from me, turns his back, kneels, bows his head and prays. And I pray too, hoping that he will choose the right words, that there will be no special rules that we don't know about that will allow Tiger to send him straight to hell.

"The best thing," Señor Popcorn whispers to me, "would be if Tiger were never to capture Carlos to begin with. We can guard against that."

I nod, then turn to my old benefactor and suddenly have a terrible understanding that makes me cast daggers at him with my eyes. "This is your sin too, Señor," I say. "Better prepare *your* soul for forgiveness too."

The popcorn man nods and walks slowly away. I hope he is praying for forgiveness. I do not know. He enters the hacienda, and after a few moments Carlitos joins me and we follow the old man into the building.

#

"Maclovio," Señor Popcorn calls moments later as he pushes open the door to our enemy's office... just off the entryway to the main house. There, slouched in a chair behind a big mahogany desk is El Mago. The Wizard.

"No magic to save you this time," the popcorn man says softly as he pulls away the pistol that El Mago still holds. Much of Renta's face is still there, but the back of his head is splashed against the wall behind him.

"Suicide?"

"Of course," Carlitos says.

"He was trapped by ghosts and monsters," Mr. Foo tells us. "There was probably no way for him to escape, and so, rather than face the horror that stalked the rest of his people, he quickly ended it all."

"Coward," I say, and I spit on him. "Cabrón."

A squeal suddenly sounds down the hall, and Carlitos and I immediately run to see what is causing such a sound. More exactly, we want to know who and what is still alive in this place of death and horror.

We open the door to the great room, and a naked baby boy in big white shoes toddles across the floor squealing as he goes. He sees us as we enter; he stops where he is, sticks his fingers into his mouth, and begins to cry. His baby sobs echo throughout the hacienda.

Carlitos gets down on one knee and holds his arms out to the kid who runs to him with crazy tumbling steps. Carlitos grabs the baby in his arms and squeezes him.

"Tranquilo, Niño," he whispers; calm down little boy. And the baby quiets, curls up in my husband's arms, and rests his head on his shoulder.

Carlitos holds the baby close to him and rocks him back and forth. His tears drench the little one's dark curly hair. His cheek presses tight against the fat baby cheeks.

"Forgive me," he whispers to the kid. Perhaps God will hear this plea too.

And then there is a great stirring, as up from behind the backs of couches, from inside closets and cupboards, and from behind the great curtains that hang over the windows, come the wives and children of the soldiers. I can see that many of them watched through the windows as all that death happened in the courtyard. They watched their husbands and fathers killed.

"I will have my men search the house for survivors," Señor Popcorn says softly. "We will offer sanctuary to anyone we find. We will treat them as our brothers and sisters."

I sniff back a ghost tear or two. El Patron is a good man, I think. Even though he benefits from this destruction, he will be generous with his old enemies.

"We must find out what Tiger plans to do next," Mr. Foo tells us.

"Try and capture Carlitos," I say with certainty.

"She may lay a trap," Mr. Foo answers. "But I am sure that she also has a plan for further destruction."

"Won't she be satisfied with all this evil?" I ask and immediately know the answer.

"Not a chance," Carlitos whispers through the curly hair of the baby he still holds. "This will just whet her appetite for greater, crueler, more evil crimes."

"So, we must find her," I say, "and put an end to her once and for all."

"If only we knew the exact nature of the *thing* that Tiger unleashed on the poor people of this hacienda." Mr. Foo adds.

"What do you think it is?" Carlitos asks.

"I have my fears."

"And what are they?"

Mr. Foo's eyes grow wide with terror. He strokes the tiny strands of hair that grow from his chin and pretend to be a beard.

He closes his eyes and gives a tremendous sigh. "Yao Guai," he whispers so softly that I can hardly hear him. "Yao Guai, the shape shifters... the soul suckers."

He trembles, and I remember the expressions on the faces of the dead... as though their very souls had been sucked out of them.

Chapter 43

I am crazy with fears for my Carlitos, fears that some rat-creature overheard me accuse him of committing a mortal sin and then reported it back to Tiger, who will suddenly become encouraged to send assassins after Carlitos... so that he will die and go straight into the pit of Hades.

I am especially crazy with this fear because we will now be taking el Patron's private jet back to San Francisco from his estate in San Martin, and everyone knows that there is no better place for assassins and terrors than on a jet plane.

Carlitos is already on board, as is Mr. Foo, but I have chosen to remain outside, praying with all my ghostly strength that God will forgive Carlitos for his mortal sin. But also I hope that God will not forgive him so much that he will go straight to *heaven* and miss all the fun we would be able to have together as ghosts. This is all so complicated that I finally decide that the very best thing to do is just keep Carlitos alive and safe, and then I will not need to worry about his after lifes.

I float up the steps into the plane that already feels too small to be carrying my love such a great distance, and I gasp out loud. I swear I see the wavy hair and handsome back of the head of our friend who has now become our enemy... Carlyle August. He is sitting beside Carlitos who has the seat near the window.

I rush down the aisle. Carlyle turns, sees me, and instantly disappears.

"What is this?" I ask my husband. "Are you bargaining with el diablo?"

"The devil?" Carlitos says. "No, just talking to Carlyle."

"Estúpido!" I say. "Carlyle is either the devil or he works for the devil. And what does he want, anyway? Did he come here to threaten us and say that he will crash our plane and drop you right into the inferno?"

"Can he do that?"

"Carlitos, I do not know everything. Maybe he can, maybe he cannot. But I don't want him or his evil ideas around us."

My husband smiles a silly smile as though he were listening to the babblings of a baby. And then he holds out his arms and says, "Com'ere, girl. I appreciate all your concern, but I'm okay... really. Let me just hold you, okay... help you forget all about Tiger and her friends. I'll give you better things to think about."

"I would like that," I say. "But not when we are flying over mountains and deserts in a plane where assassins can blow you up at any time."

Carlitos sighs. "Just close your eyes, beautiful," he says. "Pretend that you're human and can sleep... and I'll give you beautiful dreams."

"You will weave a spell on me?" I ask hopefully.

Carlitos pulls me to him, buries his nose in my hair and holds me tight. I give myself as firm a body as possible, just in case Carlitos needs things to hang onto on our bumpy flight. Because I am a ghost, I don't even have to fasten my seatbelt. I can just sit on his lap, feel his sweet breath, listen to his steady heartbeat, feel his hands on me, and become excited and know that I am safe.

Carlitos is murmuring something to me... something that is putting me to sleep... I know that it is some witch's spell, and it makes me happy. I like his spells. They are so sexy.

In my sleep we are flying over the Yucatan, over the ancient temples, and Carlitos appears like some kind of God as we fly. He is dressed in a great headdress full of feathers and silver. He wears a small fluttery cloth around his waist. His chest is bare and I feel his muscles ripple against me. They feel so strong that

I catch my breath, and I look below to find some place where we can land safely and make love right away... some place with soft grasses... near a lake... where no wild animals will bother us.... I really am falling asleep, I realize.

And then I am awake because Carlitos is no longer holding me.

I look over at him, and he is pulled back against the side of the plane. His jaw is locked. But I can barely see him because he is bouncing around so. The plane is bouncing around too as it flies straight DOWNWARD!

During my dream we must have taken off, flown high into the sky, and suddenly had some terrible problem. But is it a problem with the plane, I want to know, or assassins, or the pilot, or what?

Since I am a ghost I am not flying straight down. I am floating smoothly within the plane as it dives toward the ground. And so now I give my husband's hand a squeeze so that he will know that I am going to do something about this diving plane... then I fly into the cockpit, where one of Señor Popcorn's models is the pilot. Of course she only looks like a model, because she knows exactly what she is doing... struggling to pull the plane out of a terrible nosedive... which she does, just in time to send us flying directly toward a mountain. She jerks the plane up, and we barely skim above the snowy surface.

"WHAT IS WRONG WITH YOU, SEÑORITA PILOT?" I shout at her as calmly as I possibly can.

The woman looks up at me and tries to appear in control even though she is jerking a steering wheel that is also jerking her.

"Just a little turbulence," she answers through teeth that are locked together very tightly... over a neck and shoulders that are shaking almost without control.

I try to pull myself into the co-pilot's seat, but there is someone already there, slumped forward almost onto the floor.

"What happened to the co-pilot?" I ask. "Who did this? Some assassin?"

"That isn't exactly a very flattering word for your friends," says a smooth, gentlemanly voice, and I know whose voice it is.

"Carlyle!"

"Yes, beautiful lady?"

The pilot is now zigzagging across the sky, dodging around and over mountain peaks that threaten to tear us apart.

"Thank God for simulators," the pilot gasps.

"You practiced this stuff?" Carlyle asks.

"A lot," the pilot grunts desperately.

"So you're beautiful *and* competent," Carlyle sighs batting his eyes, as though he has just fallen in love. "I find that very attractive."

The plane is shaking now as though it is going to spring itself apart from all that bouncing from mountain peak to mountain peak.

Carlyle and I stand peacefully in mid air while the pilot, the plane, and everyone else on board is shimmying wildly across the sky.

"Are you trying to make this plane crash," I shout at Carlyle, "or is it trying to make itself crash? Or is it perhaps God trying to get even with all of us? And what about the co-pilot?"

"It's a mystery," Carlyle answers sweetly, and then disappears.

Just then, as the bouncing and shaking get more terrible than I can imagine, Carlitos pushes his way onto the flight deck. He looks far better than he did before... far better even than I feel, and I'm already dead.

"What is this, Grand Central Station?" asks the pilot.

"Nope, just a little spiritual assistance," my husband answers.

"Like that's what I need right now," the pilot grumbles.

"I think it will be beneficial, don't you, mi amor?" he says to me. All I can do is nod.

"So then," says my husband as he uses his hand to pound out a little rhythm on the front edge of the plane's control panel.

"Careful or you'll break something," says the pilot. This heroic flying is making her pretty bitchy, I think.

"Don't worry," answers Carlitos. And he continues to pound a very nice Latin rhythm on the controls. I like the beat.

I start to sway with it.

One – two – three – yes

One – two – three – yes

Suddenly the little plane stops jerking wildly and gets itself under control. It catches the beat and starts bouncing along to the same rhythm.

The rattles are now in tempo. The plane goes up and down to the beat.

One – two – three – yes

One – two – three – yes

Even the pilot is now moving her shoulders in time.

Little by little everything begins to come under control: the swaying, the bouncing, the rattling, the shaking, the shimmying. I shake the co-pilot, and he opens his eyes, smiles at me, and begins to tap his foot.

"Ummmm," he sighs, and he smacks his lips as though he has just awakened from his afternoon nap.

Carlitos softens the beat. It grows gentle, then very, very quiet, and at the same time everything smoothes out. The turbulence goes away. Perhaps Carlyle goes away too.

"Latin magic," my husband says with a grin. "Everything under control, Captain?"

The pilot smiles at him in happy confusion, then just whispers, "I'll take it from here."

Carlitos nods. "Care for more dreams, Mrs. Mann?" he asks as he takes my hand and leads me back to his seat.

"Will the plane and the air and everything stay calm for the rest of the flight?"

"Guaranteed."

"Then, yes, mi amor," I answer with an eager smile. "Pues, sí."

Chapter 44

"I don't have time for any more games," Tiger hisses at Uncle Lum as their ghosts stand in the foggy streets of Chinatown.

"That cunt has fucked up my life for the last time. Now it's my turn to do it to *her*."

I hate the word she uses to describe her sister. But I want you to understand how much anger fills the ghost of Tiger Joy.

"She's talking about Amy," Carlitos says as he stands next to me. He is still alive, so he feels the cold and dampness of the San Francisco night, which I cannot. Even with my ghost body fully formed, I can only sense it. I am not shivering with the cold. And I must admit that even Tiger's words do not bother me. Like Señor Popcorn and Carlitos who secretly wished for the destruction of their old enemy, Maclovio Renta, I know that I will do nothing to stop Tiger Joy from killing her sister, Amy. Carlitos likes her, maybe even *loves* her... and that is why. Yes, I know if I were alive it would be a sin. But I am not alive, am I?

Now, a new more terrible idea enters my mind. Tiger has talked to rodents; she has learned that Carlitos has committed a mortal sin. She knows that he is ripe for murder that will lead to damnation. Perhaps, she is saying the words we hear to lure my husband into a trap!

I turn to Carlitos to tell him these things, but he is already gone, running down Grant Avenue, to the old Joy Lum family compound where he will try to save the girl who wants him so badly that I had to come back from the dead to stop her.

"Carlitos, wait!" I call. "There is death and damnation waiting for you in there."

Carlitos does not even look back. He reaches the doorway of the family compound and uses the big round knocker to ask for entry. He must trust that his prayers were good enough to buy him paradise. I know that he has not yet gone to confession, and I am so, so worried.

One of the Joy sisters answers the door and guides him inside. Carlitos does not even look back to see where I am. At this moment he is not thinking of me or his soul, and that makes me even angrier. He simply allows himself to be pulled inside, and I can hear music and laughter as though there is a party going on.

I become invisible and follow him, through the walls, through an entryway with carved ivory and dusty Buddhas crowded everywhere. Pictures of roosters and horses and monkeys hang from the walls. Carlitos follows the Joy girl into a large room where many family groups sit at round tables. They drink tea, or wine or cocktails. Men in business suits spin whisky and ice in their heavy glasses. Some of them have wives who eye them unhappily. They are counting the number of drinks their husbands have had and wishing that they would have no more.

The women wear formal gowns of silk and taffeta; younger girls wear sexy short skirts and low-cut tops that show off their bodies. The younger men do not all wear suits and ties as their fathers do; some are in t-shirts and sport coats. A small rock band in the corner plays very quiet tunes... *lite rock, less talk.* Four lion-dragon dancers with enormous eyes and long scaly bodies dance in the corners. They rear up to an enormous height and then drop down and cock their heads like eager puppies. Their mouths flap open. I can see the young men inside of them, manipulating the lion costumes so skillfully. I stand close to the window not daring to do anything at all for fear of bringing danger to my husband. And so I watch.

I spot Amy Joy in one corner of the room. She is wearing a tight silk gown with a slit up the side. Her heels are higher than they have ever been before, and they make her legs look better than I would like them to be. My husband goes up to greet her and kisses her on the cheek. They talk. Carlitos looks so worried... excited, anxious. He must be telling her of the danger she is in. But Amy does not seem to care. She gestures around the room, as though everyone there will protect her from the things that Carlitos is warning her about.

Amy takes my husband by the arm and leads him into the very middle of the party where I see other Joy sisters and their partners. My husband tries hard to warn everyone that the ghost of Tiger Joy will soon threaten them all. But Carlitos is unable to convince anyone of the danger, and he seems to have forgotten that he should also be warning himself. So he sits down with the others and even accepts a drink. Still, he looks so uncomfortable.

"What's going on here, anyway?" I ask Mr. Foo who has just appeared beside me.

"A party of some kind," Mr. Foo answers. "Maybe Uncle Cosmo and Auntie Emily are celebrating their 50th Anniversary." He points to a couple in their seventies. They are sitting together and nodding to the good wishes of the crowd. The couple smiles at each other happily.

"Were all these people supporters of the slave trade?" I ask.

"They were at one time," answers Mr. Foo. "Though, like so many who are part of a great evil, they pretend that they are not. Unfortunately, there is something else going on here tonight, I think."

I nod my head. Yes. This is the audience for the execution of my husband.

A gong rings. The table visiting ends, the lion dancers step into the shadows, and people rush back to their seats.

The rock band surprises everyone by replacing their guitars and drums with classical Chinese instruments, which I have never seen before, but which sound very familiar. Then, from the far corner of the room, a tall, lovely young woman in a green silk dress strides into the room leading a huge white tiger on a leash. The beast moves from table to table, sniffing the food and scaring the guests. But the girl somehow keeps it under control.

"Yet another Joy sister," Mr. Foo says as he points to the tall woman. "Her name is Anastasia, also known as Kitten."

"Kitten Joy," I nod. "Tiger, Bunny, Kitten. Are they running a zoo here?"

Mr. Foo does not laugh at my poor joke. He only sighs. "A zoo full of monsters."

Kitten Joy and the big cat now make their way toward the table where Amy and Carlitos sit together. The tiger is a ghost. I can tell. As it passes before some of the tables I look right through its black stripes at the faces of guests who might understand. But it only makes them more terrified.

I can see Tiger Joy, who shimmers into appearance at an empty table in the very center of the room. The entire crowd gasps as she does. Several groups suddenly get up and run for the door. But Tiger claps her hands, the beast roars, and Kitten calls out, "Please return to your seats, honorable uncles, aunts, and cousins."

The families hesitate but then one by one they return to their places. There is growing fear in their eyes, which makes Kitten smile as she walks the big cat into the center of the room. She kneels before it, unfastens its leash, but points at its face and the cat becomes very still.

"Very obedient tiger," Mr. Foo says. "Far more obedient than the girl who bears the same name."

Kitten snaps her fingers and the tiger bounds toward the table where Auntie Emily and Uncle Cosmo are sitting. It dives right at them, its claws extended toward their throats as if to tear them apart. The ghost claws do not draw blood, but the couple pulls back in such horror that their screams begin to build and build until the couple falls motionless onto the floor.

"Scared to death," Mr. Foo whispers.

The crowd murmurs in terror, but somehow they do not move.

Carlitos does. He jumps from his chair like the hero that he is, forgetting all about his own safety. He rushes toward the tiger, but it has already turned and headed off across the room to another couple... this one is much younger. They stare at the charging cat in terror. Carlos tries to grab the tiger, but it is far too fast for him. The couple tries to run away, but the tiger corners them against the wall. It roars, bears its huge fangs, and swipes its claws at them again and again. The pair's eyes grow wide; the raging claws come closer; the two cower, gasp, and press themselves into each other in great fear. The girl covers her eyes and begins to mumble prayers. Then she lets out a shrill little shriek, gasps, and she and her companion slump into death at the tiger's feet.

The big cat strides away from them without even looking back. Then it jumps up onto the biggest table in the room, crouching on top of it, turning from one group to another, growling at everyone.

Tiger Joy's ghost nods to her sister Kitten, and the tall girl walks up to Amy, pulls her up from her seat, and begins to lead her toward the cat. Carlitos grabs Kitten by the wrist and stops her until what seems like an entire army of Tiger's boys rush in from the doorways and drag him back to the outside of the room.

Now, Kitten Joy jerks Amy forward and up to the big cat. Amy bites her lip so hard that it draws blood. She digs in her heels but Kitten pulls her forward. The big cat bends down and studies Amy carefully, and then it throws its head back and roars.

Amy jumps at the sound. She begins to sob out loud, but the cackle of her sister, Tiger, soon grows louder. Tiger marches up to Amy and immediately slaps her hard across the face.

"How dare you?" she hisses. "You were going to the FBI, weren't you?"

Amy shakes her head, raises her hand in front of her face to protect herself from another blow, and whispers, "Of course not, Sis. No."

"Sure you were," Tiger sneers. "You put together the details of all our operations, and you were going to turn them over to that Marinara goon. You were going to rat out all our partners, all our secret locations, all of our inventory... thousands of slaves."

Tiger turns and faces the rest of the people in the room.

"Everyone here is an accomplice," she shouts as she points from one group to another. "As soon as I died, you all panicked. I'm looking at a room full of traitors."

There is a loud slam as all the doors are suddenly bolted from the outside. Tiger's boys now take up positions in front of each one. Two of them march forward and grab Amy by her arms and move her even closer to the tiger, which remains on the table snarling. Amy's eyes turn to Carlitos pleading for help.

Tiger Joy smiles at my husband as though she has a terrible secret. Her eyebrows arch. Then she turns back to Amy.

"You're not the reason we're gathered here, little Amy," she says scornfully. "Nor is this room full of traitors... all of whom will die today."

The crowd panics, screams, shuffles wildly about, but somehow they are frozen in their seats unable to tear themselves away from Tiger Joy and her evil words.

"We're here to execute my *greatest* enemy who at last has shown a weakness so evil that even his own God can't forgive him."

My heart falls through the floor. My ghost hands tremble. I want to flit forward and tear the eyes out of this evil bitch, but I cannot. Mr. Foo restrains me with such a strong ghost-hold that even I understand that he is right in telling me to wait.

"Oh, Carlitos," Tiger singsongs like a playful little schoolgirl. "Won't you come over and play... pretty please?"

The boys let go of my husband, and like a fool he shakes himself for a moment, smiles like some happy martyr, and walks toward the evil woman.

Tiger crinkles up her nose with joy. She taps her toe impatiently. But it doesn't take long until Carlitos is standing right in front of her.

"I have more than a big cat to devour you, Mr. Mann," she says as she sweeps her arm in front of the tiger.

The beast lets out a roar, and Carlitos stares hard into its face as though he were staring down an opponent in the boxing ring.

Tiger raises herself on tiptoes and shouts:

"I'VE BROUGHT YOU A *DEMON!*"

Suddenly the tiger's body shifts, stretches, wavers, and turns into some kind of monster far bigger than any cat. It looks like a giant bear, with spikes for fur and nasty, drooling jaws.

The table collapses under its weight, and the beast steps out to stalk around the room, gurgling deep and terribly in its throat. One couple slumps over in their chairs as it approaches them, and they too die instantly from fear.

The thing stops for a moment, moves its massive body over them, noses about the mouth of first one person and then the other. And then it breathes in with a terrible sucking that draws the very souls out of the pair. Their bodies turn hollow and pale. The beast gurgles, swallows, and burps, then moves on around the room, eyeing each of its victims as it does, snarling at Amy as it passes her. And then it returns to Carlitos.

"Yao Guai," Tiger tells my husband, "the shape shifter, the soul sucker... here to suck out *your* soul, handsome."

The thing leans in toward Carlitos, and I know that my husband can smell blood on the monster's breath... worse than that, he can smell the decay of souls. He sees the thing's lips ripple hungrily. Its teeth chatter. Then it opens its mouth.

Tiger squeals with delight. Amy glances down at her hands and sees her fingers knotted together in prayer. She closes her eyes. Carlitos hears the hiss of the demon's breath as it sucks in air, ready to draw out his soul, and then...

NOTHING!

The Yao Guai does not move.

I look at Tiger, and her hand is over her mouth, holding back a scream.

Carlitos has one hand stretched out toward the monster; his fingers are twisting into some terrible sign. Blood pools in his eyes. He looks crueler than he has ever looked before. He steps toward the beast slowly but gracefully as though he is dancing toward it. The monster is motionless.

And then... OH NO! It springs to life... jumps backward and begins shaking its ugly head. It pounds the floor with huge feet that shake the building with every stomp. Carlitos looks surprised as though this was the last thing he expected. The beast is so great that it can shake off his spell.

"Look out, mi amor!" I cry as the beast turns on my husband and begins marching toward him across the room. Carlitos looks everywhere, perhaps for a weapon he can use against the monster. It is now drooling hungrily and sucking in powerful drafts of air, as though it is hoping to draw my husband's soul out of him.

Tiger is jumping up and down like a cheerleader. Amy is white with fear. Carlitos though is smiling. Why is that? He flashes his hand across his eyes, and there is a ringing sound. Then the scaly lion costumes fly off the dancers in the corners and advance toward the beast of their own free will. They glide closer to the Yao Guai, which tries to ignore them but cannot.

The lion shapes split, and now there are eight of them, not just four. Then they split again: sixteen. Carlitos moves his hands gracefully and is leading the dancing of the lion costumes as though he were conducting an orchestra. Another twist of his hands and the lions split again: thirty-two, and again: sixty-four. The monster begins to swat at the lions and every time it does they multiply once more... 128... 256.

The lions move in and out around the huge creature like mosquitoes around a great bull. The beast swats at them but they merely fall back, reform and fly toward it again. The Yao Guai bellows, swats at its own face to push away the swirling lions that are brushing over it, perhaps stinging it... biting it. And the lion dancers keep coming.

"NO!" shouts Tiger as she runs around the writhing mass of lion dancers. But there is almost no room on the floor. Couples are pressed back against the walls. The Yao Guai is up on its hind-legs swatting away at the lions.... now tearing its own demon flesh as they zoom in and out around it.

I see Carlitos across the way. He is smiling, laughing as the great beast begins to stumble around the floor swatting at now nearly a thousand lions. They have grown much smaller I think, and now they are flying in at the creature, biting it every time they draw near.

While this is happening Carlitos wraps his arm around Amy, pulls her away from the stumbling horror of the Yao Guai and the swirling lions. He pulls her away from the crowd and leads her slowly from the room. He points at the guards near the far door and they move out of his way. We hear levers and pulleys working and the door grinds open. Carlitos and Amy walk slowly through the entryway, and out into the streets of Chinatown.

I turn back to Tiger Joy. She is wild with rage.

"Your husband is a witch!" she screams at me. Then she runs up to the Yao Guai, as it stumbles around the room.

"WHAT GOOD ARE YOU?" she shouts as the thousands of lion dancers suddenly flash into nothingness and disappear. She pounds her fists into the side of the demon. "YOU'RE A WORTHLESS PIECE OF SHIT!"

And now the shape of the Yao Guai begins to shimmer and flutter as it turns slowly from a beast into... a beautiful young woman. She's dressed in a fairy gown so thin I can see all of her young body through it. She giggles, looks at Tiger with a smile, blows her a kiss, and dances off barefoot into the night. But as she does, her fingers carefully brush the edge of a guestbook that sits on the edge of a small table. The pages instantly flame. Then the tablecloth catches fire, the fire jumps up onto the wallpaper, and suddenly the walls are burning.

The crowd panics even more than at the sight of the Yao Guai. They rush for the doors trying to jam through them as flames eat up the whole room. The fire burns through the draperies that hang from the ceiling and rains fire down on everyone. Then the loud machinery of the doors comes to life again. It whirs, and crunches, and lowers doors that hold the crowd inside. The Joy Lum ballroom is now a trap of death.

I have seen enough. I don't want to watch these people burned alive, but I know I cannot save them, and so I grab Mr. Foo by the arm and together we fly through the walls and away from this place of death. As we reach the streets of Chinatown, the Joy Lum compound explodes behind us. And then it burns to the ground for the second time in a year.

Chapter 45

The burning remains of the Joy Lum building add warmth to the night in Chinatown. There are also firecrackers, fog, incense, and wind... not that ghosts care about the wind, except when we want it to carry us away... as I am starting to want right now.

This is because up ahead I see Amy Joy and mi Carlitos. The evil girl has her arm on his shoulder. Her fingers are sliding up his neck, and I know that soon she will be hugging and kissing him.

"Do you really want to see this?" Mr. Foo asks me.

"Yes," I answer, "I want to see if my husband can be faithful."

Amy's nose brushes over the cheek of my husband. Her lips are rising to meet his.

I stomp my foot, cross my arms, look at Mr. Foo, and know that he wants to disappear and maybe even go back into the burning Joy Lum building rather than be here when I finally come face to face with Carlitos.

And then something happens.

Carlitos brushes his fingers over Amy's cheek. It is just a gentle touch, one that I would like to feel. But there is a strange twisting motion to his fingers. They form a kind of sign as they move. Amy closes her eyes, brings her lips closer, waiting for the dishonorable kiss from my husband. But it does not come. Carlitos steps away from the girl instead, and she freezes there... just as I froze when Carlitos did not want me to go into Tiger's chamber... just as the monster froze only moments ago. Amy has now turned to stone as she tried to tempt my husband into cheating kisses.

"Hola, Alicia," Carlitos says as he turns toward me.

"What have you done to her?"

Mr. Foo is keeping his distance because he does not know whether or not there will be a terrible fight.

Carlitos shrugs. "I'm letting her rest."

"She deserves more than a rest. I would like to slowly *strangle* her."

Carlitos laughs and puts his arms around me. "No need, mi amor. She never even completed the kiss."

"And why did she not?"

"Because I didn't let her."

"Aha! Now we are getting somewhere." I stamp my foot again and barely miss bringing my ghost heel down on my husband's toes... we are standing that close together.

"And why did you not let her?"

Carlitos pulls me to him and looks into my eyes. God, he is a gorgeous man. I do not say that often enough.

"You and I are married, Alicia," he says as he breathes in deeply, though I do not know what kind of sexy smell he can get from a ghost.

"Married men should not allow beautiful young women to kiss them on the lips. Therefore, I didn't let Amy kiss me."

"QED?" I ask.

"What has been proven, yes; you're learning your syllogisms well, Alicia."

"I'm learning that my husband can turn things to stone."

"I wonder how he does that?" Mr. Foo asks as he comes flying up to us. The old man has decided that we are not going to have a fight right here in the middle of Chinatown, so he might as well join us.

"Witchcraft?" Carlitos whispers. The look in his eyes is spooky.

"Do not try to scare ghosts, Carlitos," I say. Then to Mr. Foo I explain: "My husband is descended from witches... on his mother's side... his Mexican side."

Mr. Foo nods. "And from his father's side he gets...?"

"Polish logic," I answer, and Carlitos breaks out laughing. So does Mr. Foo.

I stamp my foot. "What is so funny?"

"Which would you rather have, logic or magic?" Carlitos asks.

"Ideally both," Mr. Foo laughs. "Logical magic."

"Or magical logic," Carlitos is laughing even harder.

I don't understand any of this. Though I think my English has become much better lately, there is a meaning here that makes no sense to me. Who cares? Let them have their jokes.

I walk up to Amy Joy and pinch her cheeks. They are soft and doughy. But she does not move. She has turned to stone... soft stone. Putty. All right. I kiss her on those lips that are so hungry for my husband. And she still is without movement. Not so tasty either, I think. So what is the big temptation? I do not understand. So, I slap her. "Bitch!"

"Hey no, Alicia," Carlitos calls as he runs up to me. "Amy has helped us a great deal."

"It may have been a great deal for you, Señor," I say, "but it has been no great deal for me."

I pull my hand back to slap Amy again, just because I can, and because I want to teach her a lesson. But Carlitos snaps his fingers, and Amy suddenly comes to life.

"I was having the most beautiful dream, Dr. Mann," she sighs. "And it was all about us."

"Cabrón," I scream at Carlitos. "You have been unfaithful to me in *her* dreams. And how did you just wake her up, anyway?"

Carlitos smiles the way he does when he is going to tell me one of his silly syllogisms.

"It was a simple spell. I just broke it."

"I see. And was there someone who actually taught you these spells and how to break them?"

Carlos stops and looks very puzzled. "From my grand-mother, Ixchel? Although, I don't think she actually taught them to me. I guess they're in my blood, my DNA."

"Of course, the blood of witches," Mr. Foo says.

I ignore Mr. Foo and scowl at my husband. "Well, anyway, stay out of *her* dreams, marido!"

Carlitos laughs. "It's a deal. But I don't want *you* to stay out of mine, Alicia. In fact why don't we go home right now, and you can haunt my dreams all night long."

That sounds nice. "Where is your car?"

"St. Mary's Square Garage."

"Well, get into it and drive home. I have some official ghost business to take care of, and then I will join you."

"Should I be asleep when you get home?"

I smile. "That would be perfect. Then I can start my sexy haunting right away."

"Great. Only, don't hurt Amy."

"Don't worry, mi amor," I say as I fly away from all of them. "I will have much bigger fish in my frying pan. Adios."

"And look after Carlyle," Carlitos calls after me so that I can barely hear him.

"What?"

I want to turn back to my husband and ask him what he means by this. Look after our enemy? I don't think so.

Fortunately I do not have time to go back and question him.

· · · · ·

I flit along Grant Avenue and up to the China Trade Center. It has many stores and restaurants built around a stairway that winds down to an old souvenir shop at the bottom. Just before you get to the store, in back of the stairway, is a big cupboard that looks like it is a thousand years old. No one ever opens this cupboard, I think, because it is so big and scary looking. Who knows what might jump out at you?

Actually, *I* know, because this cupboard is at the end of the secret passageways under Chinatown. This is how Carlitos escaped from the Joy Lum Clan the first time they tried to murder him. Mr. Foo showed us the way. There must be others who know about it too. And, just as I am thinking this, Tiger Joy and Uncle Lum come flying out of the cupboard without even opening the doors.

I have the power to make myself invisible to other ghosts... though the trick does not always work, especially when they are looking for me. But Tiger and her uncle are too busy going back to the cupboard, opening it, and helping a very dirty Kitten Joy and several of the Joy boys out of the secret passageway. Tiger and her uncle have shown them how to escape the fire that killed everyone else in the compound.

Uncle Lum is very mad. I can see it in his eyes, and then I can hear it in his voice.

"You didn't have to burn down the whole damn place, Helen."

He calls Tiger by her real name.

"It was that stupid demon and that fucker, Mann," Tiger says through teeth that are locked so tight that I wonder how she can even talk.

"Yes," Uncle Lum agrees. "That was unfortunate. But still you said that you had mastered the Yao Guai."

"Duh," Tiger says as she gives her uncle a very disrespectful cross-eyed look. "*You* try and master a demon."

"Well, someone in that room did."

"Yeah, Carlos Mann, the son of a bitch. But who the hell knew that he could do it? Who knew that he had gotten so good at witchery?"

Uncle Lum just sighs and shakes his head.

"I mean, what are the chances?"

Kitten and the Joy boys sit on the bottom steps of the stairway listening. Kitten's dress is ripped up the side, and she bends over to rub a giant bruise on her thigh. She is a big girl and her breasts and legs are big too. She will not grow into a frail little Chinese grandmother, I think, but into a big tough warrior that I may have to fight some day. I do not look forward to it.

Several of the Joy boys look hungrily at Kitten. In spite of all they have been through, they still have their dirty thoughts about her. Kitten looks up and smiles. She is not trying to hide anything that her torn dress reveals. I guess she likes their dirty thoughts.

"You'll have to rebuild the compound," Tiger tells Kitten, who just shrugs, yawns, and studies her fingernails.

"Yeah, sure." She hardly answers.

"And you'll have to help her, Albert."

The tallest of the Joy boys nods his head and smiles at Kitten. I think he is telling her that he will help her and make things very easy... if she will do the same for him.

Tiger fades into her full body and struts around the stairs in her high, high heels. "In the meantime, I'll be planning my next big hit," she says.

Uncle Lum turns his back on her. Tiger doesn't even notice.

"I want to do something really important," she continues. "I think it's time we show the world how powerful we really are. Don't you agree?"

Kitten nods, but Albert *really* nods, as though he will follow Tiger anywhere and bring Kitten along for the ride. He eyes the other boys and says, "We're all with ya, boss." They all agree.

"See, Uncle Lum," Tiger says. "Why can't you be as supportive as Albert?"

"Because, unlike Albert, I know you're nuts. We have a very profitable business going, so why fuck it up?"

"Because we have people who are stealing from us, who don't respect us."

"I think after tonight we'll have all the respect we need in Chinatown."

"But we have partners all over the world... not just in Chinatown."

Uncle Lum slides up beside Kitten. He turns and smiles at her and then frowns back at Tiger.

"So, who will you take on next?"

Tiger bats her eyes at him. "I haven't quite decided who's a bigger threat, the Russian slave trade underground, or Carlos Mann."

"Great!" Uncle Lum rolls his eyes. "The Russian underground is in fifty-six countries scattered over five continents. It would take several dozen coordinated hits to get them. If those are your choices, then go after the logician."

And now I remember how Carlitos once beat Uncle Lum in a logic contest to free Amy Joy and her sister. I think it is time that I stick up for my husband.

"It will not be mi Carlitos," I say as I appear in front of them all. I have chosen to show myself at my sexiest, wearing clothing that would even embarrass Sylvia Morales (may she rest in peace).

My heels are high. My little black dress is short and tight. My neckline is low; my cleavage is spectacular. Albert's jaw falls to his feet and his tongue hangs out. I do not even look at him. Instead I march right up to Helen Tiger Joy and stand with her toe to toe.

"Go attack your Russians, bitch," I say. "Burn down the rest of the world. Carlitos and I will not stop you as long as you leave us alone."

Helen cocks her head and gives me a funny look. Finally she laughs. "He'd never do that."

"Don't listen to her," Uncle Lum tells Tiger. "You're not ready to take on the Russian underground. Do you think one Yao Guai can eradicate them all?"

Tiger just smiles, "Carlyle is at the gates of hell right now. He's putting together the greatest army of demons the world has ever known."

These words disgust me. My ex-friend Carlyle is a traitor of the worst kind... the kind that makes bargains with devils. (And yet Carlitos said to look after him. Why?)

"Pooh on Carlyle," I say as I spit on the ground. "I wash my hands of him. I wash my hands of you too, Helen. Leave Carlitos and me alone, and we will do the same for you."

"You can speak for Carlitos?" Tiger sneers.

"Of course I can. We are man and ghost."

Suddenly, Mr. Foo is beside me. He takes me by the arm

and pulls me just out of Tiger's hearing. He trembles with fear.

"Alicia, wait," he says. "Think about the terms of this agreement."

"What terms?"

"The Russian underground, the war that will be waged."

"Señor Foo, right now, I would sacrifice everything to save Carlitos from this bitch."

"You don't mean that."

"I do mean it. Carlitos and I have had enough. All we want is to be left to ourselves."

"I'm not sure that Carlos would say that if he knew that Carlyle is dealing with the devil right now."

"It's just another devil," I sigh. "We have conquered many of them... even the Spanish Inquisition. What do we care?"

"This is not just another devil, Alicia. This is *the* devil, Satan, the prince of darkness."

"El diablo?" I ask. "I do not think the king of devils will even give Carlyle an appointment."

"You're wrong," Mr. Foo says. "Satan has been trying to take control of our world for millennia. All he needs is an entre, and that may be just what Carlyle is offering him."

"Look around you," I say. "The devil is already here... he is everywhere... he is in charge."

"But not as completely as he wants to be," Foo says. "Once Tiger offers the devil an open doorway to our world, we may never be able to contain him again."

For a moment a vision appears to me, an army of los diablos sweeping across the world, spreading greed and cruelty everywhere. As bad as things are now, this is so much worse.

I wonder for a moment if it is Carlitos who is supplying these visions. My mind reels. Perhaps I have been oversimplifying again. Better forget all the things I have just said. So, I step back and turn to everyone.

"I must go," I shout.

"We're not finished bargaining," Tiger answers.

"Oh, yes we are," I say. "There is someone I have to see."

"Carlitos?" Tiger asks. "If so, don't bother. I'm sure between the two of us we can make him do anything we want. Pretty soon we'll have him eating out of the palms of our hands."

"I don't want him anywhere near your palms, Tiger, or your hands," I say.

And I am off.

If only I were going to see Carlitos. But I am not. I have another destination in mind, one that terrifies me. And so I disappear from sight, and rush off into darkness.

Chapter 46

Carlyle August stands at the very gates of hell, at the same cave of hopelessness where he met Tiger and became her slave. Before him, a great waterfall dives all the way into the underworld.

Inside the raging waters, he sees the souls of the damned traveling downward on a one-way trip. A dictator (the murderer of thousands of people) screams as his body is pounded and twisted by the waterfall. Haters and liars fall together, slamming into each other, clawing wildly whenever another body is close enough for them to grab. But the rush of the waterfall is too powerful for any of their actions to help. They will dive into a bottomless lake at the base of the fall, and there they will be fished out, dragged ashore, and then driven into the deepest parts of hell.

Carlyle is fearful, I know. He thinks of all those hopeless souls and the power of the monsters that rule them. They are the creatures he has to deal with. Can he do it?

Before Carlyle can answer the question, a great mist swirls up through the waterfall, and a three-headed demon towers above him. In each of its mouths it is chewing on a sinner who wails with pain. Blood spills down the devil's three ugly chins. Still it grins, picks one of the damned out from between its jaws, nibbles away at an arm as though it were a chicken wing, and then tosses the sinner aside.

Carlyle is terrified, and yet he still dares to speak to the demon. Tiger's hold on him is that great, I think.

"I need your help," he calls above the roar of the waterfall.

"Of course you do," the monster says.

"Help us destroy our enemies."

The great three-headed devil laughs like a thunderstorm. "And where have I heard that before?"

It pulls a second scarred body from its mouth, bites off both legs, and pushes the face of Adolf Hitler in front of Carlyle.

"See this fool?" the devil asks before it pitches Hitler's body down into the pit. "He wanted the same thing you're asking for. And he got his wish... for a little while anyway."

"We want our victory to be permanent," Carlyle calls.

The devil laughs.

"Of course you do. But nothing is permanent, except perhaps hell itself. I'll give you what you want, but eventually you will have to pay the price."

Carlyle is soaking wet from the waterfall. I see the cold water washing over his face and chilling him. He closes his eyes, and I know that he pictures eternal damnation.

"Who must pay?" Carlyle is finally brave enough to ask.

The devil shakes its head with a look of disgust. "Why are you asking such stupid questions? You know the answer... ALL OF YOU MUST PAY."

Carlyle is more frightened than ever.

"I have to discuss this with my mistress," he says.

The devil laughs another great evil laugh. "Yes, do that," he answers. "Set her up nicely for me."

"What?" Carlyle and I say the word out loud at the same time.

"Do you know the penalty for trying to trick the devil?" he asks.

Carlyle gives the monster his most dignified look. "I'm sure I don't know what you mean?"

"Nice acting, boy," the devil bellows. "I'd haul you down here in a second if you weren't delivering that sexy bitch right into my very own hands."

"You mean...." Carlyle begins.

"Take your time. You know where to find me. Only, think of this: No matter what you think you are doing... how noble your intentions... you are still making a deal with the devil."

The monster's fingers close on the third victim it has been chewing. It pulls the mangled corpse from its mouth and holds it up in front of Carlyle so he can see who it is.

Carlyle screams like a crazy person as he recognizes...
HIMSELF.

• • • • •

El Diablo disappears, but Carlyle does not leave this horrid place. Instead, he just sits down on one of the great boulders surrounding the cave, and he shivers. He looks so lonely that I know I must go to him. And I do.

I fade in beside him as he sits there shivering on the rocks. And I notice that the water passes right through me. Why does it not do the same to Carlyle's ghost?

"Have you been making crazy, dangerous plans with my husband?" I ask.

Carlyle is startled when he hears my voice.

"Beautiful!" he whispers with as much of a smile as he can give, "Why are you here?"

I see how his body shakes in the cold and damp. "I came because I feared that my friend was selling his soul for the love of a cheap puta."

Carlyle says nothing, but he does shake his head.

"But that is not it, is it? You and Carlitos were working together all along... to bring Tiger to the place where she really belongs."

Carlyle is silent, then after a moment he says, "It still won't be easy."

I smile at this foolish self-doubt.

"You are a great salesman, Señor, and a great seducer of women. Even the powerful Tiger Joy will be Jello in your hands."

Carlyle shrugs unhappily. "I haven't been able to seduce you, beautiful."

"Of course not. I am a married woman. It would not be logical."

Carlyle laughs. "I don't think you have any idea what you're talking about."

"QED," I answer proudly.

"Yes right, quad erat demonstrandum... what has been proven. And what have we proven? That you can't fool the devil. In the end he always wins."

"He *says* he always wins, you mean," I say.

"Okay."

"He does not seem to be such a winner to me... not if he has to spend forever in hell. We can outfox him, Carlyle. We have logics on our side."

Carlyle looks at me again as though I'm just some silly, giggly teenager using words she does not understand. And maybe he is right, but I do know one very important thing.

"He doesn't really care about you and me," I say, "or even Carlitos. He wants Tiger!"

Carlyle is quietly stunned for a moment. And then his eyes suddenly brighten. "Damn, Alicia, you're right."

"Of course I am, Señor. Think about it. If you deliver Tiger to him, he may be so happy that he may just forget about you... after all, you are already a ghost."

"So's Tiger."

"Sí, she is, but oh how he *wants* her!"

Carlyle's eyes suddenly sparkle. "YES!"

"So there. And now, I have an even better idea for you."

Carlyle is suddenly fascinated by me, I think... and not just my body... by my ideas. How wonderful is that! Only Carlitos who has loved me since I was an ugly little bundle of mud has admired me in this way.

"I have another girl for you," I say.

Carlyle looks disappointed. "Oh," he answers. "I've given up on girls."

He shivers, but I take him by the hand and pull him farther away from the waterfall, into a bright patch of sunlight, and slowly he begins to dry and warm. He smiles, enjoying the sunshine. Then finally he says, "Tell me about the girl."

"The one I have in mind for you?"

"Sí, Señora." His artificial Spanish accent sounds silly.

"Creo que es muy bonita," I sigh.

"Huh?"

"I think she is very pretty."

"Is she innocent or as evil as Tiger?"

"Oh, she is very innocent, Señor, though I cannot really understand how or why."

"And she's a ghost, of course."

I smile. "No, Carlyle, she is living. But Carlitos and I have already proven that the dead can marry the living very successfully, remember?"

"Yes, you have," he says. "So, tell me her name."

I giggle like a gossipy little girl.

"Amy," I say. "Her name is Amy Joy."

Carlyle flinches. "Amy?" He closes his eyes for a moment as though he does not really know what to say. And then slowly he smiles. "Yes."

His eyes widen as he thinks about the possibilities. "I've had my eye on her for quite some time. She's wonderful. I just never thought you wanted her around."

"Around Carlitos, no," I say as I cross my arms.... and then I uncross them and smile.

"Around *you,* Carlyle, married to you, I think that would be perfect."

"And you think she'd be interested."

"Cabrón, you are one of the handsomest ghosts in the afterlife," I say. "And besides, if she isn't interested at first, then I will insist that Carlitos cast a spell on her. He needs to keep practicing his sexy witching powers... his very best ones. And what better sexy witchcraft than cooking up a love potion that will give Amy Joy the hot panties for *you.*"

Carlyle's eyes are fiery. But then he shakes his head in doubt. "I'm not sure he'll do it. I mean...."

I interrupt him quickly. "Señor, do you think that I can control my own husband or not? He does whatever I tell him to... as it should be."

Carlyle smiles, and I can see that now he is becoming very excited.

"If I can convey the devil's message to Tiger and get her here..." Carlyle whispers hopefully.

"You are a natural flatterer and seducer, Señor," I repeat as I bat my eyes at him.

"I hope so," Carlyle answers. "God, I hope so."

"So, come on then I say. Let's leave this terrible place and make all of these good things happen."

Carlyle gets to his feet, feels the warmth of the sunshine, the brightness of hope, and he follows me back into the world of the living, where my husband, and perhaps his future bride await.

The End

Epilogue

Tiger Joy stands at the same windblown cave that Carlyle and Alicia visited nine months earlier. She has a lot to be angry about. She's lost Carlyle August to her simpering sister, Amy. And next week, the two are going to be married at Señor Popcorn's estate in Cancun.

In spite of the efforts of Albert and the Joy boys, her other sister, Kitten, has proven to be a poor manager and even a poor figurehead. She eats mountains of sugary pastry every day, drinks bubble tea by the gallon, and has become fat and lazy. She refuses to carry out the punishments that Tiger orders, and so the partners of the Joy Lum Clan have begun to challenge her authority and cheat more openly. The Russian underground is especially troublesome.

Tiger Joy's enemies, Carlos and Alicia Mann, are prospering. He's back teaching at Leland University, and she's flitting between continents enjoying all the friends she's made in the ghost world. She's already taken several trips back to Vienna to enjoy the opera and the great balls held at Schönbrunn. Sometimes her handsome husband goes along with her.

Still, Tiger has been looking forward to visiting the gates of hell and bargaining with the devil as Carlyle encouraged her to do. And so now she stands in the drenching mists of a waterfall that drops straight to damnation.

She wears a skintight latex pantsuit that seems to flow right into high, stiletto heels. They lift her well above six feet tall.

280

The wetness beads harmlessly on the suit but might rust the big zipper that runs from her neck, between her legs, and up her back to her shoulders. Other zippers cut across each breast and up her wrists and ankles. She wonders how she'll ever get out of the outfit, and then she remembers that she's a ghost and can just make it all disappear. Meanwhile, her long black hair is sodden from the mist... so much so that it's pulling back on her neck and making it hard for her to hold her head forward. It hurts, and Tiger wonders why a ghost should even feel the dampness. Oh well, Carlyle mentioned it, didn't he? And he said there was a reason. Though she couldn't remember what it was.

Tiger calls to the demon that said it would help the Joy Lum Clan, and instantly the enormous figure of Satan rises up out of the mist.

"Ah, Mistress Joy," it coos as though it were her lover, "I'm honored that you've finally come to see me."

The words surprise Tiger. She steps backward awkwardly, and the heaviness of her hair almost makes her fall from the huge boulder on which she's standing. But she catches herself.

"I need your help," she says.

"Anything, sweet mistress, anything."

Tiger looks up at the creature through her long lashes. The reverence in his voice confirms the words of Carlyle August. But Tiger now thinks the handsome ghost is really a traitor. Yes, he told her such promising things about the devil and his eagerness to help Tiger, but then he began courting her wimpy sister, Amy? What was that all about?

"We have a growing world of enemies that demand subjugation," Tiger says.

"One of our specialties, mistress. I'm sure that we can help you with that."

The size and strength of the demon's personality fascinates the young woman, but she's still very cautious.

"I hear that you demand a great deal of your partners."

"Don't you?" Satan asks.

Tiger lowers her eyes coquettishly and shrugs. Then her

gaze returns to the monster. The two stare at each other for a long moment, and both of them start breathing heavily. They're both getting turned on. Tiger's sure of it.

"And just *how* will you help me?" Tiger asks.

"By giving you all the power that a woman of your beauty and accomplishment deserves."

"Power!" The words trigger something deep in Tiger. The feeling is delicious.

"What kind of power?"

"The power to rule, the power to conquer, the power to subjugate."

Tiger is becoming intoxicated by the sound of it all, and by the amazingly erotic creature looming in front of her. For all his monstrosity, he is handsome.

"Perhaps we should go somewhere more comfortable and talk about all this," the devil says.

"I think we should do more than talk," Tiger sighs.

"Of course."

The beast smiles in seductive anticipation. He waves his hand, and a platform rises up out of the mist.

Tiger considers it for a moment and then steps onto it.

The devil smiles at her even more warmly... very warmly.

"Welcome," he croons.

And just like that, Tiger Joy allows herself to be lowered straight into the very depths of hell!

Available Now

The prequel novella to the Alicia Trilogy

Avenging Adelita

A tender romance with a ticking time bomb at its heart!

Supermodel Alicia Mejias meets the aging but still very beautiful Adelita at a party thrown for the faculty and students of Benito Juarez University in Mexico. Adelita seems happy this evening, but only hours later she will tell her American husband, Tom McKeever, that she is dying of cancer.

Tom and Adelita, will spend the next year trying to find enough money for a treatment that they believe will save her life. But the dean of Tom's college, a hard man known to the faculty as The Butcher, will deny Tom's request, and Adelita will eventually die sadly and quietly in his arms. Tom blames the University faculty and administration, for her death, and so he obtains a bomb, and carries it onto the train they are all taking to an outing in the mountains. He intends to blow up the train, the faculty, himself and everyone else onboard... including Alicia and her fiancé Carlos Mann who are passengers too. Though Tom regrets it, he realizes that the young couple will have to be part of the collateral damage of his revenge. What else can he do?

Read on for a special preview chapter.

Avenging Adelita

Chapter 1

Countdown: 358 minutes (Approximately 6 hours)

I take a seat near the rear of the train and wait for the other passengers to board. My attaché fits neatly into the space in front of me, and I imagine that others will think it's filled with articles of clothing: a tie, spare shirt, socks, and underwear. It's not, and I know that within six hours I'll never need those things again, nor will any of my companions.

There are a lot of ways to gain revenge, of course. If I were a younger man, taller and stronger, I'd simply corner my enemy and beat him half to death. I like the idea. I can see his face smeared with blood, teeth broken, eyes swollen shut, a deep gash across his neck. It's what he deserves.

Unfortunately, I'm not tall or strong. I'm old. My arms hurt whenever I try to move them too quickly. If I punched my enemy in the mouth, it wouldn't even draw blood. And he'd retaliate immediately. He knows the martial arts. I'd be screwed.

Murder then seems like a much better solution for a guy my age... a murder/suicide. He dies, I die; no loose ends, at least not for me... only for those who are left behind, and I don't care about any of them since I've lost Adelita.

I stare out the window of the Canyon Express... the luxury train that's supposed to take us to the wonders of Mexico's Grand Canyon. Most of my colleagues are just now getting out of the sleek school buses that brought us all the way from Benito Juárez University to the railway station in Chihuahua, Mexico.

Macario Huerta, Dean of the School of Philosophy, a man we employees have started calling *the Butcher*, now leads his frail little wife off the bus and into the blinding sunshine. He's dressed in a Western style sport coat, well-pressed jeans, and cowboy boots. Her outfit matches his. They each breathe deeply and smile as they smell the glorious aroma of huevos rancheros, breakfast burritos, and refried beans being prepared by the venders up on the station platform.

Huerta eyes it all hungrily; then he turns and greets the other passengers. He's really feeling full of himself this morning. I can see it in his puffed up chest, his exaggerated gestures, and loud laugh. It carries all the way up to the platform and into the train.

Huerta has arranged this outing for his entire faculty, a chance to do a little team building, restore old friendships, have fun together, and take the famous tourist train into the mighty Sierra Madre Mountains.

"The canyon is even more spectacular than the one in Arizona," he tells his guests, and they all nod excitedly.

It's an odd trip to be planned by someone whose employees like to call *the Butcher*, don't you think? But here he is, a man who can reconcile team building and soul destroying as part of the same philosophy.

It was only a few weeks ago when the Butcher changed my life completely, transformed my sorrow and depression into a detailed plan for revenge. He did it at one of our weekly staff meetings.

The faculty of the School of Philosophy gets together every Tuesday morning to discuss departmental issues. But lately these meetings have become rituals of public humiliation, sort of human sacrifices, presided over by Huerta.

On the day I'm remembering, the staff eyes each other cautiously as we take our seats at the big table in the Philosophy Department's conference room. Old plaster busts of famous thinkers and leaders look down on us from pedestals mounted high on the grey stucco walls.

Each of us wonders who'll be this week's victim. But on this day, my life is so full of sorrow that I tell myself Huerta's words won't matter to me. I'm wrong.

I stumble into my usual spot at the back of the room, under the busts of those old enemies Montezuma and Cortés. I nod up to them, to the other professors, and then I drift off, imaging that I'm once again sharing experiences good and bad with my late wife, Adelita. I'm so caught up in these memories that I'm sure my expression keeps changing from joy to pain and back again.

"Pay attention, Dr. McKeever!" Huerta calls, and I jump at the mention of my name. He's standing as he always is, pacing back and forth against the far wall, in front of a long credenza with its tray full of mismatched mugs and crusted pots of coffee, tea, and chocolate.

I look around the room, and everyone's seated, already involved in the meeting. They all look at me, then suddenly realize that I'm going to be this week's victim, and they're glad.

"Sorry," I say to the Butcher. "I haven't been myself, since Adelita...."

"We all know that your wife is dead, Professor," he interrupts, and the corners of his lips curl up sarcastically as though he thinks this tragic fact is somehow amusing.

Several other members of the faculty join in, if only to keep the Butcher's attention focused on me. Handsome, blue-eyed Federico Contreras, who caused so much sorrow during Adelita's last days, speaks up.

"It's been over a year, my friend," he reminds me. He runs his fingers through his wavy hair and smiles in false sympathy.

I sigh... that long? A few weeks allowed for mourning, and then back into the classroom where my lectures, I have to admit, have turned more and more negative. I speak on chaos theory and how seemingly unrelated events can interact to trigger a disaster somewhere else in the world... like maybe in my own life.

"We have talked about all of this before, Dr. McKeever," the Butcher says. "Perhaps you need to move on."

"Move on?"

"Retire," clarifies Alma Hernandez, the University controller. She's sitting directly across from me, surrounded by bright red folders thick with bureaucratic bullshit. "It'll give you all the time you need to mourn."

This stuns me. I shake my head. "No. I need to lecture. I need my students."

I think of my classroom and all the kids who sympathize with me. They enjoy my lectures. They tell me so. One student especially, Michelle Gomez, the most brilliant of them all, seems as heartbroken as I am.

"You may need your students, old man," Huerta says as he continues to pace around the table. "But they don't need you. Some of them have complained that your lectures are pointless. They're starting to call you *the mumbler*."

Contreras laughs out loud at that. "You do go on and on about the University," he says, "and how it has wronged you."

"We can't have you speaking ill of our institution," says Huerta. "This is a great school. This is the Harvard of Mexico."

Right, I think bitterly, a great school... whose faculty helped destroy my beautiful wife.

At the very end of the table, aging, hollow-eyed Professor Alejandro Blanco speaks up on my behalf. "I think there's a lot to be learned from grief," he says. "The students can observe...."

"Nonsense!" Huerta interrupts.

Alma flinches, and then she turns to me and speaks with such insincere sweetness that it's almost worse. "It really may be time to consider stepping down, Dr. McKeever."

I look around the table and see the others (all but Blanco) nodding in agreement, grateful to have the attention of the Butcher directed toward me and not at them.

"Perhaps it *is* best," I sigh.

"Consider, my friend," Contreras says, "that it took me *two weeks* to get over the death of my favorite aunt, and then I was back at work, giving the greatest lectures of my life."

"An aunt is not a wife," I remind him.

"That's not the issue," Huerta continues. "Tell me, Dr. McKeever, will you be able to regain your focus in the very near future? Will you be able to give the University its due, or should you simply retire and go back up north where you belong?"

I glance up at the bust of Aristotle on the far wall. The old philosopher appears to be as shocked as I am. Huerta's asking for my resignation right here in front of the rest of the faculty. And that phrase, *"go back up north where you belong?"* That's racist, isn't it?

"I'm tired," Huerta continues, "of employees and suppliers who take the University for granted. You remind me of one of our vendors, McKeever. He was a guy who had been paid well by the University for a very long time. He sold us clothing; you know, uniforms, sweatshirts, and logo wear. Oh, his products were good, but I thought he started acting a little too comfortable, and I didn't want him to get complacent. So, my Committee for Quality Purchasing canceled his longstanding contract just to remind him who was boss. It might have cost the guy his business; I don't know... who cares, right? It's the principle of the thing."

I really can't believe what I'm hearing.

The Butcher's staff meeting begins to give a whole new meaning to the events of the last two years. That last phrase about canceled contracts rings especially true, and suddenly I realize that Huerta's the person most responsible for the death of my wife. Not the direct cause of her death; cancer did that. But he sure as hell poisoned her last days... he and his damned faculty and committees.

I smile now and feel the bust of Aristotle almost nodding in agreement.

No one in the room knows what to make of my smile except perhaps old Dr. Blanco.

"I *will* give the University its due," I tell Huerta. Then I turn to my colleagues and add, "Forgive me for grieving so openly. I apologize to you all."

Almost everyone nods at those words, except the Butcher.

"Still, we will have to revisit this discussion at our next staff meeting," he says. "If we do not see a significant improvement in your attitude and the quality of your work, I'm afraid I will have to *insist* on your resignation."

Blanco shakes his head at the statement. But I don't mind... not any more.

"You'll see a change," I say, and I smile even more broadly. Huerta recoils as though he suddenly recognizes something very threatening in my expression. And he's right, you know. He should feel threatened.

They all should.

About the Authors

Nick Iuppa began his career as an apprentice writer with famed Bugs Bunny/Road Runner animator Chuck Jones and children's author Dr. Seuss. He later became a staff writer for the Wonderful World of Disney. *As VP Creative Director for Paramount Pictures, Nick did experimental work in interactive television and story-based simulations. He is the author of seven novels,* Management by Guilt *(Fawcett Books 1984—a Fortune Book Club selection) and eight technical books on interactive media. He lives in Northern California with his wife, Ginny. For more about Nick, visit www.nickiuppa.com.*

John Pesqueira*'s studies at the University of Arizona, Columbia, and Stanford prepared him for an impressive career in media design and development. His passion for the visual arts and popular culture continue to inform his creative efforts and still inspire his writing and photography. John grew up in the Sonoran desert and his love of the history, legends, and people of the American Southwest and Mexico remain a major focus of his work. John lives with his wife in Northern California.*

We love hearing from our readers and learning what
they like or don't like about our stories. We'd be very grateful
if you would send us a quick e-mail and tell us what
you think of *Alicia Bewitched*. We promise we'll
answer personally and directly.

Tell us who you are and let us
thank you for reading our books.

Contact Nick and John at
dosmilagrospress@Gmail.com